DEAD-END JOBS

A HITMAN ANTHOLOGY

DEAD-END JOBS

A HITMAN ANTHOLOGY

ANDY RAUSCH, EDITOR

All Due Respect Books
an imprint of Down & Out Books
3959 Van Dyke Road, Suite 265
Lutz, FL 33558
DownAndOutBooks.com

Cover design by Zach McCain

ISBN: 1-64396-212-4
ISBN-13: 978-1-64396-212-2

For Vincent and Jules.

TABLE OF CONTENTS

INTRODUCTION

Andy Rausch

Before anyone was writing about hitmen, hired guns (and swords) were prevalent in Western films and novels as well as Japanese samurai films (an Eastern variation of the American Western). Some of these hired guns killed for good, others for bad. But all shared a singular trait—they did these things for compensation. Actors Toshiro Mifune and Clint Eastwood famously played hired killers in Akira Kurosawa's *Yojimbo* and Sergio Leone's *Yojimbo* rip-off *Fistful of Dollars*.

Alain Delon played a hitman in 1967's *Le Samouraï*, and then Charles Bronson did the same in Michael Winner's *The Mechanic*. Despite these films, and despite hitmen having long been an organized crime fixture, hitmen hadn't appeared much in fiction (and certainly not as protagonists) prior to Max Allan Collins's groundbreaking Quarry series, which debuted with *The Broker* in 1976. Collins's popular series was the first to feature a hitman protagonist, and the series continues to thrive today, almost fifty years later. While it's true that Warren Murphy and Richard Sapir's *The Destroyer* series had featured an assassin protagonist half a decade earlier, their protagonist, Remo Williams, was a completely different animal. Remo Williams was a fantastical, almost superhuman character who killed out of what he believed to be patriotism. Quarry, on the other hand, was a real man living in a very real world and killing to survive. He carried out his assignments without glory or jingoism. (Also, there

1

should be a distinction made here between government assassin and hitman. While some might argue that these men are the same, they are not. There is one key difference: one is a criminal murdering for criminal reasons and the other kills as civic duty.)

And how can we forget Lawrence Block's magnificent Keller series about the stamp collecting hitman?

Contract killers continued to pop up occasionally in popular culture, but they reached their zenith in the 1990s. John Woo's Hong Kong thriller *The Killer* kicked off the hitman craze in 1989 and was soon followed by a slew of contract killer films. These included *Pulp Fiction*, *The Professional*, *Assassins*, *Gross Pointe Blank*, *Things to Do in Denver When You're Dead*, *2 Days in the Valley*, *The Big Hit*, and others. There were also films like *La Femme Nikita* and its American remake, *Point of No Return*, which, again, focus on the similar but different occupation of government assassins. During this period, hitmen also appeared in fiction like Elmore Leonard's *Killshot* (adapted to film a decade later) and Max Allan Collins's *Road to Perdition* (which originated as a graphic novel and then grew into a book series and a popular film starring Tom Hanks). Although the craze has died down some, hitmen have never gone out of style.

Today, we live in an era in which John Wick has become arguably the most famous fictional hitman ever to pull a trigger. Max Allan Collins continues to produce new books about Quarry, and indie authors like Paul D. Brazill, Nikki Dolson, myself, and others craft new books about new contract killers. So, in short, hitmen are alive and well (but their targets are not).

Why are people fascinated by contract killers? I myself am a fan of every book and movie mentioned here. I believe the primary reason I'm enthralled by (and write about) hitmen is because I find the concept of morally corrupt protagonists absolutely delicious. And who better represents the morally corrupt protagonist than someone who does the unthinkable—murdering other humans—simply for monetary gain? Then there are the questions about what make these people tick; how they do it, why they do it, and how they live with themselves.

No matter the reasons why audiences and readers are fascinated by hitmen, the fact is that they are. When it occurred to me that there were no hitman anthologies, I set out to rectify that right quick. The result of this epiphany is this collection. It contains eighteen gems by some of the finest writers working today.

There are stories of every stripe here. Stories about all kinds of hitmen (and hit-women). There are contract killers employed by mobsters, drug dealers, lovers, and businessmen in settings and scenarios as different as the writers who crafted them. There's even a supernatural-themed hitman story.

It is my sincere hope that you enjoy the hitmen you find within these pages, but be sure to watch your back. You never know when one might be lurking in the shadows behind you, ready to put two slugs in your head.

TRADE FOR THE WORKING MAN

Matt Phillips

I LIKE TO use me a over and under.

Stevens-make, what I prefer.

A shotgun is a messy way to do it, but it's about a sure thing. If you can get close enough, that is. There's a little town out there in the Mojave—Baker, it's called. I had me a contract to do a motel owner out that way. He got in some business with the Mexicans. Cartel men, you see. What he tried to do was get himself a raise. He tried to say it was all *his* risk, using *his* place as a safe house. That he deserved more of a cut, all them people paying good money to get into the good old United States. These men that paid me—the same ones that paid him—didn't see it that way. No, sir. They did not.

The Mexicans had a lawyer draft the man's will under false pretenses. Stole his signature and made up some eyewitnesses to the will's signing. All official, you see. Holds up fine in a court of law. They got the motel for themselves—free and clear. There's people all around out there who got this kind of power. I been doing this long enough, I got no illusions about what can happen in this life. About who can do whatever-the-hell to you. No, sir. There's lots of evil out here, and it runs deep.

Take me, for instance.

I drive a little Honda and wear velcro shoes. My socks get stretched out real easy and hang around my ankles. People say I got a red shade to my skin. I ain't had many women, but the

5

ones I did—they didn't stick to me none.

Damn near sixty years old and my gout burns like hell. But I still got good aim.

You'd never see me coming.

If I was to come for you.

What I did with the motel man: I made like I was going to check into the motel. Kept the shotgun hidden under a coat draped over my duffle bag. This was around midnight. He comes out all blurry-eyed and drowsy. Like he was sleeping. He asked my name and looked down at the little keyboard there, started to type. I put the Stevens over the counter and right under his chin, brought his eyes up to look into mine. He knew what it was. Not just the shotgun, but the whole thing—me being there with him.

He said, "I take it back, how I said it."

"It's too late for that, buddy-O."

"Without me they wouldn't have had—"

"Without you," I said, "they would have found them somebody else."

That's one I had to make like a suicide. Because of the will and all. It didn't go too bad, how I did it. Kind of messy though, like I said. I work for the Mexicans, I get about five large a head. I can charge extra, see—it's because I'm a white man and it throws off law enforcement. Always has been easier for a white man to get away with things, you understand. I do a job for the motorcycle gangs or some kind of domestic job, I keep it to three grand.

A fair price for honest work.

Any case, it's about all I do these days. Run around killing people.

That's a long way from how I came up in this life.

I know me the Lord's prayer. Got me some work history, too. Hell, I even got a little pension, but doing this is what keeps me going. They say you retire and you die. I'd just about agree with that, except some people die long before they get a chance to retire.

I should know, and I tell you true.

I GUESS IT started simple enough.

I needed the work.

Seems like most of what I done in life, that's how I came to it. Those four words: I needed the work. Of course, not everybody is lucky enough to get himself a trade. Lots of guys I know—women, too—end up living off overdraft accounts and disability. We all got us sore backs and beat-to-shit shoulders. It's a damned epidemic. You won't catch me saying all them broken backs ain't true—it's either the bones or the heart, but rest assured…something's broke.

Plus, who else is it can get the lawyers paid, if not us?

Talk about work: We used to have us an assembly plant in this town. Big gray box building off the north side of the highway. Had us a break room and insurance, too. Still got my uniform in the closet. My name stitched right over the pocket: Cody Ropes.

Nineteen years in a row I bolted plastic propellers onto outboard motors made in China. Every bit of horsepower you can dream up, but all of them motors was made in China. From the aluminum screws right down to the smallest rubber gaskets—made in China.

Assembled in the good old United States.

That's a deal the union got us. Them business dudes can make whatever the hell they want in China, but it gets fully assembled and shipped here in America. No goddamn exceptions.

Got us that deal after '08, and we was proud of it, too.

Of course, the Chinese found a cheaper way to get things done.

And the union couldn't do shit about it.

Now we got us an empty, big gray box building in this town.

I took to drink and burned up a Visa card. Those first few weeks, after the assembly plant closed, I wasn't sure I'd stick around. Not that I'd leave Dixon. I thought about leaving the good Earth itself. But coming up in the church, I know that do-ing it to myself is no way to go—my luck, I'll end up counting grains of gunpowder in hell.

I drink in Bucky's Bar—that's the one off Gunn Free Road.

I owed Visa about three grand—with interest—and, well, I needed work.

One Sunday, a man I never seen bellies up to me at the bar. He's got pilot sunglasses on and a mustache like a dirty toothbrush. I'm about done with my beer and—ain't it my luck—he orders me another. I said, "Hey, I appreciate it. But I ain't interested."

"What's that?" He sniffed real hard through one nostril.

"Whatever you want to buy out of me with this beer."

He pinched his nose with his thumb and index finger, kind of chuckled.

"You think that's funny?" I didn't need a broken hand, but I'd get me one if I needed to. Never did shy away from putting my fist into somebody's face. Of course, it didn't need to come to that. Nothing ever does. It's just that I was in a bad mood. My Visa debt and all.

"You the one pointed that .45 at Willie Roof back in '08?"

He got my attention. Willie Roof was a union breaker for the people in China. He grew up on a ranch in Texas, made a few bucks throwing his fists around as an amateur. Somehow he ended up working for a foreign government here in the Califor-nia desert. Can't say I understand his journey. I promised to kill him one morning in the assembly plant parking lot—took a .45 along for authenticity.

"I got you thinking about it," he said.

"Willie's still breathing, if that's what you mean."

"Only because you let him."

"Right as rain," I said.

"You really think you could kill somebody?"

I took a sip of my beer, pretended to think about it. "Mis-ter—I do anything that pays me well. I'd stand on my chair and tell nursery rhymes naked, if you gave me a hundred-dollar bill to do it." It was about the most honest thing I ever said.

He grunted. "This ain't no nursery rhyme."

"What is it then?"

"It's a man that needs killing—worse, he deserves it."

"You just point me in his direction," I said. "And make sure the check don't bounce."

I STILL DREAM about the first man I killed.

He was a little guy, maybe five-six. And he wore a Carhartt cap pulled low across his face. A few days of beard there on his cheeks, and real saggy jeans like he'd been wearing them his whole life. He worked at a feed store off 247. Drove a forklift truck at the place, stacked bales of hay into pickup trucks all day long.

You start out, and you think it's easy.

No big deal.

But it's killing. And killing is a whole lot of work.

Do it right. You got to follow the man, make sure he don't come at you with no surprises. Me, I ain't one to walk up and shoot a dude—not without making sure he don't carry. Or, if he do carry, I got to make sure he ain't got the piece on him. I knew exactly what was behind the counter in that Baker motel. Believe me. But that's only the first part. Doing the thing, that's a whole book in itself. Let me tell you. I don't want to get into that here—not enough time.

After you do it, that's what I hate the most. Do it right and you leave the sucker bleeding on the street. Or burning up in his pickup truck. Or drifting out to sea. Or wrapped up a suicide by some shit-for-brains county sheriff. But sometimes them ain't your options. You might have to cut a guy to pieces. You might have to dump him bit by bit in dumpsters along I-10. That's a thing I had to do before.

But the first man I killed—he was a fighter. I can give him that.

9

What I did is I followed him to a bar. Not Bucky's, but a place just like it. Same sad stories drifting around and asking for free booze. I waited until he wobbled out, stumbled to his truck. Soon as he gets in and starts fumbling with the keys, I slide in beside him. Had a .45 for this job and I had it out and ready, right on his belly. But he goes to work on me—I got a flash of fists in my throat. Air shooting out of me like coolant from a busted hose. He got his foot up and pressed it right into my crotch, held me against the door while we grunted and swore.

The fight was over the gun, as you might imagine.

It took all I had, but I got it from him. Fell back hard and busted the passenger window with my damn skull, glass shattering into a thousand pebbles. He knew what it was and he opened the door, got two feet on the ground before I plugged him twice in the back. Knocked that Carhartt cap clean off. Got messy because I had to get him in the back of the truck, put him in the dirt out past Amboy. But that's too much information, maybe.

Point is, I did the killing.

And all because that guy in the bar—the one who bought me a beer—was pissed as hell the little guy got into his wife somehow, sweet-talked her ass one lonely country night.

Happens like that more than you think.

I'll tell you. It sure as shit does.

Another thing: That job paid off them Visa people.

HOW I GOT to the cartel contracts is your regular small town coincidence. Man knew a guy who knew a guy who talked about what I done for him. One day out of the blue, I get a call from a notary in town. Man who goes by the moniker of Solemn. Good name, you ask me. Solemn Jones—notary public. Old Solemn says he's got a business opportunity I might like.

Did I want to come down and meet him about it?

I needed the money.

The meeting consisted of me and Solemn shaking hands. He had one eye that fluttered. Kept blinking and he couldn't stop it. That set me uneasy a bit, but I know most men got flaws.

I let that pass.

He gave me the gun on that job, a nine millimeter. What I call a gangster gun, but it's one that does the job okay. You can aim the thing, that is. Had me out to Fontana. Some of us still call it Fontucky. If you ever been there, you'd know why. This hit was a big California redneck called Scheft. He did one job or another for the Mexicans—moving drugs, I think—and got greedy somehow. Or fucked up some big way. I slept in my Honda and followed him around for two days. Biggest itinerary of fast food joints and booze spots you'll ever see. Man was big as a power forward and ate like a cow. I never did find out if Scheft had a gun or not. What I did is pull up beside him at a chicken shack near the highway, one of them franchise joints. I shot through the passenger window of his Camaro, got a good look at the holes in his head. What I made of him. I ditched the gun in a sewer grate in Moreno Valley. Let *them* cops sort it all out. God knew it wouldn't get back to me. But that's what started me on the five large. These cartels—I'll tell you—they pay more than fair for what they need.

I bet folks wonder—if they ever knew—what I do with the money. I got most of it in a couple them rolling suitcases. All stashed in the crawl space under my trailer. I been meaning to put the money in fireproof money boxes, but I ain't got around to it. Of course, where I hide it ain't the point neither. I said how no woman ever stuck to me, and that's true.

But there was a lady I took a shine to from the old outboard assembly plant.

We never had us a romance, but we shared a laugh or three during a cigarette break. Had more than that at Bucky's after work most nights. Sunny was her name, and she had a son. Well, still does. I remembered her son looking at me whenever I saw them two in the grocery store or wherever. He was three years old when I first met him. Got to be about seven or eight before the plant closed. He'd be along about eighteen now. I seen him working in a barbershop downtown, talking about he wanted to ride a motorcycle down to the tip of South America. You believe that? What a dream. He remembered me, too. Once I got in the chair.

He said, "How you doing, Mr. Ropes?"

"Hey, call me Cody. How's your momma?"

He went to buzzing and said, "She passed about two years back."

It got me right in my stomach—you know that feeling. Like it's hardened cement down there. "Shit, buddy-O. I didn't know that. You mind saying what happened?"

The kid put a finger under his chin and pretended to squeeze a trigger.

I can't tell you how that felt. Of course, my mind flashed on that motel man I put down, all the blood and brains from inside him. What I put on the walls. But I saw his face, too. Those shiny eyes looking at me. Begging. That purple tongue darting out to wet his lips.

I heard his voice—all prayer and desperation.

Since then, I got it in my head to give Sunny's kid the money. Whatever I could earn.

Maybe follow him home, drop it on his doorstep. Not like money could ever bring Sunny back, but it might tell her kid there's something left for him in this world.

No matter it came from death. Or doing wrong.

Just that it was his, and nobody wanted nothing for giving it to him.

SOLEMN HANDED ME a new piece in a brown paper lunch sack. I peeked inside—a Smith & Wesson .45. The M&P Shield they call it. It's a smaller gun and runs, what, five hundred dollars or so off the shelf? I said, "I only need this, huh?"

Solemn bit his bottom lip, scratched at his right ear with a long fingernail. "I give you what they give me. You need some other tool, something else, that's on you."

"You know, I watched a documentary about these cartels. On the streaming video, buddy-O. Them guys walk around with AKs. Why can't I get a big gun that makes people piss their pants?" I looked down at my velcro shoes and loose socks. Brought my gaze back to Solemn. He stood there and stared at me, thumbed a few papers on his desk. That eye fluttered like the wings on a bird. "Might do my image some good," I said. "That make sense to you?"

He didn't respond to that, but said, "This one's a cop."

"Won't get in line and take the payoff, huh?"

"It's something like that," Solemn said.

"You got the name, or I got to pay you for it?" He slid a three-by-five index card across his desk. I picked it up and read the name. Below the name was a city and an address—I was familiar with the city. I slid the card back across the desk and Solemn lit it on fire with a red Bic. We watched it burn there and leave another black mark on the old gray steel. I yawned and said, "Because it's a cop, I want double."

Solemn said, "They'll go up to eight large, but that's all."

"Well, I guess I got to be okay with that." I stood, cradled my lunch sack under an arm, and walked out into the rest of my day.

NOT A COP, but a sheriff's deputy.

Town of Brawley, down near the Mexican border. Man worked for the Imperial County Sheriff's Office. Nice domestic life and wife and new baby. Sad he had to go, but I knew there was a reason. I guessed he didn't want to fall in line, play ball with the Mexicans somehow. One thing I learned doing this job...It's best you fall in line. Play ball.

Or you get somebody like me on your ass.

13

Or worse. One of them they call *sicario*. That's a real Mexican hitman. Not like me, a white man moonlighting for part-time wages. Though I got to say, eight large is no joke. That's good money. The cop worked the first day I got down there. Turned out he was a special detail man.

Narcotics task force.

Raided two houses that day. Kind of funny, me watching the task force watch two houses. All from my little brown Honda. Next day was a day off, the man at home with his wife. Out front mowing a brown patch of grass. Banging around in the garage half the day.

The wife was pretty and the kid liked to cry.

Just starting to toddle.

The cop was okay it seemed to me.

A guy got on the wrong side of things somehow. There was nothing I could do about that. Hell, I couldn't live my life for him. Had me a job to do. When you got a cop, you got a man with a gun. I needed to be careful about that. What I did, I put a couple roofing nails under each of his rear tires. He drove a little Toyota—parked it on the street—and I figured, chances were, the tires go flat before he made it to the department next morning. It happened on I-8, the cop about two miles from his exit. Only one tire flat. Driver's-side rear. I watched him put on the hazard lights, pull to the shoulder. I pulled in behind him, both of us getting out at the same time. I had the .45 on the passenger seat, scooped it into my right hand as I was getting out. Kind of hid it behind my open door as he turned back to face me. Smile on my face—*I'm stopping to help you.* He lifted his chin, started toward the rear of his car. I caught the bulge of his piece on a hip, but I came out fast and plugged him three times in the chest. He reached for that hip, but came up short, went to his knees. Purple blood coming through his polo shirt. I got back in my Honda and floored it, got off two exits later. Circled back to Highway 86—saw and heard the sirens going in the opposite direction—and was halfway to Indio before they even started looking for the killer.

Pretty easy.

I tossed the gun into the aqueduct near the Salton Sea. Just an easy shot over chain-link and barbed wire. To steer clear of my own nasty guilt, I ignored the newspaper for a few weeks. Nobody ever came calling—I got away free.

And I put that eight large in my suitcases.

For Sunny's kid. That's who was going to get it.

EVERY FEW WEEKS, I'd get down to the barbershop in Dixon.

Sit in the chair and talk to Sunny's boy.

We never did mention his momma, but the kid always called me Cody, like I asked of him. Funny, how much you get to know somebody, you spend ten minutes listening. The kid really did plan on South America. Hell, he was saving up for it. And he wanted Europe after that. Maybe later, Southeast Asia. Look, I never been anywhere in my life but California, Arizona, Nevada, and Tijuana. I don't understand these kids who want to get on airplanes. Or ride motorcycles halfway to hell. I just knew the kid's momma. And she was good people.

Her boy liked him some Johnny Cash.

Snickers bars.

Miller High Life.

And he liked him some Stephen King, too.

Sunny's boy. Regular old kid who knew how to cut a man's hair.

I wondered how he'd take it, finding a hundred large on his doorstep?

SOLEMN HAD A smirk on his face when I sat down across from him. Last time he had that smirk, it was a job I'd like to forget. Not pleasant. I mentioned chopping somebody to pieces?

That was the job. The Mexicans call it sending a message. Pays a bit more, but it's harder work.

Anyway, this was my last job. I settled up with myself, decided to retire. Live off the pension from all those years assembling outboard motors from China. Comes down to it, I'm grateful I ever got to put those propellers on—thankful to all the Chinese who did the real work. Me, I just had to turn a socket, work a torque wrench. But that's something else that's coming over me. It's not what matters. What I wanted was to get Sunny's kid the money. I wanted to be done with it, to get those suitcases out from under my trailer. This was it—the last job.

I said, "You got that shit-eating look on your face. What is it?"

He slid an index card across the desk.

I took a look, sighed. I flipped the card back at him and it hit him in the chest, flopped into his lap. He didn't move, but instead held my gaze.

I said, "You know I came up in the church."

Solemn nodded. "We all come up somehow."

They wanted me to kill a pastor. "How much this going to net me?"

"Eight, again."

"What the hell did the man of God do to deserve it?"

Solemn's right eye blinked uncontrollably until he put a hand over it. "I imagine it's what he didn't do. What he refused to do. But that's not for—"

"I know it ain't," I said, interrupting him. "We just the suckers putting this shit together and sending it out. Got us a good deal and we stick to it."

"You going to do it?" He watched me, that one hand still pressed over his glitchy eye.

I thought of dropping the suitcases at the kid's house, how that might feel. I thought about how so much evil—some way or another—can turn into good. I believe that's true—evil can turn into something good. You got to make it yourself though, turn that water into wine. Find a way.

"Yeah," I said. "I'll do it."

I walked out of there with another gun. Another name. For the last time.

Forget Sunny's kid for a second. I tried to see the pastor in my mind, imagine him dead. What in shiny hell could he have done? Nothing, probably. But that don't matter in this world.

No, sir.

When you think about it that way, it's kind of easy to add it all together.

You'd never see it coming.

If someone like me was to come for you.

Matt Phillips lives in San Diego. His books include You Must Have a Death Wish, Countdown, Know Me from Smoke, Three Kinds of Fools, The Bad Kind of Lucky, *and* Accidental Outlaws.

INCIDENT AT A DINER

Chris Miller

THE PLACE SMELLS of grease and misery, of fried food and apathy. Fitting, I guess. I shouldn't be here. Not that there's anything wrong with here, but *why* I'm here is no good. I was raised better than this. But am I turning around and leaving? Not a chance. I'm too far in to turn back now. I've had a taste, and I liked how it went down. How it lingered on my tongue.

I'm not turning back.

I scan the room. Pretty typical crowd for a dive like this. Blue-collar guys, mostly. A couple of elderly women with their equally elderly husbands. There's one guy at the end of the bar shoveling eggs that I think started out as sunny side up but now are a pulverized ruin of yolk, the sun having crashed into all and obliterating it. He's eating fast and sipping at his coffee. He winces as he sets the mug down. It's hot, but he seems to like it. Asks for a refill. The briefcase next to him is black and looks like leather. He has a tie on, but it's thrown over his shoulder to keep it out of his eggs and sausage and toast. This guy isn't blue collar, but he fits right in just the same.

A couple of old men nearer to me at the bar are grumbling back and forth, laughing occasionally. They sip their coffee as their too-big bellies push against the bar inside their bib overalls. A few others litter the diner. I look down the row of booths to the right, mostly empty but for a couple leaning across their table talking—they don't look happy—and two guys who don't seem to fit at all. They're big, but not like the men in the bib overalls. They're wearing suits like the guy at the end of the bar, but these are much nicer. Their hair is slicked back and oily. They're from out of town, no doubt. They seem jovial enough, though. Cracking jokes back and forth, though I can't make out what is so funny.

Then I see her. She's at the back, in the corner, and she's already seen me. Her face is light and happy and mine matches hers as I move down the aisle between the booths. I ignore the arguing couple as I pass.

"This isn't fair and you know it," the man is saying.

"It's not about fair, it's what's best for Kendall and Kerry," the woman replies and then I can't hear them anymore.

I'm halfway to her booth now, just past the arguing couple. I pass the two guys who don't fit. They're chuckling about something and one of them glances up at me. I nod a hello. He doesn't nod back. He looks at the other guy.

"Waylon's a fuck up," he says, and now I know they're from out of town. His voice tells me New Jersey or New York, but that's just based on movies. I've never been to either. What the hell they're doing in small town Texas is a mystery.

"Fuck ups still cause problems," the other guy says as I keep moving. The first guy mumbles something, but I can't make it out.

And then I'm only a few feet from the booth and *her*. My heart ticks up a notch. My internal heat, too. My mouth feels dry and I'm glad I can see the waitress making her way toward me as I slip into the booth and take in the smile still beaming at me beneath those eyes that I swear are sparkling.

"I'm so glad you came, Sam!" she quietly squeaks.

I open my mouth to respond when the waitress arrives with a weary smile and her pen poised over the ticket pad.

"Mornin', hun!" she says and pushes a lock of hair over her ear. "What can I get you folks?"

"Coffee," I say, and Millie orders the same with a side of

scrambled eggs and sausage and hash browns. I tell the waitress to make that two and she's off down the aisle. One of the Jersey guys barks something at her as she passes and holds up a mug that's clearly empty. She smiles—still weary, but giving it her best—and nods in the affirmative.

I look into those sparkling eyes and I want to dive into them, get lost and drown in their depths. So beautiful. So sweet. So tender. She's incredible in every way and she is here with *me*.

I shouldn't be here.

I push away all the things telling me to leave. I don't want to leave. This is new and exciting and I know the grass is always greener on the other side, but I don't care. Even if the *reason* it's greener is because it's covered in shit, I don't care. Not right now. I wonder if I ever will.

"I only have an hour or so," I say, and I think she's disappointed. I like that. But then she smiles again and it's radiant.

"I'm glad for any time we can spend together," she says and slides her hands out and clasps mine. "I've missed you."

Her words are intoxicating, and I don't care how toxic they are. Toxic to my soul. Toxic to my heart. Toxic to my—

My phone buzzes on the table and I can feel it through my arms. We both make a startled jump, then we smile at each other as though to apologize for being so silly. I pick up the phone and my smile vanishes.

What are you doing? the text message says, and my joy is instantly sucked dry. I don't have to look at who sent the message. I know exactly who sent it, and this is a problem. It's both why I'm here now and why I feel I shouldn't be.

It's from Cheryl, my wife.

"What is it, babe?" Millie asks, and I see her furrowed brow when I glance up for half a second and then look back at the text message. I haven't opened it, it's just there on the home screen notifications.

I click the screen off and lay the phone facedown on the table and smile at Millie.

21

"Nothing," I say with a wave of my hand. I'm getting better at this, and I feel both pride and shame at this fact. But it's the excited little boy in me doing something he knows he shouldn't that seems to rule me now since this tryst started. "Did you get the package I sent you?"

She blushes and I think it's the most beautiful thing I've ever seen. Then her expression changes to something more seductive, something like the face she made at me that first time we met at the motel outside of town and we rutted like pigs in slop.

It makes me stir.

"I'm wearing them," she says and winks at me, and I can feel my face matching the color of hers.

My shade deepens and the smile fades when the phone buzzes again. I don't pick it up this time. Millie's eyes glance at it and then back to me.

"Is it her?"

I consider lying, but decide there's no point.

"Yeah."

She leans back and pulls her hands into her lap, the concern on her face changing to something like shame. She's human. I'm human. The shame reminds us of that.

"I'm a bad person, aren't I?" she says to her lap.

"No," I reply immediately. "I'm the bad guy. Not you. You're just…"

I don't know how to finish the sentence, don't know where it was going. Like you have an idea and it's a light at the far end of a tunnel, but you never get there no matter how long you run toward it. Finally, you just give up and try to find your way out.

"I should go," she says and starts to grab her purse. I don't want her to leave. I want her to stay, and I want to throw caution to the wind and take her to the motel and make us both feel like we're someone else for a while.

"Wait," I say and reach out and touch her arm. "Don't go. It's nothing. I'm going to tell her soon. It will all be over then. No more sneaking."

She smiles, but her eyes never fully accommodate it. She's thinking something. I might know what it is, too. I'm thinking that the sneaking is precisely why this feels so good and exciting. Will I think she's so amazing once we're in the open?

Her hand covers the one I'm grabbing her arm with, and that electric tingle is there, and I don't care about the future or my wife or any of it because *now* is all that matters to me.

"Hey!" a man's voice shouts, and I jerk as I look up the aisle. One of the Jersey Boys is looking at the couple who were arguing quietly. Millie turns to see what's happening, then looks back at me, her face confused.

"You know we can hear yous over here, yeah?" one of the Jersey Boys says to the couple. I can barely see the woman from my angle and all I can see of the man is the side of his face. He puts a surrendering hand up, waves it a couple times.

"Excuse us," the guy says. "We're having a conversation."

"No shit you're having a conversation," Jersey One—the one with his back to me—says. "We can hear every goddamned word. Christ! Keep it the fuck down, will ya?"

The guy with the woman tenses, and his shoulder muscles draw together.

"Hey, who do you think—"

The second Jersey Boy whips his fork around and points it at the guy.

"You know who the fuck we are, little man? Huh? You shut your cock-holder, you know what's good for ya."

Jerseys One and Two drop words like "if" sometimes, and I instantly feel freaked out. They seem like gangsters. Like *real* gangsters. They have the look down pat. Voices, too. What the hell are they doing in East Texas?

The lady with the guy at the other table is saying something I can't hear to him, probably trying to get him to back down. He doesn't want to. But I think she's right. They aren't the types you want to mess with.

The clatter of forks on plates resumes as the Jersey Boys begin to eat again, absolutely no concern on their faces whatsoever. I'm watching the other guy—the one with the lady—and I think he's working up the nerve to say something else, but if he does, I don't hear it because my attention is drawn to my phone again, which buzzes three times in quick succession.

"Fuck," I grumble and pick it up.

It's Cheryl. Of course it is.

I glance up at Millie and my face is pained. Hers is, too. We're bad people. The worst kind. Total asshol—

The phone buzzes in my hand again and I nearly jump out of my skin. Millie's face is etched with concern when I glance up at her and make a pitiful attempt at a self-deprecating smile. She makes an equally pitiful attempt in return.

"I, uh..." she says, then loses whatever thread she had. She's messing with her hands, clasping them, then interlocking her fingers, then spreading her palms flat on the table between us. Guilt warms my face and chest and I lift the phone so the notifications will show.

There are four more messages.

Sam, we need to talk.

Are you ignoring me?

Where are you?

Why won't you answer me?

I sigh so harshly it makes me cough. I'm laying the phone down when Millie speaks.

"I care for you, Sam," she says, and her eyes are pained. This isn't going to go well. She's feeling it, too. The guilt. The crushing weight of self-inflicted pain that seems worth every bit of it when we're in bed. But now...

"We're both adults," she goes on and I can feel a different weight descending on me. "We've done some things most people would find unforgivable. I think even *we* find it unforgivable, if we're totally honest. I know I do. We both know this is wrong. But, the thing is, when I'm with you I...I just don't care."

Her eyes are still pained, but they seem to light up here.

"I don't know what I'm trying to say here, just that I know this is putting you through hell. You don't deserve that and neither does Cheryl. God, I feel like such a bitch sometimes. I wasn't raised to do anything like this. But with you…" She reaches a hand out and touches mine, the one holding the phone. "…with you it all seems worth it to—"

My phone starts buzzing again and I drop it as we both jerk our hands away with quiet gasps. Our eyes fall on the screen, the one showing the Memoji of Cheryl in the background, announcing her call.

"Shit," I mutter and Millie covers her mouth with both her hands.

I pick up the phone, look at it for a second as though it's a venomous snake readying to strike, then glance up to Millie. She's dropping her hands from her face and her eyes are wide and her mouth is opening.

I answer the phone as a bell chimes over the front door, announcing a new patron. It's an old cowboy, big hat and even bigger dentures on display as he smiles and waves to the waitress as he comes in.

"What the hell is going on?" Cheryl's voice barks in my ear, and I forget all about the cowboy.

"Cheryl, what are you—"

"*No,*" she says with authority, and I unconsciously obey. "I know you, Sam. I know you better than you know yourself. Something's going on and you need to tell me what it is."

I swallow and my throat clicks. I open my mouth to answer, but the waitress is here with our food and she's noisily placing it in front of us, and the racket sounds enormous, and I start clearing my throat in hopes of covering the sound.

It doesn't work.

"What is that sound?" she asks, and I'm thinking *fuck-fuck-fuck!*

"I, uh, it's just—"

"Can I get you two anything else?" our waitress asks, and

25

she's loud and smiling too much and Cheryl hears it.

"Are you at a restaurant? Who are you with?"

"I'm not with anybody," I lie terribly with a squeak in my voice and Millie is about to freak out.

"Goddammit, can I get a cup of coffee here?" one of the Jersey Boys says. The waitress turns red and Millie dismisses her with a smile. She saunters up the aisle to them and I absurdly look at her ass that might have been something to look at three kids ago.

I really am an asshole.

"I feel like such a fool," Cheryl squawks in my ear, and I snap back to the moment. "Things have been rocky, but now—"

"Cheryl," I say curtly and sigh. "Look, you're freaking out over nothing. I'm just getting breakfast, nothing is going on, I'll talk to you—"

"Don't do this to me, Sam!" she screams in my ear and gooseflesh ripples my body as I quickly end the call and turn the phone off, sweeping the dust under the rug.

I'm an asshole *and* a wimp.

I sigh again and pinch my eyes shut. I can hear the faint grunts of the Jersey Boys talking about something and I hear that name Waylon again. I hear a southern accent asking what someone would recommend on the menu.

"First time here, darlin'!" the words float to me and I open my eyes and see the cowboy ordering something from the waitress. The couple that was arguing before are leaning in close and I can't hear them, but it doesn't look pleasant.

"I'm sorry, Sam," Millie says, and I blink a few times and take in her face. She really is pretty, but not abandon your marriage and throw your life away pretty. Only, there are moments where she seems to be just that attractive. Moments that lead to lines being crossed and carnal desires being satisfied.

I'm not a good person.

"You've got nothing to be sorry for, Mill," I say. I want to say so much more, want to get out of this place and just vanish somewhere where Cheryl can't call and interrupt us ever again and we can do all those things my wife won't.

Millie smiles weakly and scoops a bite of food. I sip some coffee and it's hot and scalds my lips. I take another sip. The food is better than the coffee, but that isn't saying much. The eggs are runny and the sausage is overcooked, but it's passable. Hash browns are okay. It'll keep you fueled and going. We eat in silence for a couple of minutes and I think she tries to say something once or twice, but I can't be sure and she never speaks.

Jersey One gets up from their booth and he's on his cell phone. His olive face is fat and scrunched and his cheeks are flushed. His eyes are darting around as he walks down the aisle, and I feel uncomfortable suddenly as he comes near us. He isn't looking at me or Millie; he's staring beyond us to the restrooms.

"The fuck you talking about?" Jersey One says as he moves past us. "That pain in the ass is supposed to be handled."

He doesn't say anything and I'm suddenly mesmerized by the man, still flabbergasted at why he and his friend are *here*, of all places. Fish out of water doesn't quite cut it. It's more like finding a McDonald's on the moon.

He vanishes into the restrooms and I can't hear anything else from him.

"You from out of town, friend?" I hear a cheerful and friendly voice and instantly know it's the cowboy. I glance up the aisle and see he's talking to Jersey Two, who looks annoyed.

"What's it to you?" he replies, turning to the cowboy and staring over the bridge of his nose.

The cowboy laughs. "Oh, hell, ain't nothin' to me, I's just asking. 'Round here folks is friendly."

Jersey Two mumbles something and turns back to his mostly gone meal and starts picking at the remains with his fork.

"Yeah," he grunts, "well, we ain't from *'round* here."

He's mocking the cowboy's accent but the cowboy doesn't

seem fazed by it at all. He's still smiling and his teeth are big, white things. He's not a young man, but now I'm not sure just how old he really is. He seems so nondescript other than his voice and clothes.

"Fuck you, Brandon!" suddenly explodes from the woman at the booth with the guy, and she stands up. He's reaching for her arm, but she yanks it away from him before he can get a hand on her.

"You're just the same as you always were!" she spits. "Take it up with my lawyer."

"You can't do this, Ang!" he says and starts to stand.

Millie is turning around to see the commotion I'm mesmerized by.

"Hey!" a fat man behind the counter barks at them. He's wearing a stained apron over a white undershirt and there's a sheen of sweat on his brow. "Knock it off or take it outside, you hear me?"

Brandon looks like he's been dipped in red paint. Everyone is staring at him and a hush has fallen over the room, leaving only the crackling sound of bacon and fat sizzling on the griddle.

Ang—*is she an Angela or an Angel?*—turns from him and storms out the door, the bell chiming loudly as she leaves. Jersey Two is staring up at Brandon, and I can't make out the meaning of the look on his face. Maybe annoyed, maybe interested. Almost like he's just waiting to see what this guy might do, if he's going to make a scene. Maybe he *wants* there to be a scene.

"Shit, Millie, we should get out of here," I say, and she nods.

Before we can stand, the restroom door makes a sucking sound and opens as Jersey One steps back into the aisle. He's still on his phone and the color is drained from his fingers when I glance up at him. He's right next to me. He isn't paying any attention to us, but he's stopped and staring straight down the aisle at Brandon's back. A bead of sweat trickles down the side of his temple.

"One of Waylon's guys?" Jersey One says, and I finally think of Waylon Blackshear, the only Waylon I've ever heard of. I don't know him, but I know *of* him. Owns a bar on this side of town where I normally would never be if not for Millie and my inability to stop cheating on my wife who doesn't deserve any of this.

I shouldn't be here.

Waylon is a strange guy. In the news a lot, at odds with police, but never shut down. I don't know what he does, but most folks don't *want* to know. He's not the kind of guy you talk to when you see him. In fact, you don't *see* him at all.

"Take a load off, partner," the cowboy says to Brandon with a big smile. "Let her cool off, it'll be alright."

Millie is nudging me to go, but Jersey One is still blocking our exit from the booth. Brandon is shaking his head and I can see him trembling from here. He's wound up like a spring and he buries his face in his hands for a moment.

"Sit the fuck down, kid," Jersey Two says to Brandon with that same annoyed look he'd given the cowboy a few minutes ago. "You don't wanna make a scene."

Brandon drops his arms to his sides and clenches his fists a few times. Then he nods and collapses back into his booth and lays his head on his forearms.

"Say, feller," the cowboy says and Jersey Two's head swivels around, annoyance projected masterfully, "that's a nice suit ya got there, can I ask—"

"Listen, hick," Jersey Two says with unhurried aggravation, "I ain't here to have a fucking conversation, get me? Why don't yous talk to your new pal here and leave me the fuck alone."

He gestures to Brandon who's still got his face down. Jersey One is still listening to whoever is on the phone and he's breathing faster now. Another glance up at him and I can see his face is red and his brow is furrowed and he's got the beginnings of a snarl forming over his mouth. I look away quickly and see the cowboy is still unfazed and smiling at Jersey Two. Jersey Two is still glowering at him with an aggravated aura.

I grab my phone to check the time and remember I turned it off. I hold the switch down to turn it on and the Apple symbol appears. Millie leans close.

"We should go," she whispers, glancing sidelong at Jersey One. "This was a mistake. This was *all* a mistake."

My phone comes on and nine new messages start machine-gun vibrating. They're all from Cheryl. Of *course* they are.

I ignore the messages calling me a pig and a terrible husband and see it's almost eight o'clock. I drop the phone as Jersey One says something.

"Listen to me, goddammit, this ain't our mess. You get me? We was sent down here to this god-forsaken hellhole to strike a deal with that redneck son of a bitch, and he ain't interested. When he ain't interested, we create some incentive. He still don't wanna make a deal, so fuck him. Boss says make it happen one way or another, so that's what we're doing. We'll be on our way in a few minutes and this whole thing will get put to bed."

He turns and sees me looking and I jerk my head away so fast bones pop. I can feel him staring for too many seconds, and Millie is looking up at him with wide eyes. I turn back slowly and see his eyes zeroed in on me with the phone placed against his chest.

"Mind ya fuckin' business, you know what's good for ya," he says and I gulp and nod and he puts the phone back to his ear and starts to walk up the aisle.

"Come on," I say and Millie and I slip out of the booth. I dig some money from my pocket and throw it down amongst the mostly untouched food and cooling coffee. I grab the back of her arm and start to move, but Jersey One is blocking us and still not sitting down. *Excuse me* might be customary, but right now I don't want to say anything to this guy. I don't want to be anywhere near him or this place. The Jersey Boys don't belong here, and I've got a really bad feeling and I don't need any of this in my life.

"We'll call when it's done," Jersey One says and hangs up

the phone and slips back into the booth with his companion.

The path is finally clear and we start to move.

"But they're my babies," I hear Brandon mumble, and I think he's crying. I feel for him. He's me in a week and I feel some shame at that, but he's not our problem, and we move past when the cowboy turns his head in the direction of the Jersey Boys.

"Big plans, fella?" he says, and Jerseys One and Two turn to him as Millie tugs on my arm.

I turn to her, still trying to leave, and she says, "I forgot my purse."

I sigh and we move back down the aisle to our abandoned booth and she starts grabbing up her things.

"Fuck off, hillbilly," I hear, and I think it's Jersey One.

"Order up!" someone says behind the counter and there's a clatter of plates.

"You boys ain't too friendly, are ya?" I hear the cowboy say, and I urge Millie to hurry up.

"Goddammit," Jersey Two says, and he turns in the booth, throwing an arm over the back of the seat, "would you just fuck off, already? What, yous hard of hearing? Or are you just too stupid to know when to shut your fucking trap?"

"Okay," Millie says, and I look at her and see she's got her bag and is ready to go.

Good.

I place a hand at the small of her back and start leading her up the aisle. Brandon is openly crying now and the Jersey Boys and the cowboy are in some absurd standoff, the cowboy's teeth still showing bright and large behind his friendly smile, and the guys who shouldn't be here at all are red in the face looking ready to pounce. My phone is vibrating again in my pocket and I can tell by its cadence that it's a phone call this time. My heart is starting to hammer in my chest. I'm an asshole and I shouldn't be here, and I shouldn't be with Millie, and *why am I so nervous?*

"I can hear ya just fine," the cowboy is saying as he scoots to the edge of the booth with some effort. "Ain't stupid, neither."

"Yeah?" Jersey One says. "If you're so smart, then mind your business and piss off."

We're nearly to the back of Brandon's booth and he starts pounding his fist on the table.

"Why, why, why?" he's saying in time with his fist.

"That's just what I'm doing, fellas," the still-smiling cowboy says as his hand comes up from under his table. "Waylon says for you boys to get a message to your boss."

I pull up short when I hear that name again and now it's starting to make sense what these Jersey Boys are doing here and a thousand pieces start falling into place at once, especially when I see the wide, angry eyes in their fat sockets.

"Millie, get down," I gasp, and we both fall to the floor.

"He says to tell your boss to fuck off."

I see the gun in the cowboy's hand, and Brandon is hammering his fist so hard the plates and silverware on his table are bouncing and dancing, and I think my chest is going to explode.

Jersey One has a hand reaching into his jacket when his throat explodes and blood starts spraying all over Jersey Two. He's clawing at himself and gurgling, and Jersey Two is in too much shock to do much of anything but blink.

That stops when the side of his head comes apart in a meaty pulp and he slumps over in the booth. Millie is screaming now and the phone in my pocket is *still* buzzing. Jersey One is slapping at his throat, trying to contain the spurting crimson but failing miserably. The cowboy turns back to him, the small revolver in his hand smoking.

"We got a certain way of doin' business down here," he says to the dying, terrified man, "and we don't need no yankee interference."

The final shot takes the back of Jersey One's head off and a lot of it lands on me. All *over* me. I'm shaking and dripping with another man's blood and brains. I can hear a faint scream from Millie, but my ears are ringing, and Brandon isn't slamming his fist anymore. He's staring at the whole thing in shocked awe.

I turn back and the cowboy is tucking his gun in his waistband as casually as he might put away his wallet. He's also smiling at me.

"Sorry 'bout that, partner," he says and winks at me. "Dirty job, sometimes."

Then he's leaving, and Millie and I are shaking and the other patrons are getting off the floor and the employees are peeking over the counter and from the window to the kitchen. The bell chimes as the cowboy exits, and all I can think is that any hope I had of keeping Cheryl from knowing what I'm doing is gone. I'm going to be interviewed by the cops and TV vans are going to show up and everyone who's ever known me is going to wonder what the hell I was doing at this diner and who the hell this woman with me is.

I look at the dripping cavity at the back of Jersey One's head again and I begin to laugh. I'm an asshole. A *cheating* asshole. But in this moment I realize that I just got everything I wanted and cut through all the bullshit. I don't have to explain things to Cheryl. I don't have to lie and sneak anymore. All of that is over. The cowboy with the big teeth just dashed all the red tape of ending a marriage for me.

I laugh all the harder for a few moments as my bones begin to tremble and Millie's screams get louder. Brandon is joining her now. I settle again on the open wound of Jersey One's skull and feel tears sting my eyes and my howling laughter turns to howls of horror. Then I remember what I'm covered in and look down at myself.

My screams are louder than all the others.

Chris Miller lives in Winnsboro, Texas. He is the author of such novels as Dust, The Hard Goodbye, *and* The Damned Place.

THE SILVER LINING

Andy Rausch

ORLANDO WILLIAMS WALKED into the Sacred Heart Catholic Church with a heavy heart. He was pleased to feel the warmth of the church since it was cold this morning—sixty, which was cold for Los Angeles—but this was not enough to raise his spirits. He looked at the wall to his left, seeing the reflection of his black face in a mirrored crucifix with a small gold Christ hanging in its center. The church had a unique smell—a smell he'd never smelled before; although he couldn't explain why, he believed it the smell of history and tradition.

Orlando looked ahead at the hallway, carpeted with a gaudy lavender carpeting with white spots, and saw three connected mahogany confessionals on the left side, against the wall just ahead of the entrance to the sanctuary. The two farthest booths were roped off, but the first was not. There was a long gold-framed painting above the confessionals depicting Christ in the center, flanked by angels, looking down at what appeared to be a family on their knees praying.

Orlando was not Catholic, so he was unsure exactly how confession worked. He stood there for a moment, studying the ornately decorated wooden booth with its gold-colored trim and purple curtain, trying to decide his next move. He saw no one else in sight, and was unsure whether the booth was manned or if he needed to track down the priest he'd spoken to on the phone.

He stepped slowly toward the booth with his head slightly cocked, listening intently for sounds inside. Hearing nothing, he stepped closer to the curtained door and knocked on the wood beside it.

"Hello?" came a man's voice from inside the priest's side of the confessional.

"Father Giordano?"

"Yes, Mr. Smith," said the priest, addressing him by the fake name he'd given him on the phone. "Please step inside."

Orlando pulled the curtain back and stepped into the booth. The inside was completely bare save for a wooden cross on the wall directly ahead and a hard wooden bench on the left, which faced the priest's side. Orlando sat and pulled the curtain closed. Now he was staring ahead at a wooden lattice, which hid the priest who was sitting on the left, out of sight.

The priest waited for a moment. When Orlando hadn't said the things he was expected to say, Father Giordano finally said, "Are you okay?"

"Yes," Orlando said. "I apologize, Father. As I told you, I've never been to confession before. I've never so much as stepped foot inside a Catholic church before."

There was a pause. "Do you know how to make the sign of the cross?"

"I do."

"Okay, you do that and I'll say the prayer for you."

Orlando made the sign of the cross, touching each of the four points of an imaginary crucifix over his chest with his right hand. As he did this, Father Giordano said, "'In the name of the Father, Son, and Holy Spirit, Amen.'" The priest paused for another moment before saying, "May the Lord help you to confess your sins. Amen."

The priest then said, "Okay, my son, tell me why you've come today."

Orlando sighed. His elbows rested on the tops of his thighs and his palms curled over his knees. He slumped forward, feeling tears welling up in his eyes.

"I'm..." He'd started the sentence but now found himself unable to finish. Father Giordano must have heard the distress in his voice—in that single word—because he said, "What troubles you, my son?"

"Everything," Orlando said. "Everything troubles me."

"The world?"

"Not *the* world, not exactly. *My* world."

"In what way do you find it troubling?"

Orlando made himself sit upright again, exhaling hard as he did. "My little girl...My six-year-old daughter...was...killed..."

The priest moved closer to the lattice so Orlando could see his partial profile.

"Killed?" the priest asked. "Was she murdered?"

"No. It was an accident."

There was a pause before the priest asked, "Was this an accident that you were responsible for?"

"No," Orlando said. "She was hit by a car, out in front of her school."

"I see."

"My wife has fallen apart. She's devastated. I think she's going to leave me. And even if she doesn't...we're through."

"You must work to stay together," Father Giordano advised. "The Lord does not approve of divorce. Marriage is a sacred bond in the eyes of the Lord, and it is an oath that is made to be kept."

Orlando exhaled hard again. "I don't want to get a divorce, Father, but it's not up to me. And my wife...she's not Catholic either."

"Whatever religion she practices, there is no God who approves of divorce."

"She grew up Baptist, but that doesn't matter. She's tired of me. She was tired of me before our daughter's death."

"I'm sorry, but..."

"But what?"

"A man must strive to find the silver lining in the darkness of life, my son. I'm sorry you are having a rough time, but this is not what confession is for. Confession is for you to confess your sins. This isn't counseling."

"I understand that."

"So then, have you sinned?"

Orlando stared at the lattice, where only a portion of the priest's nose was visible. "Doesn't everyone sin?"

There was a brief silence before the priest said, "Yes, most definitely. But is there a particular sin or sins you want to discuss?"

"I'm sorry, Father," Orlando said with tears in his eyes. "I was getting to that. Anyway, my life is in shambles. I feel like Job. I feel like all of this is more than I can bear."

There was a long silence. Orlando expected Father Giordano to speak, but he did not. So Orlando continued. "I don't think I can handle this anymore. I know the Bible says God never gives you more than you can handle, but I don't believe that." He paused, trying to collect himself and rein himself in. He decided to get to the point: "I'm giving serious consideration to suicide."

The priest leaned forward again so Orlando could see the right side of his face. "How often do you consider this?"

"Every day. I go to the cemetery and sit at my daughter's grave and think."

"About suicide?"

"Yes."

"You mustn't commit suicide," Father Giordano said. "Suicide is a mortal sin. It is a sin you cannot be forgiven for. The catechism is very clear about that. In fact, Judas betrayed Jesus and that betrayal led to Jesus's death. I'm sure you are aware of this. But then Judas hung himself. Despite his turning on Jesus, the suicide is considered a far greater sin."

"The world just seems so bleak right now," Orlando said. He took a breath before saying, "I don't know how long confession is supposed to last..."

"Confessions are generally only a few minutes."

Orlando looked at the lattice and pleaded. Orlando Williams was not a man who pleaded. Ever. He wasn't even sure he would plead for his wife to stay when the time came for her to leave, but in this moment he pleaded. "Father, can you just stay and talk to me for a few more minutes. I..."

"What?"

"I need to talk to someone right now," Orlando said. "I feel like this could be the day."

The priest leaned forward again. "The day you cause yourself harm?"

"The day I kill myself," Orlando said flatly.

"I don't have another appointment for a while," Father Giordano said. "I can talk to you, but only for a bit."

Orlando felt more tears spring from his eyes. "Thank you."

The priest said nothing.

"I have something to tell you, Father."

"What is it, my son?"

"I'm a bad man," Orlando said. "I do bad things. Really bad things."

"What sort of bad things?"

"Look Father, this is a different thing from my wanting to kill myself, but it's related. It's part of the reason I'm considering it."

"Alright, I'm listening."

"I do bad things, and I do them for money."

There was a pause. Then the priest said, "What kinds of things?"

Orlando sat there, trying to figure out how he should proceed.

"Are these bad things sexual in nature?" Father Giordano asked.

Despite his tears, Orlando chuckled lightly. "No, no, nothing like that."

"Then what?"

"I hurt people, Father."

"You hurt people for money?"

39

"Yes," Orlando said.

"How do you hurt them?"

Orlando sat in silence again, trying to decide whether or not he should lie. No, he decided, he would tell the truth.

"I murder people for money, Father."

Orlando actually heard the priest gasp. Then there was a long silence.

The priest leaned forward so Orlando could see his entire face peering through the lattice. "Is this real? Are you...are you telling the truth?"

"Yes. I kill people for money."

"An assassin," the priest said in a manner that suggested the words just popped out of his mouth on accident, as a revelation.

"Yes, Father."

"How many men have you killed?"

Orlando cocked his head, his eyes moving upward as he tried to calculate a total. Finally he gave up and said, "I'm not sure."

"You're not sure?" the priest asked incredulously.

"I didn't keep count."

"Okay..." The priest sat there for a moment, trying to process this. "How do you feel about these murders? You said the job contributed to your wanting to kill yourself, so I'm assuming you feel guilt?"

"I do," Orlando said. "But not the way you think."

"What do you mean?"

"I guess you could say I feel guilty for...*not* feeling guilty."

"So," Father Giordano said with bewilderment, "you feel no remorse?"

Orlando felt bad when he heard the judgment in the priest's voice.

"Father, is it possible that God didn't equip me with the proper tools to feel remorse? And if that's the case, then is it my fault?"

"That is not the case, I assure you," Father Giordano snapped. "God gives us all the proper tools to navigate through life and live

40

a godly life. It's up to us to see those tools and acknowledge them as such and use them. If we commit sins, and most assuredly you have, then the fault lies squarely on our shoulders, not His."

Orlando considered this, weighing the priest's words.

"I'd like to ask you something, my son," Father Giordano said. "And I'd like you to carefully consider your answer before speaking."

"Okay."

"Has the thought ever occurred to you that the Lord may have taken your daughter's life as punishment for your life of misdeeds? After all, in the grand scheme of things, one life is fairly insignificant in contrast to the countless lives you claim that you yourself have taken."

Orlando stared at the lattice, the tears coming fast and heavy now. His voice trembled when he said, "I have considered that. Many times. More than you could possibly know. But then I think, what kind of God would take the life of an innocent child because of her father's actions? That...that doesn't seem like a just God to me."

"It may seem that way, but God's ways are not our ways. We are not capable of fully comprehending His plan. We don't always understand what is and is not justice in His eyes."

Orlando wiped his tears away with the sleeve of his jacket.

"Do you believe I can be forgiven for my sins, Father?"

The priest exhaled. "Yes, yes, you can. Even you can be forgiven. Anyone can except for, well, the suicide. But before we discuss that, I must implore you to turn yourself into the authorities at once. Go and tell them what you've done. You'll feel better too. As John 8:32 tells us, 'the truth shall make you free.'"

Orlando stared at the small portion of the priest's face he could see through the lattice. The priest's words made sense, but Orlando knew he would not be turning himself in. Suicide might be an option and quitting his job as a hitter might be an option, but turning himself in and going to prison was not.

"I'm considering quitting my job," Orlando said.

"That…that would be a good thing. But even then, I think you should turn yourself in at once."

"I'm not entirely sure I'm going to quit, but even if I do, I have one last job to carry out."

"Murder is a sin, my son," Father Giordano said. "You must reconsider. I know you have taken many lives, but although you cannot take those sins back nor return those lives, you have the chance to save a life here."

Orlando thought of something. "A moment ago you said that one life is fairly insignificant—those were your words, 'fairly insignificant'—in contrast to all the lives I've taken. What good would saving this one man do?"

"Think of this man's family," the priest said. "Think of your own soul. Do this man a favor…do *yourself* a favor, and spare his life. Spare his life and go to the authorities at once and confess your crimes."

"I have to do this one last hit no matter what."

"Why? What compels you to do more killing?"

"I believe God would approve of this one," Orlando said.

The priest leaned forward again, making himself visible through the lattice. "I assure you He would not. God does not approve of *any* killing."

Orlando thought about this. He considered reminding Father Giordano of all the people the Catholics murdered in God's name during the Crusades. He thought about pointing out all the killing the Bible. The number of people, including innocent babies, God supposedly killed in the great flood. But he didn't. Instead he said, "This man is a bigger sinner than I, Father. He hurts people."

"You shouldn't compare one man's sin to another. Either way, it's not up to you to punish this man. It's God's place, not yours."

"Except it's my job," Orlando said. "I'm pretty sure my boss would have a shit fit if I didn't follow through."

"So what?" asked the priest. "Who would you rather have angry at you, your boss or the Lord?"

Orlando chuckled. "You don't know my boss."

Orlando heard the priest suck his teeth.

"My boss really wants this man dead," Orlando explained. "He and his family trusted this man, but he took advantage of his nephew and made him do terrible things."

"Your boss makes you do terrible things. How is that any different?

"Oh, it's definitely different. My boss pays me to do the things I do, and like you said, I'm responsible for my own actions. And I'm a grown man. My boss's nephew is nine years old."

"Oh my," the priest said.

"Their family trusted this man," Orlando said. "You're not gonna believe what this scumbag does for a living."

"What's that?"

"He's a priest," Orlando said. "Can you imagine that?"

Father Giordano leaned forward to take a good look at Orlando. When he did, he found himself face to face with the silencer on Orlando's .45. His eyes got big and he said, "God no!" These would be his final words.

"This is for Dominic Vitelli," Orlando said as he squeezed the trigger. He then opened the curtain and stepped out of the confessional, walking around to put a second bullet into the priest's head. Orlando then returned to the other side of the confessional to wipe everything down with a handkerchief. When he was finished, he stepped back out onto the tile. He looked both ways but saw no one. He buttoned his suit jacket and strode toward the exit, his Bruno Maglis clicking with each step.

As he stepped out into the cool November wind, Orlando reflected on the conversation he'd had with the priest. He wasn't sure he'd gotten all that much out of the exchange, and he knew damn well he wasn't going to turn himself in to the police. As he walked down the sidewalk to where he'd parked his Escalade, he thought of his little girl, Keisha, again. He pictured her swinging in his mind's eye. He felt a sickening pain in his heart and a churning in his stomach. He wondered if he would ever be able to remember her without hurting. He doubted it.

He thought about the two slugs he'd put in the priest's head and felt a little better. The cloud of depression would not be lifting anytime soon, but at least he could feel good about a job well done.

Father Giordano had been correct when he'd said a man had to strive to find the silver lining in all the darkness. Orlando's life was incredibly dark these days, but he'd found a silver lining in Father Giordano's execution.

He unlocked the Escalade, climbed in, started it, and headed for the cemetery to pay his daily respects.

Andy Rausch is the author of more than forty books, including the hitman novels The Suicide Game, Layla's Score, *and* Let It Kill You.

THE BODY COUNT

Tom Leins

I'VE ALWAYS HATED the word hitman. Too gauche. Assassin. Too extravagant. Hired gun. Too out-dated. Dreary clichés in search of coherent job descriptions. In my world, the day you willingly describe yourself as a hitman is the day you kneel in the weeds and wait for the pop of a silencer behind your right ear. Never draw attention to yourself. Never stand out. Self-aggrandizement is your enemy. Anonymity is your friend.

If pushed, I would describe myself as a contract killer. The term is dry and methodical—much like myself.

While there is no industry regulator comparing the quality of service offered by myself and my rivals, market forces provide a clear indicator of our respective statuses. By my reckoning, I'm currently the third most sought-after contract killer in Exodus, Florida. And when you're the third best contract killer in Exodus, Florida, you have two options for self-improvement—each of which involves a headshot.

BARRY UDALL WAS a gaunt, distrustful man. The best hit-men are—distrustful, not gaunt, that is. Gaunt is no good. Gaunt is rotten in this line of work. Too healthy, you stick out. Too unhealthy, you stick out. Barry Udall was far too creepy for close-quarters work. A guy like that, he would never get close enough for blade work, close enough to use a sidearm.

Even the most inexperienced target would immediately recoil at the skeletal figure in the off-white shirt, his lazy eye drooping, his oversized forehead bulging in concentration. In a way I felt sorry for the guy. Here was a man who would never reach the same dizzy heights as me, and I've barely got started. I'm forty. I'm in my prime.

9 a.m.

I ALWAYS SAVE my first-generation Walther WA 2000 for special occasions like today. Only 176 were ever manufactured due to the high production cost. It's a semi-automatic bullpup sniper rifle. Wooden frame and stock. Quick-detachable scope mount. Long-range accuracy. The model in my hands—more alluring than any lover—has a resale value of fifty thousand dollars. Of course, you can acquire illegal, two-handed, high-damage weaponry almost anywhere these days, and the model has been relegated to a curio. Personally, I would never dream of paying that much money for a firearm. The previous owner was a client. Paid for a hit on a political rival. He was a freak. A ghoul. A tourist. A goddamn collector. He had no business owning a gun as beautiful as this and I was forced to liberate it from his possession.

Half-empty parking lots are a particular preference of mine. I deal in contracted casualties, not bloodbaths, so wide-open spaces work well. Barry Udall is outside the Active Shooter Rifle Range fiddling with the lockbox in his trunk when I decorate the interior of the SUV with his grey matter—raising myself up the list in the process. Number two—with a bullet.

I MAKE MY way down the wrought-iron fire escape and drop to the asphalt—finding myself within spitting distance of Udall's cooling corpse. The overwhelming smell of shit and blood means that I have no need to verify his status. He's deader than disco, and I'm now the second most sought after contract killer in Exodus. I head to my car—just another office drone in his cornflower blue Oxford and chinos—on his way to work. Inconspicuous to a tee.

I find Dominic Danilo leaning on the hood of my butter yellow 1974 Impala Sport Sedan. The most sought after contract killer in Exodus.

"The old man wants a word."

"Which old man?"

He shakes his head. "My fucking uncle, dickwad."

I'm not a people person. My sole interaction with most people is shooting them in the head from long range. I have no interest in meeting with a snake like Desmond Danilo—no matter how lucrative the prospective payday.

Dominic is dressed like a rent boy, but I suppose that is the fashion nowadays. Skin-tight jeans and a scoop-neck T-shirt. You go into a meeting with the Bartorelli Family or the Swamp Town Reapers dressed like that you'd have your neck slashed over a stainless-steel trough and your vital organs nailed to your parents' front door.

He removes a lump of gum from his mouth and sticks it to the hood of my Impala. That'll leave a mark. He raises himself to his full height. At six-two he has a good four inches on me.

"I said to him: Uncle—forget this chomo-looking punk. Whatever you need doing, I'll take care of it. I'm a motherfuckin' hitman, y'all!"

I drop the kit bag holding my gun on the concrete—hating myself for tossing such a glorious weapon aside like a side-street hooker, and turn to face Danilo. I'm confident I won't need a gun to finish this guy.

"But you know how my uncle's generation likes to do things. They like to put some distance between them and their targets. Plausible deniability, or some such bullshit."

He stretches his arms in a way that shows off his musculature. He's gym toned and doesn't have a fighter's muscles. I edge closer, looking him in his bloodshot eyes as I drift across the parking lot.

He removes a Glock from the back of his jeans—no holster—and holds it sideways as he aims it at me, making sure to take in his own reflection in the window of my Impala.

While he's admiring the view, I step in and rip my switchblade across his stomach, leaving it there until I feel the hot collapse of his guts on my wrist as his insides unspool. The Glock clatters against the asphalt, and I take a step back.

Within seconds, a Crown Vic eases alongside me, windows down, and I feel a shotgun barrel press against my kidneys.

"Drop the knife."

A grating Florida accent.

I wait a beat and then toss the blade—kicking it across the lot.

"Now, turn around slowly. Try to shoot me or stab me, and I'll fucking destroy you."

I turn slowly and face the driver. He has oversized sunglasses and a crewcut. A thick pink scar that runs from his left eyebrow to the corner of his lip seems to twitch involuntarily. His enormous arms are thickly corded with veins. In his black leather gloves, he holds a combat shotgun.

"You come hard, or you come easy, tough guy. Either way you come."

I nod and hold out my wrists, expecting cable ties.

What I get are military-grade handcuffs.

"Now throw the Walther in the trunk. You don't want to leave a piece like that outside a place like this."

I crouch down and retrieve the gun, circling round to the back of the car.

"How do you know the make of my gun?"

He chuckles darkly. "Pal, you're gonna realize that there's very little that myself and my employer don't know about you. Now hop in. In case the penny hasn't dropped yet, you really don't wanna keep Mr. Danilo waiting."

11 a.m.

DESMOND DANILO FLASHES me a bullshit grin and places a squat glass in front of me. He dumps in some ice and tops it off with cheap vodka. Grins even harder when I notice the obscure label.

"Thank you, but I don't drink."

He grunts and pours the unwanted drink into his own too-full glass. Clear liquid splashes across his oak desk.

He raises his glass to his lips with trembling, liver-spotted hands and gulps an inch off the top.

"To the dearly departed."

Desmond Danilo, it has to be said, is not a picture of health. His skin hangs off his bones like an old suit that no longer fits. He pauses for a rattling coughing fit and then sips at his vodka. Today's going to be a long day.

The house is a gaudy Miami Beach McMansion that's been transplanted into the middle of some blasted swamp or other. When the hired hand bundled me into his study, Danilo's teenage companion melted into the background. Her skin was smooth and unblemished, like a department store mannequin. No fear in her eyes, but no obvious signs of pleasure either.

Danilo offers me a sour smile and clasps his tumbler in snake-veined hands.

"Son, when you're in my line of work, it's important to maintain a front row view of hell. It allows me to keep tabs on this town's malcontents."

I nod.

"Frankly, I like my killers to look like killers. Court-martialed military personnel with hate in their eyes. Ex-con bikers with raging drug habits. Bareknuckle fighters one broken bone away from their last ambulance ride. Hell, I once hired a damned pro wrestler. Killer McHann. You ever heard of him?"

I shake my head.

"Me neither, but he did a good fucking job. I look at you, and I think to myself: what the fuck is this pen pusher gonna do to impress me?"

I briefly consider removing the fountain pen from his desk and jamming it in one of his glaucoma-stricken eyeballs, but his glasses are too thick.

"I'm a very capable man, Mr. Danilo. I'll make this right. Your nephew, he was a fine young man and he didn't deserve to die facedown in a parking lot, like a dog."

Danilo burps gently and smiles. "Son, my nephew was a piece of shit. His father—my brother—was a piece of shit. He still is for all I know. Let me be clear: I do not blame you for ending his life, but I do need you to work for me. Not forever, just for the duration of the assignment."

I say nothing.

"As I'm sure you are aware, large portions of this fine state are rural and agricultural in nature—ideal sites for the production of methamphetamine and the cultivation of cannabis. Florida has fourteen major deep-water ports on the Gulf and Atlantic coasts. It ranks second among the US states for having the longest shoreline and third in terms of square miles of inland water..."

"This is starting to sound like a pitch," I joke.

He takes a breath and plows ahead—sounding like he's reading from a brochure.

"...In addition, Florida has over seven hundred private airports, airstrips, heliports, and seaplane bases, alongside hundreds of small, unregulated airstrips on ranches. There are more drugs in this state than in any other state in the southern United States. I've always hated the phrase 'drug dealer.' Far too gauche for my liking, but a drug dealer is exactly what I am. Competition in my industry is savage. I want you to kill three...individuals for me."

I nod, feeling more comfortable. "Sure thing, Mr. Danilo. Let me know the timeline and the targets and I'll set things in motion. Do you have a window of opportunity that you'd like me to exploit?"

He turns to the muscleman, still chuckling. "Window of opportunity? Where'd you find this guy, Cleland?"

The bodyguard, Cleland, shrugs.

"Your window of opportunity just creaked open, young man."

"Sorry, Mr. Danilo. I don't follow."

"All three kills must happen today, son."

I scratch my temple. "Sir, with all due respect, people hire me for my methodical planning—not for my impetuousness."

He removes his chunky glasses and massages the bridge of his nose. "I ain't hiring you, son. I'm instructing you. This stopped being a conventional drug dealer-hitman interaction the moment you gutted a family member of mine in broad daylight."

He turns to Cleland. "Bring him in."

He turns back to me. "Are you sure I can't tempt you with that drink?"

I shake my head.

Cleland returns moments later, pushing a hospital gurney.

"We all get it, Mr. Jackman. We all fooled around with our cousins back in the day. Mr. Cleland here told me that he fingered his cousin, Sandrine, in the shallows below Testament Falls three times one summer. He was ten at the time."

Cleland smiles sheepishly, ripping the white sheet of the gurney with an ill-judged theatrical flourish.

My cousin, Jamie, lies flat on his back like an unconscious angel.

Danilo continues: "Where I come from, back in the old country, boys should never do the things that you two boys do to one another."

I feel my cheeks color with shame, even though I have no

reason to feel ashamed. What consenting adults do to one another behind a locked door is their business. And anyway, Jamie is a third cousin twice removed. We're barely related.

"If you fail to complete your assignment, I won't harm you. Instead, I will inflict your punishment on your cousin. Don't worry. He's heavily sedated, so he won't feel a thing—until he wakes up. And I'll make sure he wakes up."

I glance across at Jamie and exhale. "What exactly is my assignment?"

"Skull. Fists. Feet. I'll leave the precise running order up to you."

I remove my glasses and wipe them on my slacks. "Excuse me?"

"Three kills. One with your skull. One with your fists. One with your feet."

"You've got to be fucking joking."

"I've never been more serious in my life."

"What are you, some kind of sadist?"

He beams at me. "Yes, Mr. Jackman. That's exactly what I am."

1 p.m.

"VICTIM NUMBER ONE."

Cleland reverses his Crown Vic into one of the empty management parking spots next the Tenderloin Bar & Grill. It's a gloomy, low-ceilinged building that used to be a fried chicken joint, Mothercluckers. Unsurprisingly, it wasn't in business for long, but it was my late father's final workplace. He rose to the rank of assistant manager, and they made him wear an embossed badge that read "ASS. MAN. Here to help" while he scrubbed the bathrooms, unclogged the deep-fat fryer, and stomped the dumpster rats with his taped-together slip-on shoes.

Now it's a drag king club half a kilometer outside of Exodus. Cleland—who is well-briefed if nothing else—tells me that it's owned and operated by Tonya "Tendril" Tucker, the first woman in Florida to pass Ranger School. Five years ago, she paid good money for a black-market sex-change operation that left her with nothing more than an empty bank balance and a fleshy tendril between her legs. Desperate to get out of debt, she now forms part of a statewide heroin distribution network controlled by the Swamp Town Reapers. The Reapers are outcasts from other gangs who have washed up in Florida. A posse of violently unhinged career criminals who retain little or no affiliation to national street gangs.

I unbuckle my seatbelt. "Will they let us in?"

Cleland shrugs and gestures to the gun across his lap. "You know what this is?"

I nod. "Franchi SPAS-12 combat shotgun. Illegal in the United States since 1994."

"Then you know what it can do to you?"

I nod again. It can rupture my world.

He slides the weapon into a kit bag and zips it shut.

"Do as you're instructed and you'll remain intact."

We each pay the cover charge and stride into the building.

It's not even lunchtime, and the venue is deserted. As Cleland briefed me, Tendril Tucker is sitting next to the bar on a customized throne nursing a Michelob.

The girl on Tendril's lap is naked apart from her earrings. The boss probes the girl lazily, with fingers and thumbs, barely acknowledging Cleland or myself.

Cleland signals to the meaty Latino bartender with the pencil mustache and strapped down breasts.

"Drink?"

I shake my head. "I don't drink."

"Sorry, it slipped my mind."

He shrugs and hands over a crisp twenty-dollar bill, turning to face me, heaving his kit bag onto the polished bartop.

"Well, what are you waiting for?"

I stare at him.

Am I really going to do this?

Sensing trouble, Tendril bounces off her throne, tossing the naked girl aside like a rag doll.

I know I have a reputation as a triggerman, but I *can* fight. I just choose not to. Most of the time.

I feint with my right, and bloody Tendril's nose with a left hook, splattering her pearl-buttoned cowboy shirt.

The naked girl is shrieking behind me—a shrill noise like fake nails down a blackboard. I slam my right elbow into her face as I line up another punch.

This one knocks Tendril off her feet. She's a thick-necked boozer. Fifteen years older than me. Sluggish. Ill-prepared. She tries to reach for the knife handle protruding from her boot sheath, but I slam a heel into her knee and put her back on the dancefloor.

Behind us, the bartender emerges from behind the chrome counter with a cut-down baseball bat. She swings at Cleland, putting some heft into it and he catches the bat in his gloved fist—twisting it out of her hands effortlessly, and slamming the bat through her teeth.

I keep Tendril down with a flurry of punches, as she gasps for breath through her mangled nose.

This feels horrible. Grubby and pointless. Then I think of Jamie on the gurney—and what Danilo might do to him.

I aim a headbutt at Tendril's already-ruined nose and it lands with a vicious crack. It sounds like she's gargling blood.

Behind me, I hear Cleland take out both security cameras with his SPAS-12.

I try to shatter her skull with another headbutt, but we're both slick with viscera, and my head skids off hers.

I glance over my shoulder at Cleland. He looks blank. Serene.

I start punching and don't stop until I have brain matter on my fists.

I slump to my knees on the empty dancefloor.

Cleland hauls me to my feet, thrusting a sodden bar towel into my hands.

"Interesting choice."

"Huh?"

"Your fists. Most men in your position would save their fists for the endgame, rather than…frittering them away so soon."

I wipe the worst of the blood off my face and climb into the passenger seat of his Crown Vic.

"Don't worry, Cleland. I'm not most men."

His thick scar wrinkles in amusement, but he says nothing, just slips the car into drive and leaves the scene of the crime.

3 p.m.

THE SUN LOOKS like a hot blur on the horizon. Warped trees sag in the midday heat.

"You know him?"

I nod. The man in the mugshot is known as Daddy Badwater.

"Then you know he's a fucking animal."

Daddy Badwater's reputation precedes him. I've heard that he's a major meth chef who operates out of a trashed trailer lab in the badlands. I've also heard that he runs a small crew of stick-up men who hold up four or five places a night.

His family owns nine acres of swampland—won in a bet more than a hundred years ago—outside of Dogtown. About a mile south of the Florida-Georgia state line, deep in hymn country, it used to be home to a carnival. Long before I was born, Badwater's father, a paranoid schizophrenic, built an ark using pilfered carnival money—right in the middle of the swamp. He died hammering in the final nail seven years later. The rotted ark sits behind us, shielding us from the brutal August sun. The whole area is scattered with ruined and rusted carnival rides, all decrepit with disuse.

My father once brought me to the carnival here as a child. He was a weak man—shaky hands and an unquenchable thirst—but he tried to connect with me, in his own hopeless way. He left me outside in the weeds while he screwed a carnival hooker in a warped-looking single-wide.

"A body built for loving—a face only a mother could love," he said with a wink, as he rejoined me afterwards. There was no money left for me to go on any of the attractions. That evening put me off booze and women for life.

We follow a well-trodden path toward the ark. All I can smell are the dirt and rotted vegetation. We climb a rickety ladder that takes us onto what's left of the boat. On the top deck, Daddy Badwater lounges in a wheelchair—a stooped, ungainly specimen. He's so laconic he resembles a stroke patient. He spits a wad of chewing tobacco out of the side of his mouth, but it lands on the thigh of his cut-off denims.

I turn to Cleland. "I'm not killing a man in a fucking wheelchair!"

He sighs and removes an old iPhone from his pocket and swipes it open, opening an encrypted app.

Onscreen, Danilo stands hands-on-hips, facing the camera. He changed since we met earlier. Now he's wearing a peach pullover knotted around shoulders over a lime green golf shirt.

"Mr. Cleland, do we have a problem?"

Despite the rural location, the audio is crystal clear.

"Yes, sir. It appears so. Our friend Mr. Jackman is reluctant to murder the cripple."

Danilo swivels the handset towards Jamie. "Use your goddamn hands, Mr. Jackman. Some people no longer have that luxury."

Then he goes to work on Jamie's fingers with a lump hammer.

I stride toward Badwater across the rotten planks.

The old man spits a phlegmy wad of tobacco at me as I upend his wheelchair.

He writhes on his back, like a fish on concrete, withdrawing a small pearl-handled revolver from the pile of rancid blankets covering his lap.

I stomp his wrists until the gun falls free, following through until my footwear makes contact with his ribs, his hip bone, his wet entrails.

Cleland scoops up the revolver and climbs back down the ladder, shaking his head. He has seen enough.

I finish the old man off with a savage foot to the face—almost snapping his jaw off.

5 p.m.

"I NEED A piss."

Cleland sighs. "Then take a piss, motherfucker."

"You've been up my ass like a tapeworm all day, but you're gonna let me get out of the car and take a piss?"

He chuckles nastily and dumps his gas station coffee out the window, holding the empty container next to my crotch.

"Rock out with your cock out."

"Seriously?"

He nods and I remove my dick, placing it in the cup. I'm halfway done when he crunches the cup around my penis. Piss bubbles over my chinos—and all over his black leather gloves.

He laughs humourlessly and removes the gloves, tossing them on the back seat. I notice that he has big, calloused hands like a carny, but the nail on his pinky finger has been painted with a skull.

He shrugs. "My girlfriend. She's Vietnamese. Works in a nail bar. That nail bar."

I recognize the strip mall straight away. The place on the end used to be an Irish bar: Mulligans. I went there with my father on my twenty-first birthday, for my first legal beer. Halfway through his second drink he offered me the chance to snort badly cut cocaine off the palm of his hand in the disabled bathroom. I never saw him again—not alive at any rate.

Cleland passes me another photograph. A sixty-year-old man with aviators and thick, windswept hair.

"Do you know how dirty you need to be to get kicked out of the CIA? Man, this guy was dirtier than J. Edgar Hoover's Friday night panties!"

I clear my throat. "Wrong agency."

"Huh?"

"Hoover was a fed. FBI. Everyone knows that."

Cleland grunts and lowers his own sunglasses, to hide his embarrassment.

He crams the photo back in the glove box.

"James Queenan Jr. Rogue ex-CIA agent. Ended his career operating a black ops training camp in the Everglades. He now works with FARC—the Colombian guerilla movement—and a number of disgraced Venezuelan military figures. They're on a DoJ watchlist, accused of flooding Florida with cocaine."

Cleland gestures across the strip mall parking lot. Queenan looks different than he does in the picture. Older. Less self-assured. A tall man with a prominent gut. His white tennis shorts are so tight you can see his whole dick. A dumpy-looking ten-year-old girl stands next to him, fidgeting in a garish designer dress.

"His daughter by his third wife. I forget her name. They're here for the pre-teen beauty pageant. It starts in fifteen minutes."

"Jesus, Cleland! This is obscene! I'm not killing him in front of his daughter!"

He waves the smartphone at me, saying nothing.

"Fine."

I slide out of the car. My clothing is encrusted with blood. I look grotesque.

"Headbutt, motherfucker. Remember the fucking headbutt!" Cleland yells.

As I round the corner, I see a crowd of at least forty people—anxious parents and queasily made-up little girls. A low murmur of disapproval ripples through the crowd as I approach.

I tap Queenan on the shoulder and he swivels on his heel, ready to shake my hand. When he sees my bloodied clothing, his right hand curls into a fist and he pushes his daughter away with his left.

"Scram, punk, or I'll give you a hiding!"

His voice is strong, but his watery eyes betray him.

The children are screaming now as the adults fumble for their cellphones.

I step toward Queenan, pulverizing his nose with a headbutt, and he drops to his knees.

"Goddamn you!"

He bangs on the door of the minivan next to him with the flat of his hand. The back door clicks open and a pale, gelatinous monster of a man oozes out onto the road. The guy is albino, dressed in a baggy white T-shirt and soiled-looking track pants.

"Globule, deal with this punk!" Queenan barks.

Globule?

Across the parking lot, I hear guttural laughter. Cleland.

Globule circles me, his enormous body undulating as he moves. He looks dead behind the eyes. The lobotomized look of a man who has witnessed true horror in his life.

Globule grabs hold of me and starts squeezing the life out of me. I hear blood pounding in my skull and hysterical children screaming. I try to prise the beast off me with my hands, but he starts biting at my fingers with rotten, broken teeth. I feel a couple of ribs crack and my limbs start to go slack. Then Cleland evens the odds with his SPAS-12—obliterating Globule's cerebral cortex and splattering me with gore. I slump against the minivan. Somewhere in the distance, sirens stain the air.

Queenan looks sunken, shrunken in front of me. I crawl toward him—ready to end this, when Cleland shoots him in the face.

I turn to face him, still on my hands and knees.

"What the fuck did you do that for?!"

He shakes his head sadly. "Believe it or not, pal, I used to have Globule's job. Queenan dragged me out of some fucking hellhole in Suriname in the '90s and put me to work for him. He found this poor bastard in Guyana. They were conducting medical experiments on him. Come on—let's roll."

"But..."

"But nothing. Danilo's stupid fucking game is over."

He starts walking back to the car.

Then I realize that Queenan has a small throwdown piece in an ankle holster tucked inside his tennis sock.

I remove the gun and start to follow Cleland. Before he can climb into the car, I put two bullets in his lower back. He pirouettes clumsily and I put another one in his gut.

"Don't do this, pal. It wasn't personal—just business."

Blood bubbles out of his gaping mouth.

I remove the iPhone from his trouser pocket and swipe it open, aiming the camera at the reddening hole in Cleland's gut.

Danilo's cadaverous face appears onscreen.

"You'll regret this, son."

He swivels the camera to reveal Jamie's prone form on the gurney.

I can hear him wheezing as he checks his gun. I know what's coming, but I can't look away.

He presses the pistol against Jamie's temple and squeezes the trigger—coating the lens in viscera.

"Not as much as you will, old man."

7 p.m.

THE CROWN VIC grinds to a halt on the gravel driveway of Danilo's McMansion. I slide out of the car and open the back door. Cleland is writhing on the pleather seats in a pool of pain. I drag him out by his collar and dump him on the gravel. Violence and chaos—the only language some people truly understand.

"Can you walk?"

His grey eyes gleam accusingly, but he nods.

"Then fucking walk."

I retrieve his SPAS-12 from the trunk.

"Try to fuck me and I will end you, Cleland."

He shuffles forward, disconsolately, his boots scuffing against the gravel, trying to hold his ruptured guts in with both hands. The man looks half dead.

I keep the combat shotgun aimed at his spinal column.

We pass an elaborate water feature in which two fat cherubs appear to be spitting water into one another's mouths.

"You have a key?"

He shakes his head.

"Fucking knock then."

He raises his right fist to knock and a fat splat of viscera slips out of his midriff and lands on the doorstep between his feet.

He knocks, weakly.

"Knock fucking harder."

My words come out in a ragged hiss.

Cleland knocks again and steps back, clutching his bloody, pulsing stomach.

Within seconds, the door erupts—the fish-eye peephole lens exploding, as a high caliber round enters Cleland's skull. He flails backwards, closely followed by a trail of fine red mist, before landing at my feet.

I center the shotgun on the door and squeeze the trigger twice.

The door slowly creaks open.

Danilo sways slightly, an oversized ballistics vest baggy over his lime green golf shirt, and staggers down the steps—nearly tripping over Cleland's corpse.

His thick glasses are cobwebbed. Blood trickles from his right ear. His Desert Eagle points at the floor. He raises the weapon, weakly.

"You'll regret this, son."

I raise the SPAS-12, aiming it at his rotten elderly skull.
"I already do."

Tom Leins is a crime writer from Paignton, UK. His books include Boneyard Dogs, Ten Pints of Blood, Meat Bubbles & Other Stories, Repetition Kills You *and* The Good Book: Fairy Tales for Hard Men.

NOTHING MORE THAN DEATH

Rob Pierce

"FUCK." SKAL SAID it to himself, he didn't have many friends. He'd just gotten his latest assignment. Strictly verbal, of course. He wasn't a guy who needed a photo or an address, not in writing anyway. He killed a lot of people he knew. And this one wouldn't be pleasant. He hated killing people he liked.

He wanted a drink. He went to Reed's. Decent place, good scotch, good bourbon, good beer. He wasn't John Lee Hooker, didn't drink them all at once, but it was nice to have options.

"Jay." The bartender ambled over, a high school linebacker who broke a knee and blew a handful of scholarship offers. Never recovered all the way. Good bartender, though; a soft word or two shut up the riff raff.

It was a scotch night. Skal ordered a double Glenlivet with a beer back. He could've said no to the job over the phone and walked away. Not once he met the guy making the offer. Paid half in front, too. And hell, this was how he made a buck.

He drank half the scotch, switched to the beer, finished the scotch and ordered another. A scotch night. Two days to pull the job. What happened if it took three, he didn't know. Didn't matter, it'd be done in two.

Farrar knew him a little, but it wasn't a business where you exchanged details. Guys who talked got killed. Farrar was a guy he'd run into at Reed's more than once. Maybe they'd met here, he didn't remember. When you meet a guy, unless something

63

big happens it's incidental.

Why he liked Farrar was the question. Mainly attitude, he supposed. Couldn't imagine what the guy had done, didn't have to either. Took too much off a score, got caught and ratted—all the same to him.

He didn't have Farrar's number, wasn't like they were phone buddies. He expected to find him tomorrow, though. Just check the regular places, the places a man goes when he doesn't work: bars, the track, illegal casinos, like that. Taco trucks, but almost as many of them as bars in this town.

He finished his second round and got the fuck out. Made no sense to wait in a place Farrar actually went. Better off buying a bottle and taking it home.

He got to the house. It was evening, not yet dark. He admired the birds flitting about the trees. Didn't know what they were, only small, nature's creatures. They would all die, and he didn't know how long they'd live before that, knew nothing about the lives of birds. Figured it was damn unlikely any of them would get shot to death. Not as likely as any human would, not in this country. He held his pistol loose, put it away fast.

He liked the feel of a .38, this one in particular. Damn reliable, but each time he bought another to replace the one he'd thrown away he had to test it, get comfortable with it. Make it the weapon he'd never toss, until he tossed it. Once you've killed a man, no sentimentality.

He opened the bottle on the porch, drank, and watched the birds while he got out his keys, unlocked the door and stepped inside. He stepped into the kitchen, took another slug direct from the bottle, set it down. Into the dining room, hung his jacket on a chair. The .38 was on a shoulder holster; he set the weapon on the dining room table then took off the holster. Back to the kitchen, poured a tall glass of scotch, carried it into the bedroom. Where he kicked off his shoes then peeled off his socks and dropped them in the hamper. Same with his shirt. Stayed bare chested and barefoot, returned to the dining room, and set the glass on the table next to his .38.

He sat, drank with his right hand, rubbed the .38 with his left. Thought about where he'd find Farrar, how. Grinned at the thought of killing the bastard, his occasional acquaintance. Nothing more than death when you thought about it. The final gift, and he was the man who would deliver it.

He got up, opened a drawer, and grabbed a burner phone. Small drawer filled with 'em. He made a few calls, got Farrar's favorite lunch spots, bars, and how he filled his time. He hung onto the phone for now. Wouldn't make it through the job; wouldn't last as long as the .38. No longer, anyway.

Done with tonight's research, he settled back to drink, took the pistol and the bottle to the living room, and turned on the TV. He'd get laid after the job was done. Would keep the pistol on him in the meantime.

SKAL GOT UP late enough his head felt fine. Farrar wasn't a morning person either, so he hadn't missed anything. None of his calls last night told him where the guy lived or a favorite breakfast place or even if he ate before lunch. He showered, ate a mountain of eggs, and drank coffee and more coffee, got in his car and parked near one of Farrar's lunch spots. Didn't see him or his car by one thirty, moved on. Now he rolled by places, looked for the car. Didn't see it outside the Chinese joint, the Mexican either. Or the burger place, the deli, the Thai place, or the Vietnamese. It was starting to look like Farrar ate lunch at home today.

He checked bookie joints, parks, districts near his favorite theatres. Hit restaurants again come dinner time. Shit, maybe the guy blew town. Or he went other places. He pulled the burner, made more calls, got an interesting answer he hadn't heard the night before. Drove in the direction of Fruitvale to look for whores. And saw the car.

He pulled over, saw it park near one of Farrar's preferred

restaurants. When Farrar got out he walked in the opposite direction. Farrar, tall, lean, dressed formal but not a suit, no jacket, no tie, just a nice shirt. Real nice, burgundy, navy blue slacks. Stepped into another restaurant. Skal gave it five minutes, crossed the street to the restaurant. No windows where he could look inside. Fine. He returned to his car.

Waited, over an hour. When Farrar came out, he was with a guy. Short, stocky, dressed like he was in a seventies crime flick, flashy shirt and green leather jacket. Skal didn't give a shit who the guy was, what the meet was about. Long as he wasn't the sort of sonuvabitch to come back at him. Skal was the only one who had seen. He followed Farrar home.

Crowded neighborhood. Farrar stepped into an apartment building. Had to be meeting his girl, no way he lived there. Nice building though, so maybe. Too crowded to get a shot off as he entered, Skal parked and waited. The job was mostly boring, waiting for a good shot at the victim. But when it happened that was the rush that made it worthwhile. That and the money. Not executive money, but not bad. And it was only a killing every now and then.

Here, though, Farrar or the girl had stamina. Long as he didn't really care about her, wasn't spending the night. Skal had no desire to stay up all night. He would, but by the time he killed the guy he'd be done for the next day. He knew Farrar well enough to wonder what kind of woman would take him serious. Knew himself well enough to know it was something he shouldn't question. Broads was broads, they used to say, and thank God for that.

It was too good a neighborhood was his problem. Sit in his car the whole time and a cop might tap on his window. After an hour he got out of the car, walked across the street with his thermos. It was empty and he'd prefer it wasn't, but there weren't any open cafés in this neighborhood. And strolling down the sidewalk pretending to sip from a thermos was not as suspicious as sitting in a car for hours on end. Plus standing helped keep him awake. So he stood and he strolled, after a while strolled back, waited for Farrar.

He showed about one. Skal watched him, stood still until he got in the car, walked casually across the street. He knew he'd have had an open shot if he'd fired from his car as soon as Farrar stepped out. Knew also that the neighborhood was too nice, an early morning gunshot would attract attention and he didn't have a hideout in the area. Plus he'd have been one of the only suspects in a car. Not his wish.

Instead he followed Farrar close as he dared, watched him pull into a driveway. The house was too nice to be his unless he was skimming. Figured he was. Again too nice an area for sleeping in a car, and that's what Skal needed. He noted the address and drove home.

NEXT MORNING HE parked across the street from Farrar's place. Not in his own car. His car was blocks away. It was only nine, long before he expected Farrar to get up. He sat there in a business suit, as though waiting to pick up his passenger.

He sat, driver's side window down, .38 under his jacket. He sipped coffee from his thermos, ready to grab the pistol in an instant. Or to pull away casually at any sighting of a cop. He didn't worry about witnesses, ill-trained for spotting details and utterly inept at remembering them. He worried only about cops and whether Farrar might see him. Either would cause him to drive away. In Farrar's case, at regular speed until off the block, then speeding to his own car.

Which, assuming he reached it unseen, he would drive casually home. He hoped that was the worst-case scenario.

It was just past eleven when the house door opened. He reached under his coat, stepped out of the car and a few steps forward, and fired. As he aimed the pistol Farrar reached for his own, but he was a step behind. Skal fired a shot to Farrar's gut, another to his chest as he crumpled, pistol in hand.

Skal returned the .38 to its holster and pulled away. People who looked out may have seen the car, but they hadn't seen the shooter. He drove the stolen car to his own, which sat parked over a gutter vent. He dropped the pistol and his burner into the gutter and drove. There shouldn't be prints on the pistol but even if there were, by the time a few toilets flushed it should wash away to the reservoir, or wherever those underground waters went.

He pulled into his driveway, would wait a few days before he collected the rest of his cash. No one wants to see the shooter too soon after the shooting. Hookers don't mind though. He grabbed another phone, called a number he knew. "Gimme a leggy brunette. Asian. The sooner the better." He gave his address and ended the call, changed into jeans and a T-shirt.

She showed up in a half hour. Black hair, tall. Long, skinny legs. A risk you took ordering Asian girls you couldn't see. Maybe he should have gone for a top of the line escort service, one where you looked up the girls online and chose, but even when he had the money he didn't want to spend it, not that much at one time.

Two hundred bucks sat on the living room table, between two glasses of bourbon.

"The money's yours, plus one of the bourbons."

"Thanks," she said. "My name is Teri." No accent. Wore easy to step out of shoes, loose blouse, and a short skirt.

"Don," he said. He liked a one syllable alias. "Sit, drink."

She sat, crossed her legs. Not a lot of thigh, but he liked what he saw.

"Nice legs."

"Thanks." She put the money in her purse, which was big enough to hold a pistol, and took a drink. More likely a blade in there for self-defense, but it was a thing you noted in his line of work.

He ran a finger down her face. "I wish I could kiss your lips."

"You know you can't, right?"

"I just wish." He dropped his hand to her thigh, held it there a minute. "I just finished a big job. Don't ask what it was. The work was a lot easier than the anticipation."

"You expected problems and you're relieved they didn't occur?"

"You could say that." He rubbed her thigh, bit her neck.

Her hand moved between his legs, rubbed his dick through his pants. The other hand dropped down, unsnapped the button of his jeans. He stood and slipped out of his shoes as she slid his pants down. None of that needless "Oh, baby," cheap hooker talk. Maybe he'd ask for her next time. Teri. He'd find out if he needed to know more—oh Jesus, she held his cock and he went hard and she slid a condom over it with her mouth. He pushed her back on the couch, spilled the contents of her purse. No weapons, she must have been told he could be trusted. Her clothes were already off somehow. And dear God he wanted her.

And he had her, but each time he was ready to burst she'd turn slightly and prolong the action, until at last he couldn't take it anymore and when she turned he turned with her and shoved, took charge like he could have done any time. He came like crazy. She seemed to also, but he assumed it was an act. Didn't care, that was for amateurs.

Thing was, she made him an idiot. He couldn't say what he felt that would make him sound like one. It was just the aftershock of great sex; wanting her to stay forever made no sense. He lay on her a while, sat up, peeled off the condom, and walked away, dropped it in the kitchen wastebasket.

He returned to the couch, still naked. "Stick around." He poured two tall glasses of bourbon, drank and she joined him. "Another hundred," he said, reaching for his wallet and removing the bills. "We go again. After this drink."

She smiled and drank. "Sure." She took the money, gathered everything that had fallen to the floor and added it to her purse.

They fucked again, she drove him crazy again, and he kept his idiocy to himself. He could have a steady whore but not a steady girl. Maybe he'd ask for a blonde next time. Or a Mexican girl.

They both got dressed next to the couch. He sat down and watched her walk to the door.

She turned. "You want me again, just ask for Teri. With an i."

He nodded. "Lock it behind ya, wouldja?"

She stepped out. He heard the doorknob turn, couldn't tell if it locked. He walked over. Yeah, she'd locked it.

Now he just had to worry about the guy Farrar met at that restaurant. He was the loose end, only Skal had no idea who he was. Job was over, he killed who he was paid to. Fine, except the reason for the job. He didn't know and had to find out. Short stocky guy in a seventies jacket and shirt. A shame so many guys loved that era.

Inside, got on the phone. Finding out all he could about Farrar. Something had to be the reason. He also asked about the short stocky guy Farrar seemed to know. One of the last people to see him alive. Little by little, it came out.

Short and stocky was a made guy. Pulled a lot of jobs, sanctioned and otherwise. Name was Caruso. The sanction Farrar could never get, no matter who he robbed. Didn't matter far as this went, the two got together. Got together tight was the rumor.

Him and Caruso hit a protected place and word got out. He didn't know who got the Caruso hit, but he wished the guy would speed the fuck up. Fuck professional courtesy, if he killed someone who someone else got paid for, he'd have to kill a killer then find out who hired him to collect. Sounded like putting his life on the line for a goddamn freebie.

Plus there was Caruso to deal with. Little fucking wop. His main concern, a short guy who stood out. Skal didn't want to get caught in the crossfire if someone came for him, mainly didn't want to deal with the motherfucker tracking him down.

Back on the phone, found Caruso worked out of a meat packing joint, Jack London Square. Finding when he'd be there would take longer. Depending on time of day, parking was either wide open or impossible. He didn't care much about parking. He'd triple park if necessary, walk in, kill the guy, walk out, and drive away.

His question, was Caruso looking for him, went unanswered everywhere he asked. Caruso's closest aides weren't worth asking, they wouldn't talk. The only people who talked at all told him he was lucky to know what he had been told; people didn't talk about Caruso.

But they'd given up his name. No one would give up Skal's. Damn few knew it. It meant Caruso wasn't a hitman, that was all, and he was. Those who knew his name were among those who hired or didn't know him as a hitman. Life was simpler that way. Not exactly a double life, just a life where he walked as one man and worked as another. The man who walked also drank and fucked, his source of income unknown. Also, unquestioned: he was clearly connected.

Caruso would never find him by his name. He would have to know his face. And he hadn't been seen that night, he knew that much. Farrar was dead, and in a couple of days he would pick up the rest of the payment for that. In the meantime, he would worry about Caruso. Over the course of his lifetime, that worry would gradually fade, be supplanted by worries about other potential witnesses. His life was not worry free, would never be. That was the extent of freedom he had bargained for with this job. He could live carefree as he pleased. He could never trust anyone.

There were times he couldn't tell how much more freedom he could take. Fear was nothing though. Nothing but proof he remained alive. Really, it was nothing at all. Nothing. Life was nothing. At times he removed it. For money. He sat in his living room with his bourbon and a glass and thought all this. Thought was also a waste, when it wasn't being used to keep him alive. Afraid. Of death, but also of life. Of living fully, which no one did. No one could.

Life was reduced to opportunities to die, and surviving. He knew it was bullshit, knew it less with each glass of bourbon. Only that if he stepped out on his porch right now, Caruso would not kill him. He could camp there for years and Caruso wouldn't kill him. Probably no one would. He refused to step onto the porch and find out. After every murder he felt like this.

He would go out tomorrow and drink. Hardly without a care, but he would be waiting for the next order. The next hit. The next chance to end the life of another and extend his own. Next opportunity to call the outcall service. Someone would kill him someday, or he'd just die. Alone and miserable, most likely. Probably better off if someone killed him. But not yet. So far, he was in charge of extending the cycle.

Derringer Award-nominated author Rob Pierce is the author of a number of novels and novellas, including Tommy Shakes, Uncle Dust, With the Right Enemies, *and* Blood By Choice.

CITY OF LEAD

Michael A. Gonzales

SINKING INTO THE quicksand of his murky thoughts, Blue Mitchell wished he could've been anywhere besides where he was. "Hurry-up with that joint," barked Micheaux as he splattered a massive canvas with a distinctive blend of blood red paint. "A brother needs his black man's Prozac right now." Laughing heartily, he swung his stylish dreads out of his face and put the paintbrush down. As he stopped laughing, he stared at the painting, sticking his mocha-hued face close to the canvas. Blue simply watched as Micheaux studied his latest mixed-media masterwork *Ghetto Bastard*, a tribute to slain street messiah The Notorious B.I.G. (aka Biggie Smalls). For his new work of art, the "genius-in-residence," as Blue jokingly called his homeboy employer, had sampled glossy images of hip-hop high life from fan magazines and combined splashes of his own trademarked textures: wild styled hieroglyphic graffiti, various copyrighted symbols, bizarre primitive art, and skeletal sketches of African masks. There were also real nine-millimeter shells glued to the canvas.

Dressed in a paint-spattered Armani suit that further perpetuated the self-proclaimed myth that he was "the Basquiat for the new millennium," Micheaux stared at his newest creation with the ego of a god. Striding barefoot across the paint-splattered floor, he walked over to the windowsill and sat down. "This painting will be dedicated to all brothers in the hood," bragged Micheaux. "This one's for the homies!" Although Blue knew that

Micheaux wasn't a real rap revolutionary, he was a Biggie fan. In fact, the two had met in 1997, a few months before the MC was killed in Los Angeles.

Back in their geek-boy days at the School of Visual Arts, back in the mid-1990s when Micheaux was still answering to his real name, Rodney Beckett, he and Blue had taken a few courses together, and, amid the majority white kids in their classes, developed a quick friendship. Years later, after the name change and Blue's decision to give up the dream of being a magazine illustrator, Micheaux hired him to be his right hand. As the assistant to the art world's black prince, it was Blue's job to roll the weed, control the steady stream of music, brew oceans of Kenya AA Grand Cru coffee, score the latest designer drug, and mix modish colors for Micheaux's palate. Unlike previous ambitious assistants who secretly wanted their own fifteen minutes of Warholian fame, Blue had long ago discarded his artistic dreams. Besides his paycheck, there wasn't anything Blue wanted from Micheaux.

As Micheaux continued to study *Ghetto Bastard*, Blue asked, "You think they know who really killed Biggie?"

Micheaux sucked his teeth. "Somebody knows who did that shit, but dead niggers are a low priority for po-po; dead nigger rappers are even lower on the scale. Pac, Jam Master Jay, Big L, they don't give a damn."

Blue shook his head. "So what you saying, if somebody killed Vanilla Ice they would've caught up."

Micheaux laughed. "Damn straight, they would've caught him and that fool would be under the jail."

Blue stood up and checked the bright yellow of the Bart Simpson faced Swatch. He wasn't surprised to see that it was almost one a.m. He knew Micheaux would slave through the night adding the finishing touches to the piece, but as far as he was concerned, the party was over.

Over the iceberg coolness of Miles Davis's trumpet wafting from the stereo speakers, Blue asked, "Is there anything else you need me to do before I leave out of here? The subway going up-town been acting funny the last few nights." The studio was on 23rd Street, off 6th Avenue, and the ride home usually took about forty minutes. "Don't want to have to get an express train operating on a local track."

Micheaux snickered. "I thought that was the story of your life," he snapped, lighting yet another thick spliff with a vintage Zippo lighter. "You can go, just do me a favor and try to be on time tomorrow. You know I have to get these new paintings together for the Studio Museum show."

"What difference does it make what time I get in—you aren't going to be up anyway. The entire art world knows the great Micheaux is the Blacula of the art world. Your ass don't ever rise before two o'clock anyway."

Suddenly, the din of the thundering telephone violently screeched throughout the loft.

"Hello," Blue answered. Through a white cloud of phone static, he could hear the roar of a passing motorcycle and cars as though the call was coming from a pay phone. "Speak or forever hold your peace." Blue doodled peculiar designs on notepad paper while cradling the receiver between his head and left shoulder; his drawing hand moved swiftly, as though unin-formed of his premature retirement.

"I got you now," a voice murmured, hanging up abruptly. Blue wanted to believe the mystery stranger was one of Mi-cheaux's ivory princesses joking around, but he had the unset-tling feeling that he was the person the call was intended. For the last week he'd had these strange feelings that he was being watched and followed but had shrugged it off as pothead para-noia. Even the most passive people have enemies, he thought. Although the call could've been anyone, something in his brain whispered, "Be careful." Placing the phone in its cradle, he stared at Micheaux.

"Who was it?" the artist asked.

"I haven't the slighted idea."

Minutes later, he went into the bathroom and changed his clothes.

STANDING AT THE loft's front door, Blue pulled on his sharp private detective overcoat on top of his black turtleneck sweater, thrift store double-knit slacks, and old-school marshmallow shoes. If he had been a slick private dick in some shoot 'em-up blaxploitation flick, he would have chosen the moniker Moses Nighthawk. Renting a shabby office in the back of a rowdy poolhall that overlooked the chaos of 125th, Moses took no shit from the man.

"Shaft ain't got shit on you," Micheaux said as Blue completed his look with a black Kangol.

"Superfly neither," Blue grunted, pulling up the leather's collar to protect him from the wintry wings of the hawk. The two men slapped each other five, and Blue finally left.

The A train was a block away and, ten minutes after pushing through the turnstile, the subway zoomed into the station. Trekking to Harlem World on the Duke Ellington Express, there were always some weirdos on board. That night there was a well-dressed dude who was shadow boxing, throwing crazy punches at an invisible opponent. Certainly, just because none of the other passengers saw the man's rival didn't mean he wasn't really there.

Blue got off the iron horse at 145th Street. On St. Nicholas Avenue the streetlights were dim and the rattle 'n' bang of the garbage men created a symphonic soundtrack of noise that traveled for miles. He turned the corner at 148th and he trooped up the long avenue blocks. Blue caught a glimpse of rats the size of cats slinking behind battered trashcans. Overhead the miserable moonlight cast complex shadows from the decaying tenements. On Amsterdam Avenue, an aged, frail derelict that looked close to death pushed a rusty shopping cart overflowing with five-cent deposit cans past a bulletproof glass encased bodega. With dirty fingers the bum counted change for a few Newport loosies.

A trio of ragged winos, two men and one woman, stood around a bonfire trading stories and gulping from a sticky bottle of Wild Irish Rose. Minding his business, a dandy black midget walked two Great Danes down the block. "Them dawgs bigger than you," yelled the toothless woman. Her laughter sounded like the Wicked Witch of the West. "And they prettier than you," squealed the midget. Blue, along with a couple of Dominican crack dealers as well as her fellow drunks, laughed loudly. "That shit wasn't funny," the woman slurred as the two dogs dragged the snippy midget away.

The wind whipped and sent a tense chill through Blue as he neared Broadway. He shivered. Again, he felt as though he were being watched. He stopped, scanned the numerous rooftops, and looked carefully up the block. He felt the heat of lingering eyes caressing his chilled body. Yet, with the exception of the drunks and drug dealers, the street was deserted. A blast of wind swirled a pile of dirt as Blue lit a cigarette. Although he had a sweet-loving, big-boned woman named Rita waiting for him beneath the warm sheets of a king-sized bed, Blue preferred being in the company of the other nocturnal nighthawks.

There were various bars and after-hour spots throughout the landscape of Harlem, where he often went to chill, sniff coke, consume cocktails, and, if he were lucky, perhaps get a little pussy. Lately, the Bliss Bar had become his newest escapist wonderland. Instead of backroom gambling, Bliss offered ghetto gal strippers. Overflowing with big-booty mamas who danced as though they were auditioning for Soul Train, that Mecca of sepia-toned flesh had become his latest thrill in an otherwise boring existence. A few feet away from the doorway, a grimy dude preached angrily from a battered bible. "On judgment day the Lord will remember you," screamed the sidewalk minister, pointing accusingly at Blue. Like a rabid dog, there was a nasty whiteness foaming from his mouth. As Blue scrabbled for the desolate doorway, he pretended to ignore the rundown reverend.

"All things weird are normal in this whore of cities," Blue said, reciting the club's password. The bored, sleepy-eyed doorman patted him down thoroughly. After slipping the no-neck rogue ten bucks for admission, Blue walked down a steep flight of rusty stairs that led to the Babylonian basement. Inside, he looked around and finally made his way to the bar. "What's up?" he shouted, greeting the grouchy dike bartender Pat. The music was so loud he could feel the bass in his balls.

"What's up your damn self," grunted Pat. Dressed in a double-breasted suit that might have once belonged to her dearly departed daddy, she looked like one of the fellows. "There was some man in here earlier asking about you. He said he might stop through later."

"Asking about me?" he repeated, somewhat concerned. Blue lifted a couple of maraschinos from the bar. Slowly he rolled the tiny fruit over his tongue before he bit into its syrupy center, cherry juice squirting down his throat. "Did he leave a name?"

"This ain't no hotel and I don't be taking messages. All I do is pour drinks and mind my business." Slapping down a thick highball glass, Pat filled the glass with ice cubes and Bacardi rum; the little bit of Coke was merely for coloring. Blue put forty bucks on the bar and waited coolly for Pat to count out a stack of singles. Leaving a three-buck tip for her troubles, Pat said, "Thanks."

Gloomily, he strolled toward the awaiting flock of sexual sirens performing perverse acrobatics in the main arena. Walking through the dense crowd, Blue overheard snatches of scandalous conversation. One dude was trying to negotiate a backroom blow job while another all-night sucker was trying to score a hit of Kaleidoscope ecstasy. Blue lit a cigarette. Easily lured into a lustful state of high-heeled hypnosis, Blue stared intensely at a down-hearted dame dancing on the stage.

Every night for the past two weeks, he had watched lustfully as that she-devil of desire fluttered in front of the aqua lights.

There was a dangerous beauty in her every movement, he thought, as he tipped her generously. Beneath the colorful lights, she sadly swayed as D'Angelo's blunted booty shaker "Brown Sugar" flowed from the speakers. With a full-figured body that was as devilishly alluring as sinful thoughts on Easter morning, he was soon lost in the crashing waves of her thick thighs and the drowning pools of her lifeless eyes.

The almond shape of her Asiatic eyes reminded him of his old girlfriend Initia. The still-healing knife scar over her left eye made her more fascinating. If Blue had still possessed a passion for painting, he would have created an entire series of watercolors consisting entirely of her fleshy image. Instead, he drew silhouettes of her on a napkin. Closing his eyes briefly, Blue wandered through the hallowed halls of his personal wet dream museum admiring his sexually charged pop art. He was a slave to this stranger's majestic image. Like most sad-eyed men living in this melancholy metropolis, Blue often fell in love with women he had never spoken to. Sometimes reality was too complex for oral communication. He preferred to be invisible, observing life without being forced to participate.

Riding on the foul subway or sitting in a diamond dog strip club, Blue created imaginary relationships with adorable strangers. In his mind they strolled through Central Park sipping white wine and admiring the gleaming skyscrapers spanning across Manhattan; in these fantasies it was always dark outside and shooting stars exploded in the heavens like fireworks on the Fourth of July.

Minutes later, Blue's daydream crashed to the ground when he heard a crowd of cursing creatures chugging pints of Olde English 800 screaming drunken obscenities at the object of his desire. "She sure look like she can take it," yelled one, grabbing his crotch. His goofy friends laughed, tossed wrinkled singles onto the stage. A thick cloud of cigarette smoke drifted from their area, gray ashes fell steadily on the table. They pooled their loot together and coughed up enough for a group lap dance. The sweaty men swarmed around the strange woman as though devouring her body. Blue was content to watch her from a distance. As her sad eyes watched the floor, she looked like the kind of broad who had grown accustomed to loneliness. He downed three more drinks before finally stumbling from Bliss Bar.

Drunk as a skunk while insisting to the doorman that he'd be alright, Blue walked through a thick fog of intoxication. Unexplainably, the four blocks leading to his crib were blanketed with immaculate rose pedals; the beautiful blossoms in various hues shrouded the sidewalk. Blue sat on the curb, removed his shoes, and toddled barefoot until reaching his building's stoop. Walking up to the chrome and glass front door, he pushed past the mute kid from the fifth floor who sat on the stone stairs. Obliviously, the boy bopped his head to a beat only he could hear. Blue was happy that the old elevator was already in the lobby. Pressing the fifth floor, he leaned against the wood-paneled wall until the slow lift reached his floor.

The moment Blue drunkenly opened the apartment door he knew his girlfriend Rita was gone. Usually the TV would be on, usually he could smell the odor of cooked food in the air, but on this night there was nothing. Across the room the telephone rang as though it had been ringing for a thousand years. The piercing noise shattered his drunken nerves as he snatched the receiver. "Yeah," he screamed into the phone. A woman's voice whimpered like a whipped dog. "Rita, that you baby girl," he slurred, dramatically falling to his knees. "I'm so sorry, I'm so sorry." Although he rarely showed her real affection, the fact that she was gone filled him with dread. "I'll do right, Rita," he lied. "I promise, baby, just come home."

The whimpering woman was soon replaced by hard man's voice. "Finally got home, huh." Obviously not the bittersweet voice he had expected, Blue was surprised. "Your promises mean nothing. All you can do now is repent."

Whoever it was hung up. Tasting the vile bile building in his throat, Blue held his stomach so as not to vomit. He dropped the phone on the floor. He left the telephone off the hook and climbed onto the couch. A haunting Charles Stewart photograph of tenor titan John Coltrane hung on the wall above him. There was a cheap radio/record player in the corner. Blue refused to ever buy CDs, but instead kept a stack of jazz and soul sides in the closet. More than a few were scattered on the floor.

With one arm hanging off the side of the ratty sofa, Blue stared intensely at the ceiling until the cracks began to resemble a strange trio of words. *Memories Are Killer.* The words flashed in his mind like neon on forty-deuce. *Memories Are Killer.* They were the same words that were sprayed on the canvas of Micheaux's in-progress *Ghetto Bastard* painting. *Memories Are Killer.* Outside the window, Blue heard footsteps racing down the fire escape. He lay as quiet as a corpse, fearing any movement would alert the prowlers of his presence. Seconds later, he heard the ancient elevator creaking upwards. He got off the couch, walked to the door, and quietly looked out of the peephole.

The hallways were painted in a light texture brown. Blue watched as the aged elevator door slowly slid open, but the wood-paneled lift was empty. Standing at the door, Blue was shocked when he felt a frigid breeze blowing through the now open window. For the second time that night, he shivered. "In your next life, you really should be careful about keeping your window locked," a voice behind him mumbled. He recognized the smoky voice from the telephone call. "You never know who might come calling."

Blue turned around slowly and saw a tall Spanish man dressed in a gray pinstriped suit, a white shirt, red tie, and a gray overcoat. The stranger was gripping a black nine millimeter. The stranger chuckled and, without warning, pulled the trigger. Shot in his right knee, Blue collapsed to the floor for the second time that night. Holding his bleeding limb, he moaned like a child. "Did you ever love her?" the gunman asked, and smiled wickedly. It was difficult being a hard-boiled hero, Blue thought. He had more respect for Cagney and Bogart than ever before.

"I have no idea what you're talking about," Blue moaned. There was a pathetic gleam in his eyes. He lay silently, watched as the shooter walked across the room. "Are you going to kill me?"

"Do you think you deserve to die?" the shooter asked coyly. "Some would say that a man without love is already dead, but I've been watching you too long to believe that."

Blue crawled to the couch, carefully hoisting himself to the softness of the cushions. "I'm sorry," he mumbled. "I never meant to hurt anyone."

"Anyone? You mean, you don't know exactly who you've hurt? It must be quite a list," he said, and shot Blue in the side of his neck. Blood spurted, splashed the wall like a Jackson Pollock painting or a spouting Dadaist fountain filled with sticky cherry soda.

"Why are you doing this?" he cried.

"It's strictly professional," the stranger joked. "I get paid to do a job and I do it, and do it well." Painfully, Blue tried to open his eyes as he heard the shooter exit through the open window.

Fifteen minutes later, as he lay closer to death, he heard a key in the front door. The last thing he saw before dying was his girlfriend Rita walk into the living room, look at his limp body, and smile. The last thing he heard was Rita's fake crying and her high-pitched scream, "Somebody help me please...my boyfriend's been killed."

New York City native Michael A. Gonzales is a journalist, music critic, and short story writer. His fiction has been published by The Root, Bronx Biannual, Brown Sugar, *and* Black Pulp *(edited by Gary Phillips).*

KILLER IN A CAGE

Tyson Blue

THE HARD PART was getting myself locked up in the Larey County Jail.

Two weeks ago, I walked into the FBI office in the Federal Courthouse in Shannon, Larey County, Georgia, and knocked on the door before opening it and walking in. It was a small office, about ten by ten, with an institutional-looking desk, file cabinets along one wall, and two chairs in front of the desk. Venetian blinds covered the top half of the window, and an American flag fluttered outside.

Behind the desk was a man in his forties, wearing a white shirt with a conservatively striped tie. His grey eyes were couched in wrinkles, as if he had spent a lot of time in the sun. Everything about him said "FBI agent posted to an out-of-the-way field office to wait for retirement." He looked up at me and smiled.

"I'm Agent Walters," he said. "Can I help you?"

I smiled back and took a seat. "Yes," I said. "My name's Ray Vincent, and you can arrest me."

Agent Walters looked a little puzzled.

"Now why would I want to do that?" he asked.

I pointed at his desktop computer. "Run my name," I told him. "You'll see."

He pulled his keyboard over in front of him and typed in my name, then hit Enter. I could tell when he read my entry because his face went pale under his tan. His eyes widened as he looked at me, his glance going from my face to my hands and back again. He started to move his right hand toward a drawer of his desk, watching me carefully.

"Don't worry," I said. "If I was going to do anything to you, you'd be dead already. I told you—I came here to turn myself in."

To show him I was sincere, I held out my hands, wrists turned inward.

He stood up, walked around his desk, and motioned for me to stand as well.

"Turn around," he said when I was out of the chair. "Hands behind you."

I complied. He clicked a pair of handcuffs on my wrists, ratcheting them tight but not too tight. They were Smith & Wesson cuffs, pretty standard issue for American police officers. I could have gotten out of them pretty much anytime I wanted to—an escape-artist trick I'd learned many years ago from Jim Steranko, a magician turned comic artist. But that wouldn't get me where I wanted to go.

Agent Walters picked up his phone and dialed. He listened for a moment as the call went through.

"Hello," he said. "Hey Roger, this is Eric Walters over at the FBI office. I just had a top ten fugitive turn himself in to me. Can you send a couple of deputies over to pick him up and put him in your facility while we figure out the next step?"

He listened.

"You can? Great," he said. "I'll see you in a few."

He hung up and turned to me. "Okay, here's how this is going to work. The Larey County Sheriff's Office is in the basement of the county courthouse, the building directly behind this one. We have a contract with the county to house high-risk prisoners—which includes you—because the facility is underground, with one way in or out, which makes it virtually escape-proof.

"You'll be there probably for the next few weeks, while the feds figure out which state has dibs on you based on the outstanding charges against you."

I nodded. "Understood."

We waited for about five minutes, then I heard footsteps on the stairs down the hall. Two deputies came through the door, both well over six feet. One was black, broad-shouldered, and muscular. The other was white with a mustache. He wore glasses. The nameplates on their tan shirts read Lucius Cole and Tim Foster.

"I thought Deputy James was coming," Walters said.

"He's still on light duty," said Foster. "He got shot awhile back and hasn't been certified to go back on the road."

Walters nodded. "Oh yeah, I'd forgotten about that," he said. "How's he doing?"

"Little sore, but not bad," Cole replied. Then, looking at me, he asked "Is this our boy?"

"Yep," Walters said. "Boys, meet Ray Vincent. He's wanted in connection with a dozen contract killings all over the country over the last ten years or so. It might take all those jurisdictions awhile to figure out who gets first crack at him, so in the meantime I hope you can find a place for him."

Cole raised his eyebrows at that, shook his head, and smiled. "I think we can accommodate him." He took my arm and guided me to the hallway.

"You're not going to make me go down those stairs with my hands behind my back, are you?" I asked.

"No," Foster said. "We'll use the elevator. Can't do anything about the steps out of the building, though. But you can take your time."

They were true to their word. We went down in the elevator, which was just about big enough to hold all three of us, and then they helped me negotiate the concrete steps that led down to the sidewalk. We turned right and walked about fifty feet, to the top of a sharply angled ramp that led down to the parking lot of the Sheriff's Department, which lay under the county courthouse building.

Foster held the door for me, and I preceded Cole into the

lobby, a narrow area in front of the metal-mesh grate that separated the lobby from the office area of the department. Another deputy, whose name tag identified him as Roger James, reached under the counter, and there was a buzzing sound as the door unlocked. Cole guided me through the door, and Foster followed. The door clicked shut behind us.

I was in the outer reaches of the Larey County Jail.

For the next twenty minutes or so, I was logged in as an inmate, with a couple of calls to Agent Walters to check details. Then I was led down the hall to the cell area. There were four bullpens, two on each side of a corridor running the length of the building. On the right was a solid metal door which led to the solitary confinement cells. At the end of the hall were two individual cells, one on each side of the central hallway. They faced west and were lit during the day by light from two barred windows near the top of the wall across a narrow corridor in front of the cell doors.

Foster unlocked the door of one of the cells with a huge brass key and rolled the door back. Cole unlocked my hands and I stepped inside. On the bunk was a set of jail scrubs, black and white striped like something out of a prison movie from the 1930s.

"Because you're federal, we can't have you in with the general population," Cole explained. "So you'll be down here. Behave yourself and don't give us any trouble, and you might earn privileges to get out some during the day."

"For now, though, put on that uniform and drop your street clothes out in the corridor," Foster told me. "We'll put 'em in a property bag that'll travel with you when you leave. Any questions?"

I smiled.

"Do you leave the lights on after bedtime?"

They both stared at me for a moment, dumbfounded.

"Do we what?" Foster asked.

"I'm just pulling your leg a little," I said with a chuckle. "I think I've got it."

"Did you stay anywhere in town before you turned yourself in?" Cole asked.

I gave them the name of the cheap motel I had stayed in for a few days when I arrived in Shannon. I told them they had my permission to search it and bring back anything they found there. With that, they left, their footsteps clacking hollowly as they went back up the main hallway. The cell block door clanged shut, and I was alone. I lay back on my bunk after changing my clothes and went to sleep.

ABOUT AN HOUR after dinner that night, a short, stocky man in civilian clothes stopped in front of my cell, along with Deputy Cole. In his hand, he held a small leather pouch with a folder top, secured by a metal snap. He juggled it lightly in one hand and looked at me for a moment with his piercing blue eyes.

"I'm Investigator Darnell," he said. "We went through your room at the motel, and this was all we found. Is it yours?"

I sat up on my bunk and looked at it, then into Darnell's eyes.

"Yes it is, sir," I told him. He struck me as the kind of person who liked that "sir" crap.

"What is it?" he asked.

"It's a set of leather working tools," I told him. "Little hobby of mine. I make gun belts, holsters, regular belts, leather armbands or bracelets, with any design you can think of. I could make some stuff for you guys while I'm here. All you'd have to do is buy the materials—my resources are kind of limited in here—and I'd do the rest."

Darnell eyed Cole's well-worn, plain gun belt, then looked at me and shook his head.

"I don't know about that," he said. "That'd be up to the high sheriff himself, and up to you. If you behave, we can maybe work something out."

"You won't get any trouble out of me," I said, trying to look as sincere as I could.

Darnell stood there for a minute, idly tossing the kit up in the air and catching it.

"We'll see," he said. Then he and Cole turned and left.

ABOUT THREE DAYS later, Deputy Foster came down and opened the door of my cell. I got up, stretched, and walked up to the door.

"Jailer wants to see you," he said. He gestured for me to come out ahead of him, so I walked out, turned right, and headed up the hallway toward the front.

"Where to?" I asked, turning back slightly.

Foster gestured ahead with his hand.

"Through the door, straight ahead, up to the front counter where you were logged in."

I went through the door and walked past a couple of interview rooms on my left and stopped at the counter. The jailer, a heavyset man wearing dark glasses, leaned on one elbow, and regarded me impassively.

"So you're Ray Vincent," he drawled. "That right?"

I nodded. "I am."

"FBI tells us you've hired out to kill a dozen men," the jailer went on. He didn't have a name tag; I never did learn his name. "That right?"

I shrugged. "That's what they say," I replied.

"Well, did you?" he asked.

"Well, sir," I said, "I haven't been tried or convicted of any of those, so I'd rather not say. Besides, I'm sure you wouldn't want to hear me say something that would result in you flying all over the country to testify at a dozen trials about anything I might allegedly admit to. Can we just say I'm the man they say I am and leave it at that?"

The jailer seemed to ponder that for a minute, then pursed

his lips and nodded slowly.

"Fair enough," he said. "Listen, there's a couple reasons I asked to see you.

"First off, you haven't given anybody any trouble since you came in, and if you promise to keep it up, I'm willing to make you a trusty. That means you'll have the run of the jail and the kitchen from first thing in the morning until things shut down for the night. In exchange, you can do the sweeping and mopping, help out with the cookin' if you're any good at it, and the washin' up afterward. Sound fair so far?"

I pretended to think it over for a minute, then nodded. "Fine with me, sir," I told him. "Anything else?"

"Investigator Darnell tells me you do leather work," he said. "Carve designs on belts and holsters and such. That true?"

"Yes, sir, it is," I answered. "It's a hobby I took up when I was younger. It helps me relax, and it makes me happy when people like the things I make. Like I told Investigator Darnell, I'd need people to buy the materials I'd need, mostly leather, maybe some buckles and things. The rest of what I'd need are in the tool kit Investigator Darnell found in my motel room the other day."

The jailer opened a slim drawer to his left and reached inside. He came up with my tool kit in his hand. He looked down at it, then looked up at me.

"I give y'all this, are you gonna dig a tunnel out of your cell or stick somethin' in one of my deputies?"

I smiled wryly. "No, sir," I said. "Your people been good to me, and I don't aim to give anybody any trouble while I'm here. As for trying to use those tools, to tunnel my way out of here, I don't think I'm gonna be here long enough to accomplish that. If you look at the tools, you'll see none of us are probably gonna be here long enough for me to get that job done."

The jailer gazed thoughtfully into the space between us, idly tossing the kit up and down in his hand. Reaching a decision, he straightened up and held the kit out to me. I took it and thanked him. I opened the kit and counted the tools; everything I needed was there, the grooving tool, edgers, an awl for punching holes for the tongue of a buckle to go through—they were all there. I snapped the case shut and looked up.

"Does anyone want to me to make anything yet?" I asked.

"Investigator Darnell said something about a gun belt," the jailer said. "And depending on how it turns out, I might want something. Just let me know what you need to get started, and I'll see about getting it for you. In the meantime, though, why don't you grab a broom and run it down that hall?"

I gave him a mock—but not *too* mock—salute and headed off.

BY THE MIDDLE of the next day, I had my first order. As the jailer had said, Investigator Darnell had wanted a gun belt and matching holster. I got his waist measurement, calculated the length of leather I would need, and ordered up a rectangular piece of cowhide about an eighth of an inch thick, just about right for a heavy-duty utility-type belt like a gun belt would be. And since he had the largest waist of any of the deputies, the leather I had on hand would make a belt for any of the others, and the extra leather could be used for other projects.

I set up shop at a small worktable in the kitchen, out of the flow of traffic but in a place where I could be observed by any of the deputies, so they would be reassured that I was working on a project and not tunneling my way out of the escape-proof jail.

When I wasn't cleaning up the jail, or helping out with the food service, I was working on Darnell's belt. All the deputies in the department came back to the kitchen at one time or another during their shifts to see the quality of my work, the intricate carving I was putting into the leather of the belts, carving, stamping, and rubbing in stain to bring out the grain of the leather and emphasize the detail of the carving.

A couple of days into the project, Mitch Dickinson, the other trusty, stopped by. He was another federal prisoner and occupied the other cell at the back of the jail. We had struck up several conversations back there, and were starting to become pretty good friends, at least as jailhouse acquaintances go. He took a look at what I was doing, nodding his head appreciatively.

"You do good work, Ray," he said. "Maybe you could do something for me, maybe a keychain or something small. I can't afford to buy the stuff for a belt, but maybe you could do something with some of the small scraps.

I glanced up at him as I worked.

"Maybe so," I said. "A keychain might be possible. Maybe I could carve your name into it, or a Western scene, something like that."

Mitch smiled; he had bad teeth.

"I'll be looking forward to it, Ray," he said. "Thanks!"

"Don't thank me yet," I told him. "Let's see how things turn out."

Mitch walked away into the kitchen and got a Coke from the soft drink machine at the other end of the room. Then he came back over to the large counter near the stove and began cutting up potatoes for fries for dinner. He hummed a snatch of an old tune while he worked. I tried my best to ignore it and concentrate on my work.

The carving work on the belt was done by the time I had to stop to work on the dinner service, so I set it on the table and went to work along with Mitch and another local trusty, an old lush named Don, who spent lots of time sobering up in jail, which was always good news for the inmates and the deputies, because he was a fantastic cook at one of the better restaurants in Shannon. Some deputies would even bring groceries in especially for him which he was there, so he could fix a meal to order for them.

After the meals were all done and the dishes had been collected, washed, dried, and put away, it was going for eight. I was back working on Investigator Darnell's belt when Deputy James stuck his head in the door. He took a look at what I was working on and smiled.

"That is some good work you're doing, man," he said.

"Thanks, Deputy James," I told him. "Can I make something for you?"

James shook his head admiringly. "I sure am thinking about it," he said. "I'll let you know."

"Glad to do it," I told him. "It helps to pass the time."

"Well, I'll leave you to it. Listen," he added, "everybody's out on patrol, so I've gotta man the radio for any traffic. So I'll be up there if you need anything."

I nodded. "I'm gonna see if I can finish this belt tonight before I turn in, so I can surprise Investigator Darnell with it in the morning."

"He'll like that," Deputy James said. Then he headed back up to the front.

I spent the next forty-five minutes or so finishing up Investigator Darnell's belt, gave it a final rubdown with oil, then left it coiled on the table to dry. I headed down the hall, then turned right to stand by Mitch's cell. His door was open, and he was lying on his bunk, reading a tattered Louis L'Amour Western.

He glanced up and saw me. "Hey, how's it going?"

I shrugged. "Not bad," I told him. "I finished up that belt, thought I'd call it a night."

Mitch sat up, setting the book down beside him.

"Hey, Mitch," I said. "You don't exactly seem like the criminal type. What are you in here for?"

Mitch glanced to his left and right, as though someone else was around. "Well, if you promise not to tell anyone," he said, then dropped his voice to a whisper. "I'm being held here in protective custody."

"Wow," I said, leaning forward and uncrossing my arms. "How come?"

"I'm a witness in a big drug trial that's coming up in Atlanta soon," he explained. "I'm a pharmacist, and a drug dealer named Luis Esparza was using my store to funnel opioids to him for street sale. I met with him in person a couple of times, so I can connect him directly to what's going on."

"Sounds pretty dangerous for you," I said. "Seems to me this Esparza guy would want to get to you before you can testify, or afterward if he can't. You know, for revenge."

"Once I'm done testifying, the feds are going to put me into Witness Protection," Mitch said. "Set me up someplace with a new identity and a new start. Hopefully, they'll never find me."

As the words left his mouth, I jumped forward and landed with my full two hundred forty-five pounds on Mitch, slamming him back onto his bunk. I clamped my left hand over his mouth to prevent him from making any noise, and reached my right hand into my shirt pocket and pulled out an engraving tool from my leather working kit. It was about the length of a ballpoint pen, but a little slimmer, with a point at one end for carving leather, and a round top like the head of a nail at the other.

Moving quickly, I stuck the pointed end up Mitch's left nostril, pushing it all the way in until it butted up against his top of his nasal passage. The skull, which houses the brain, is very thin at that point, so I moved my arm back and slammed my palm into the end of the tool, driving it through the thin layer of bone and into Mitch's brain. He pitched and bucked under me as I took hold of the end of the tool and began swirling it around, the pointed end tearing through brain tissue.

Mitch continued twitching beneath me, his body spasming involuntarily as his ravaged brain broke down. I pushed the tool up a little farther, then swirled it around some more. His spasms gradually grew weaker and weaker, then finally ceased. His breathing grew ragged, then stopped. His pupils grew fixed and dilated.

I waited a little longer to be sure, then got off him.

Mitch was dead.

I pulled the tool out of his nose and wiped it off on the inside of my pants pocket. Then I put it back in my shirt pocket and took a small piece of paper towel and stuffed it up Mitch's nostril to keep what little blood there might be from running out. Then I arranged his body on his bunk to make it look like he'd gone to sleep facing the wall and covered him with a blanket, just like he might have done it himself. Then, I slid the cell door closed, and felt it lock in place automatically.

Walking quickly and quietly, I headed back up the hall toward the kitchen. Someone in one of the bullpens called out to me as I passed, but I ignored him.

I came into the kitchen, passed the table with Investigator Darnell's finished belt on it, and scooped up my toolkit. I replaced the tool I'd used on Mitch and carried the whole thing across the kitchen to the alcove at the other end, where the soda and snack vending machines were. Moving as quietly as I could, I moved the soda machine forward, away from the wall as far as the cord would reach.

Behind the machine was a door. From studying plans for the courthouse that I had obtained about a week before turning myself in, I knew that this door connected to a service corridor that allowed access to the water pipes that serviced the bullpens and other cells. It also let out into the parking area by a small office where the school system's dietician worked. The door was locked and opened outward; it had obviously not been used for years.

I went to work with another tool from my kit, which had a wide flat end like a screwdriver. Working as quickly as I could, I pried up the pins from the hinges, until I was able to grab them with my fingers and pull them out. I put the pins in my pocket.

Then I used the tool to move the hinge end of the door out enough to grip it and eased it out into the corridor. I set the tool against the wall, then reached in and got hold of the soda machine, pulling it back into position as nearly as I could. After that, I moved the door back into position, slotted the deadbolt into place, and propped the door back into the jamb as tightly as I could. It wouldn't withstand more than a cursory examination, but I wanted the deputies to spend as much time figuring out how I vanished without a trace from the jail as possible, so I could have more time to get away.

I moved quickly to the end of the corridor and eased the door open, listening for any activity in the parking garage. There was no one there. I slid out the door and eased it shut behind me. I walked over to the ramp leading up to the street level, keeping out of range of the two cameras that covered the spaces used by the sheriff's cars when they were parked. I had scoped out the cameras and their areas of focus when I had checked the place out before turning myself in.

I moved quickly to the top of the ramp and looked left and right. There was no traffic at all. I trotted quickly across the street, avoiding the closed storefronts and heading directly for the dimly lit side street that came into the circle around the two courthouses from the north. I was a lot less conspicuous now than I had been crossing the street in my striped suit, since the traffic circle was pretty well lit, while this street wasn't.

Three doors down on my left was a small house I had rented about a week before I turned myself in, using part of the advance I'd gotten from Mr. Esparza. I found the key under the front steps, where I'd left it before turning myself in.

I let myself into the house and went back to the rear bedroom, where I quickly stripped off the jail uniform and put on the clothes I had left there when I rented the place. I picked up the cell phone I had left on a charger and put it in my shirt pocket. My tool kit went into the pants pocket.

I gathered up my jail clothes and put them into a garbage bag, then made a quick check to make sure every trace of me was gone, then went out the front door, locking the key inside. I walked quickly over to the rental car I'd parked there earlier and got in. It started up, and I backed into the street. I had the window down to listen for any sounds of alarm, but I heard nothing. Hopefully, neither my escape nor Mitch's body had yet been discovered.

I drove over to a street which ran parallel to Highway 80 and followed it down almost to the Oconee River. Then I turned right, went over a block and turned left, heading east out of Shannon. My GPS was preprogrammed with a back-road route to Savannah, where I had arranged for a quiet, fast boat to spirit me out of the country before the sun came up.

WHEN I ARRIVED dockside, it was about three a.m. by the dashboard clock. The boat was standing by, a low-slung, sleek black speedboat. I found the key taped behind the dash and started her up. The low burble of the inboard motor was quiet. I put it in reverse, backed out into the Savannah River, and headed down toward the Atlantic, passing the large container facility in Garden City on my right.

I continued on under the huge bridge that arched over the river, connecting Georgia and South Carolina, then on past the City of Savannah on my right, with its thriving waterfront of shops and restaurants along River Street, with the city itself extending back on top of a cliff about forty feet above the level of the water. I always thought of Savannah, a beautiful old town, as New Orleans designed by smart people.

I continued on down the river, passing occasional container ships heading up river to offload at the container port. I hugged the South Carolina shore to avoid their wakes, which would toss me around a lot. I increased my speed a little as I left the city behind me, passing by Thunderbolt and then the Savannah Beach area and the nearby Tybee Island lighthouse as I reached the end of the river and headed out into the Atlantic.

When I calculated I had reached the twelve-mile limit of US territorial waters, I gave the boat its head and arrowed straight into the Atlantic. I began to relax as the sky lightened to the east with the first hints of dawn. The water was smooth as glass.

Once I reached the twenty-four-mile limit for law enforcement, I pulled out my phone to call the larger boat that was standing by to pick me up and take me to my final destination, a nice tropical locale with no extradition treaty with the US. Then it was just a matter of getting the rest of my fee from Mr. Esparza, and things would be, as Deputy James liked to say, copacetic.

The sun was peeking over the horizon. It was going to be a glorious day.

A renowned Stephen King expert, Tyson Blue is the author of The Unseen King *and editor of* Hope and Miracles: The Shawshank Redemption and The Green Mile. *His fiction has appeared in numerous anthologies.*

QUARRY'S LUCK

Max Allan Collins

ONCE UPON A time, I killed people for a living.

Now, as I sit in my living quarters looking out at Sylvan Lake, its gently rippling gray-blue surface alive with sunlight, the scent and sight of pines soothing me, I seldom think of those years. With the exception of the occasional memoirs I've penned, I have never been very reflective. What's done is done. What's over is over.

But occasionally someone or something I see stirs a memory. In the summer, when Sylvan Lodge (of which I've been manager for several years now) is hopping with guests, I now and then see a cute blue-eyed blonde college girl, and I think of Linda, my late wife. I'd retired from the contract murder profession, lounging on a cottage on a lake not unlike this one, when my past had come looking for me and Linda became a casualty.

What I'd learned from that was two things: the past is not something disconnected from the present—you can't write off old debts or old enemies (whereas, oddly, friends you can completely forget); and not to enter into long-term relationships.

Linda hadn't been a very smart human being, but she was pleasant company and she loved me, and I wouldn't want to cause somebody like her to die again. You know—an innocent.

After all, when I was taking contracts through the man I knew as the Broker, I was dispatching the guilty. I had no idea what these people were guilty of, but it stood to reason that they were guilty of something, or somebody wouldn't have decided they should be dead.

A paid assassin isn't a killer, really. He's a weapon. Someone has already decided someone else is going to die, before the paid assassin is even in the picture, let alone on the scene. A paid assassin is no more a killer than a nine millimeter automatic or a bludgeon. Somebody has to pick up a weapon, to use it.

Anyway, that was my rationalization back in the seventies, when I was a human weapon for hire. I never took pleasure from the job—just money. And when the time came, I got out of it.

So, a few years ago, after Linda's death, and after I killed the fuckers responsible, I did not allow myself to get pulled back into that profession. I was too old, too tired, my reflexes were not all that good. A friend I ran into, by chance, needed my only other expertise—I had operated a small resort in Wisconsin with Linda—and I now manage Sylvan Lodge.

Something I saw recently—something quite outrageous really, even considering that I have in my time witnessed human behavior of the vilest sort—stirred a distant memory.

The indoor swimming pool with hot tub is a short jog across the road from my two-room apartment in the central lodge building (don't feel sorry for me: it's a bedroom and spacious living room with kitchenette, plus two baths, with a deck looking out on my storybook view of the lake). We close the pool room at ten p.m., and sometimes I take the keys over and open the place up for a solitary midnight swim.

I was doing that—actually, I'd finished my swim and was letting the hot tub's jet streams have at my chronically sore lower back—when somebody came knocking at the glass doors.

It was a male figure—portly—and a female figure—slender, shapely, both wrapped in towels. That was all I could see of them through the glass; the lights were off outside.

Sighing, I climbed out of the hot tub, wrapped a towel around myself, and unlocked the glass door and slid it open just enough to deal with these two.

"We want a swim!" the man said. He was probably fifty-five, with a booze-mottled face and a brown toupee that squatted on his round head like a slumbering gopher.

Next to him, the blonde of twenty-something, with huge blue eyes and huge big boobs (her towel, thankfully, was tied around her waist), stood almost behind the man. She looked meek. Even embarrassed.

"Mr. Davis," I said, cordial enough, "it's after hours."

"Fuck that! *You're* in here, aren't you?"

"I'm the manager. I sneak a little time in for myself, after closing, after the guests have had their fun."

He put his hand on my bare chest. "Well, *we're* guests, and *we* want to have some fun, too!"

His breath was ninety proof.

I removed his hand. Bending the fingers back a little in the process.

He winced, and started to say something, but I said, "I'm sorry. It's the lodge policy. My apologies to you and your wife."

Bloodshot eyes widened in the face, and he began to say something, but stopped short. He tucked his tail between his legs (and his towel), and took the girl by the arm, roughly, saying, "Come on, baby. We don't need this horseshit."

The blonde looked back at me and gave me a crinkly little chagrined grin, and I smiled back at her, locked the glass door, and climbed back in the hot tub to cool off.

"Asshole," I said. It echoed in the high-ceilinged steamy room. "Fucking asshole!" I said louder, just because I could, and the echo was enjoyable.

He hadn't tucked towel 'tween his legs because I'd bent his fingers back: he'd done it because I mentioned his wife, who we both knew the little blonde bimbo wasn't.

That was because (and here's the outrageous part) he'd been here last month—to this very same resort—with another very attractive blonde, but one about forty, maybe forty-five, who was indeed, and in fact, his lawful wedded wife.

We had guys who came to Sylvan Lodge with their families; we had guys who came with just their wives; and we had guys who came with what used to be called in olden times their mistresses. But we seldom had a son of a bitch so fucking bold as to bring his wife one week, and his mistress the next, to the same goddamn motel, which is what Sylvan Lodge, after all, let's face it, is a glorified version of.

As I enjoyed the jet stream on my low back, I smiled and then frowned, as the memory stirred...Christ, I'd forgotten about that! You'd think that Sylvan Lodge itself would've jogged my memory. But it hadn't.

Even though the memory in question was of one of my earliest jobs, which took place at a resort not terribly unlike this one...

WE MET OFF Interstate 80, at a truck stop outside of the Quad Cities. It was late—almost midnight—a hot, muggy June night; my black T-shirt was sticking to me. My blue jeans, too.

The Broker had taken a booth in back; the restaurant wasn't particularly busy, except for an area designated for truckers. But it had the war-zone look of a rush hour just past; it was a blindingly white but not terribly clean-looking place and the jukebox—wailing "I Shot the Sheriff" at the moment—combated the clatter of dishes being bused.

Sitting with the Broker was an oval-faced, bright-eyed kid of about twenty-three (which at the time was about my age, too) who wore a Doobie Brothers t-shirt and had shoulder-length brown hair. Mine was cut short—not soldier-cut, but businessman short.

"Quarry," the Broker said, in his melodious baritone; he gestured with an open hand. "How good to see you. Sit down." His smile was faint under the wispy mustache, but there was a fatherly air to his manner.

He was trying to look casual in a yellow banlon shirt and

golf slacks; he had white, styled hair and a long face that managed to look both fleshy and largely unlined. He was solid-looking man, fairly tall—he looked like a captain of industry, which he was in a way. I took him for fifty, but that was just a guess.

"This is Adam," the Broker said.

"How are you doin', man?" Adam said, and grinned, and half-rose; he seemed a little nervous, and in the process—before I'd even had a chance to decide whether to take the hand he offered or not—overturned a salt shaker, which sent him into a minor tizzy.

"Damn!" Adam said, forgetting about the handshake. "I hate fuckin' bad luck!" He tossed some salt over either shoulder, then grinned at me and said, "I'm afraid I'm one superstitious motherfucker."

"Well, you know what Stevie Wonder says," I said.

He squinted. "No, what?"

Sucker.

"Nothing," I said, sliding in.

A twentyish waitress with a nice shape, a hair net and two pounds of acne took my order, which was for a Coke; the Broker already had coffee and the kid a bottle of Mountain Dew and a glass.

When she went away, I said, "Well, Broker. Got some work for me? I drove hundreds of miles in a fucking gas shortage, so you sure as shit better have."

Adam seemed a little stunned to hear the Broker spoken to so disrespectfully, but the Broker was used to my attitude and merely smiled and patted the air with a benedictory palm.

"I wouldn't waste your time otherwise, Quarry. This will pay handsomely. Ten thousand for the two of you."

Five grand was good money; three was pretty standard. Money was worth more then. You could buy a Snickers bar for ten cents. Or was it fifteen? I forget.

But I was still a little irritated.

"The two of us?" I said. "Adam, here, isn't my better half on this one, is he?"

"Yes he is," the Broker said. He had his hands folded now, prayerfully. His baritone was calming. Or was meant to be.

Adam was frowning, playing nervously with a silver skull ring on the little finger of his left hand. "I don't like your fuckin' attitude, man…"

The way he tried to work menace into his voice would have been amusing if I'd given a shit.

"I don't like your fuckin' hippie hair," I said.

"What?" He leaned forward, furious, and knocked his water glass over; it spun on its side and fell off my edge of the booth and we heard it shatter. A few eyes looked our way.

Adam's tiny bright eyes were wide. "Fuck," he said.

"Seven years bad luck, dipshit," I said.

"That's just mirrors!"

"I think it's any kind of glass. Isn't that right, Broker?"

The Broker was frowning a little. "Quarry…" He sounded so disappointed in me.

"Hair like that attracts attention," I said. "You go in for a hit, you got to be the invisible man."

"These days everybody wears their hair like this," the kid said defensively.

"In Greenwich Village, maybe. But in America, if you want to disappear, you look like a businessman or a college student."

That made him laugh. "You ever see a college student lately, asshole?"

"I mean the kind who belongs to a fraternity. You want to go around killing people, you need to look clean-cut."

Adam's mouth had dropped open; he had crooked lower teeth. He pointed at me with a thumb and turned to look at Broker, indignant. "Is this guy for real?"

"Yes indeed," the Broker said. "He's also the best active agent I have."

By "active," Broker meant (in his own personal jargon) that I was the half of a hit team that took out the target; the "passive" half was the lookout person, the back-up.

"And he's right," the Broker said, "about your hair."

"Far as that's concerned," I said, "we look pretty goddamn conspicuous right here—me looking collegiate, you looking like the prez of a country club, and junior here like a roadshow Mick Jagger."

Adam looked half bewildered, half outraged.

"You may have a point," the Broker allowed me.

"On the other hand," I said, "people probably think we're fags waiting for a fourth."

"You're unbelievable," Adam said, shaking his greasy Beatle mop. "I don't want to work with this son of a bitch."

"Stay calm," the Broker said. "I'm not proposing a partner- ship, not unless this should happen to work out beyond all of our wildest expectations."

"I tend to agree with Adam, here," I said. "We're not made for each other."

"The question is," the Broker said, "are you made for ten thousand dollars?"

Adam and I thought about that.

"I have a job that needs to go down, very soon," he said, "and very quickly. You're the only two men available right now. And I know neither of you wants to disappoint me."

Half of ten grand did sound good to me. I had a lake-front lot in Wisconsin where I could put up this nifty little A-frame prefab, if I could put a few more thousand together...

"I'm in," I said, "if he cuts his hair."

The Broker looked at Adam, who scowled and nodded.

"You're both going to like this," the Broker said, sitting for- ward, withdrawing a travel brochure from his back pocket.

"A resort?" I asked.

"Near Chicago. A wooded area. There's a man-made lake, two indoor swimming pools and one outdoor, an 'old town' gift shop area, several restaurants, bowling alley, tennis courts, horse-back riding..."

"If they have archery," I said, "maybe we could arrange a little accident."

That made the Broker chuckle. "You're not far off the mark. We need either an accident, or a robbery. It's an insurance situation."

Broker would tell us no more than that: part of his function was to shield the client from us, and us from the client, for that matter. He was sort of a combination agent and buffer; he could tell us only this much: the target was going down so that someone could collect insurance. The double indemnity kind that comes from accidental death, and of course getting killed by thieves counts in that regard.

"This is him," Broker said, carefully showing us a photograph of a thin, handsome, tanned man of possibly sixty with black hair that was probably dyed; he wore dark sunglasses and tennis togs and had an arm around a dark-haired woman of about forty, a tanned slim busty woman also in dark glasses and tennis togs.

"Who's the babe?" Adam said.

"The wife," the Broker said.

The client.

"The client?" Adam asked.

"I didn't say that," Broker said edgily, "and you mustn't ask stupid questions. Your target is this man—Baxter Bennedict."

"I hope his wife isn't named Bunny," I said.

The Broker chuckled again, but Adam didn't see the joke.

"Close. Her name is Bernice, actually."

I groaned. "One more 'B' and I'll kill 'em *both*—for free."

The Broker took out a silver cigarette case. "Actually, that's going to be one of the...delicate aspects of this job."

"How so?" I asked.

He offered me a cigarette from the case and I waved it off; he offered one to Adam, and he took it.

The Broker said, "They'll be on vacation. Together, at the

Wistful Wagon Lodge. She's not to be harmed. You must wait and watch until you can get him alone."

"And then make it look like an accident," I said.

"Or a robbery. Correct." The Broker struck a match, lighted his cigarette. He tried to light Adam's, but Adam gestured no, frantically.

"Two on a match," he said. Then got a lighter out and lit himself up.

"Two on a match?" I asked.

"Haven't you ever heard that?" the kid asked, almost wild-eyed. "Two on a match. It's unlucky!"

"*Three* on a match is unlucky," I said.

Adam squinted at me. "Are you superstitious, too?"

I looked hard at Broker, who merely shrugged.

"I gotta pee," the kid said suddenly, and had the Broker let him slide out.

Standing, he wasn't very big: probably five-seven. Skinny. His jeans were tattered.

When we were alone, I said, "What are you doing, hooking me up with that dumb-ass jerk?"

"Give him a chance. He was in Vietnam. Like you. He's not completely inexperienced."

"Most of the guys I knew in Vietnam were stoned twenty-four hours a day. That's not what I'm looking for in a partner."

"He's just a little green. You'll season him."

"I'll ice him if he fucks up. Understood?"

The Broker shrugged. "Understood."

When Adam came back, Broker let him in and said, "The hardest part is, you have a window of only four days."

"That's bad," I said, frowning. "I like to maintain a surveillance, get a pattern down..."

Broker shrugged again. "It's a different situation. They're on vacation. They won't have much of a pattern."

"Great."

Now the Broker frowned. "Why in hell do you think it pays

so well? Think of it as hazardous duty pay."

Adam sneered and said, "What's the matter, Quarry? Didn't you never take no fuckin' risks?"

"I think I'm about to," I said.

"It'll go well," the Broker said.

"Knock on wood," the kid said, and rapped on the table.

"That's formica," I said.

THE WISTFUL WAGON Lodge sprawled out over numerous wooded acres, just off the outskirts of Wistful Vista, Illinois. According to the Broker's brochure, back in the late '40s, the hamlet had taken the name of Fibber McGee and Molly's fictional hometown, for purposes of attracting tourists; apparently one of the secondary stars of the radio show had been born nearby. This marketing ploy had been just in time for television making radio passe, and the little farm community's only remaining sign of having at all successfully tapped into the tourist trade was the Wistful Wagon Lodge itself.

A cobblestone drive wound through the scattering of log cabins, and several larger buildings—including the main lodge where the check-in and restaurants were—were similarly rustic structures, but of gray weathered wood. Trees clustered everywhere, turning warm sunlight into cool pools of shade; wood-burned signs showed the way to this building or that path, and decorative wagon wheels, often with flower beds in and around them, were scattered about as if some long-ago pioneer mishap had been beautified by nature and time. Of course that wasn't the case: this was the hokey hand of man.

We arrived separately, Adam and I, each having reserved rooms in advance, each paying cash up front upon registration; no credit cards. We each had log-cabin cottages, not terribly close to one another.

As the back-up and surveillance man, Adam went in early. The target and his wife were taking a long weekend—arriving

Thursday, leaving Monday. I didn't arrive until Saturday morning.

I went to Adam's cabin and knocked, but got no answer. Which just meant he was trailing Mr. and Mrs. Target around the grounds. After I dropped my stuff off at my own cabin, I wandered, trying to get the general layout of the place, checking out the lodge itself, where about half of the rooms were, as well as two restaurants. Everything had a pine smell, which was partially the many trees, and partially Pinesol. Wistful Wagon was Hollywood rustic—there was a dated quality about it, from the cowboy/cowgirl attire of the waiters and waitresses in the Wistful Chuckwagon Cafe to the wood-and-leather furnishings to the barnwood-framed Remington prints.

I got myself some lunch and traded smiles with a giggly tableful of college girls who were on a weekend scouting expedition of their own. *Good*, I thought. *If I can connect with one of them tonight, that'll provide nice cover.*

As I was finishing up, my cowgirl waitress, a curly-haired blonde pushing thirty who was pretty cute herself, said, "Looks like you might get lucky tonight."

She was re-filling my coffee cup.

"With them or with you?" I asked.

She had big washed-out blue eyes and heavy eye make-up, more '60s than '70s. She was wearing a 1950s style cowboy hat cinched under her chin. "I'm not supposed to fraternize with the guests."

"How did you know I was a fraternity man?"

She laughed a little; her chin crinkled. Her face was kind of round and she was a little pudgy, nicely so in the bosom.

"Wild stab," she said. "Anyway, there's an open dance in the ballroom. Of the Wagontrain Dining Room? Country swing band. You'll like it."

"You inviting me?"

"No," she said; she narrowed her eyes and cocked her head, her expression one of mild scolding. "Those little girls'll be there, and plenty of others. You won't have any trouble finding what you want."

"I bet I will."

"Why's that?"

"I was hoping for a girl wearing cowboy boots like yours."

"Oh, there'll be girls in cowboys boots there tonight."

"I meant, just cowboy boots."

She laughed at that, shook her head; under her Dale Evans hat, her blonde curls bounced off her shoulders.

She went away and let me finish my coffee, and I smiled at the college girls some more, but when I paid for my check, at the register, it was my plump little cowgirl again.

"I work late tonight," she said.

"How late?"

"I get off at midnight," she said.

"That's only the first time," I said.

"First time what?"

"That you'll get off tonight."

She liked that. Times were different, then. The only way you could die from fucking was if a husband or boyfriend caught you at it. She told me where to meet her, later.

I strolled back up a winding path to my cabin. A few groups of college girls and college guys, not paired off together yet, were buzzing around; some couples in their twenties up into their sixties were walking, often hand-in-hand, around the sun-dappled, lushly shaded grounds. The sound of a gentle breeze in the trees made a faint shimmering music. Getting laid here was no trick.

I got my swim trunks on and grabbed a towel and headed for the nearest pool, which was the outdoor one. That's where I found Adam.

He did look like a college frat rat, with his shorter hair; his skinny pale body reddening, he was sitting in a deck chair, sipping a Coke, in sunglasses and racing trunks, chatting with a couple of bikinied college cuties, also in sunglasses.

"Bill?" I said.

"Jim?" he said, taking off his sunglasses to get a better look at me. He grinned, extended his hand. I took it, shook it, as he stood. "I haven't seen you since spring break!"

We'd agreed to be old high-school buddies from Peoria who had gone to separate colleges; I was attending the University of Iowa, he was at Michigan. We avoided using Illinois schools because Illinois kids were who we'd most likely run into here.

Adam introduced me to the girls—I don't remember their names, but one was a busty brunette Veronica, the other a flat-chested blonde Betty. The sound of splashing and running screaming kids—though this was a couples' hideaway, there was a share of families here, as well—kept the conversation to a blessed minimum. The girls were nursing majors. We were engineering majors. We all liked Credence Clearwater. We all hoped Nixon would get the book thrown at him. We were all going to the dance tonight.

Across the way, Baxter Bennedict was sitting in a deck chair under an umbrella reading *Jaws*. Every page or so, he'd sip his martini; every ten pages or so, he'd wave a waitress in cowgirl vest and white plastic hot pants over for another one. His wife was swimming, her dark arms cutting the water like knives. It seemed methodical, an exercise work-out in the midst of a pool filled with water babies of various ages.

When she pulled herself out of the water, her suit a stark, startling white against her almost burned black skin, she revealed a slender, rather tall figure; tight ass, high, full breasts. Her rather lined leathery face was the only tip-off to her age, and that had the blessing of a model's beauty to get it by.

She pulled off a white swim cap and unfurled a mane of dark, blond-tipped hair. Toweling herself off, she bent to kiss her husband on the cheek, but he only scowled at her. She stretched out on her colorful beach towel beside him, to further blacken herself.

"Oooo," said Veronica. "What's that ring?"

"That's my lucky ring," Adam said.

That fucking skull ring of his! Had he been dumb enough to wear that? Yes.

"Bought that at a Grateful Dead concert, didn't you, Bill?" I asked.

"Uh, yeah," he said.

"Ick," said Betty. "I don't like the Dead. Their hair is greasy. They're so...druggie."

"Drugs aren't so bad," Veronica said boldly, thrusting out her admirably thrustworthy bosom.

"Bill and I had our wild days back in high school," I said. "You shoulda seen our hair—down to our asses, right Bill?"

"Right."

"But we don't do that anymore," I said. "Kinda put that behind us."

"Well I for one don't approve of drugs," Betty said.

"Don't blame you," I said.

"Except for grass, of course," she said.

"Of course."

"And coke. Scientific studies prove coke isn't bad for you."

"Well, you're in nursing," I said. "You'd know."

We made informal dates with the girls for the dance, and I wandered off with "Bill" to his cabin.

"The skull ring was a nice touch," I said.

He frowned at me. "Fuck you—it's my lucky ring!"

A black gardener on a rider mower rumbled by us.

"Now we're really in trouble," I said.

He looked genuinely concerned. "What do you mean?"

"A black cat crossed our path."

In Adam's cabin, I sat on the brown, fake-leather sofa while he sat on the nubby yellow bedspread and spread his hands.

"They actually do have a sorta pattern," he said, "vacation or not."

Adam had arrived on Wednesday; the Bennedicts had arrived Thursday around two p.m., which was check-in time.

"They drink and swim all afternoon," Adam said, "and they

112

go dining and dancing—and drinking—in the evening."

"What about mornings?"

"Tennis. He doesn't start drinking till lunch."

"Doesn't she drink?"

"Not as much. He's an asshole. We're doing the world a favor, here."

"How do you mean?"

He shrugged; he looked very different in his short hair. "He's kind of abusive. He don't yell at her, but just looking at them, you can see him glaring at her all the time, real ugly. Saying things that hurt her."

"She doesn't stand up to him?"

He shook his head, no. "They're very one-sided arguments. He either sits there and ignores her or he's giving her foul looks and it looks like he's chewing her out or something."

"Sounds like a sweet guy."

"After the drinking and dining and dancing, they head to the bar. Both nights so far, she's gone off to bed around eleven and he's stayed and shut the joint down."

"Good. That means he's alone when he walks back to their cabin."

Adam nodded. "But this place is crawlin' with people."

"Not at two in the morning. Most of these people are sleeping or fucking by then."

"Maybe so. He's got a fancy watch, some heavy gold jewelry."

"Well that's very good. Now we got ourselves a motive."

"But *she's* the one with jewels." He whistled. "You should see the rocks hanging off that dame."

"Well, we aren't interested in those."

"What about the stuff you steal off him? Just toss it somewhere?"

"Hell no! Broker'll have it fenced for us. A little extra dough for our trouble."

He grinned. "Great. This is easy money. Vacation with pay."

"Don't ever think that...don't ever let your guard down."

"I know that," he said defensively.

"It's unlucky to think that way," I said, and knocked on wood. Real wood.

WE MET UP with Betty and Veronica at the dance; I took Betty because Adam was into knockers and Veronica had them. Betty was pleasant company, but I wasn't listening to her babble. I was keeping an eye on the Bennedicts, who were seated at a corner table under a buffalo head.

He really was an asshole. You could tell, by the way he sneered at her and spit sentences out at her, that he'd spent a lifetime—or at least a marriage—making her miserable. His hatred for her was something you could see as well as sense, like steam over asphalt. She was taking it placidly. Cool as Cher while Sonny prattled on.

But I had a hunch she usually took it more personally. Right now she could be placid: she knew the son of a bitch was going to die this weekend.

"Did you ever do Lauderdale?" Betty was saying. "I got *so* drunk there..."

The band was playing "Crazy" and a decent girl singer was doing a respectable Patsy Cline. What a great song.

I said, "I won a chug-a-lug contest at Boonie's in '72."

Betty was impressed. "Were you even in college then?"

"No. I had a hell of a fake I.D., though."

"Bitchin'!"

Around eleven, the band took a break and we walked the girls to their cabins, hand in hand, like high school sweethearts. Gas lanterns on poles scorched the night orangely; a half-moon threw some silvery light on us, too. Adam disappeared around the side of the cabin with Veronica and I stood and watched Betty beam at me and rock girlishly on her heels. She smelled of perfume and beer, which mingled with the scent of pines; it was more pleasant than it sounds.

She was making with the dimples. "You're so nice."

"Well thanks."

"And I'm a good judge of character."

"I bet you are."

Then she put her arms around me and pressed her slim frame to me and put her tongue half-way down my throat.

She pulled herself away and smiled coquettishly and said, "That's all you get tonight. See you tomorrow."

As if on cue, Veronica appeared with her lipstick mussed up and her sweater askew.

"Good night, boys," Veronica said, and they slipped inside, giggling like the school girls they were.

"Fuck," Adam said, scowling. "All I got was a little bare tit."

"Not so little."

"I thought I was gonna get laid."

I shrugged. "Instead you got screwed."

We walked. We passed a cabin that was getting some remodeling and repairs; I'd noticed it earlier. A ladder was leaned up against the side, for some re-roofing. Adam made a wide circle around the ladder. I walked under it just to watch him squirm.

When I fell back in step with him, he said, "You gonna do the hit tonight?"

"No."

"Bar closes at midnight on Sundays. Gonna do it then?"

"Yes."

He sighed. "Good."

We walked, and it was the place where one path went toward my cabin, and another toward his.

"Well," he said, "maybe I'll get lucky tomorrow night."

"No pick-ups the night of the hit. I need back-up more than either of us needs an alibi, or an easy fuck, either."

"Oh. Of course. You're right. Sorry. 'Night."

"'Night, Bill."

Then I went back and picked up the waitress cowgirl and took her to my cabin; she had some dope in her purse, and I smoked a little with her, just to be nice, and apologized for not having a rubber, and she said, Don't sweat it, pardner, I'm on the pill, and she rode me in her cowboy boots until my dick said yahoo.

THE NEXT MORNING I had breakfast in the cafe with Adam and he seemed preoccupied as I ate my scrambled eggs and bacon, and he poked at his French toast.

"Bill," I said. "What's wrong?"

"I'm worried."

"What about?"

We were seated in a rough-wood booth and had plenty of privacy; we kept our voices down. Our conversation, after all, wasn't really proper breakfast conversation.

"I don't think you should hit him like that."

"Like what?"

He frowned. "On his way back to his cabin after the bar closes."

"Oh? Why?"

"He might not be drunk enough. Bar closes early Sunday night, remember?"

"Jesus," I said. "The fucker starts drinking at noon. What more do you want?"

"But there could be people around."

"At midnight?"

"It's a resort. People get romantic at resorts. Moonlight strolls..."

"You got a better idea?"

He nodded. "Do it in his room. Take the wife's jewels and it's a robbery got out of hand. In and out. No fuss, no muss."

"Are you high? What about the wife?"

"She won't be there."

"What are you talking about?"

He started gesturing, earnestly. "She gets worried about him, see. It's midnight, and she goes looking for him. While she's gone, he gets back, flops on the bed, you come in, bing bang boom."

I just looked at him. "Are you psychic now? How do we know she'll do that?"

He swallowed; took a nibble at a forkful of syrup-dripping French toast. Smiled kind of nervously.

"She told me so," he said.

We were walking now. The sun was filtering through the trees and birds were chirping and the sounds of children laughing wafted through the air.

"Are you fucking nuts? Making contact with the client?"

"Quarry—she contacted me! I swear!"

"Then *she's* fucking nuts. Jesus!" I sat on a bench by a flower bed. "It's off. I'm calling the Broker. It's over."

"Listen to me! Listen. She was waiting for me at my cabin last night. After we struck out with the college girls? She was fuckin' waitin' for me! She told me she knew who I was."

"How did she know that?"

"She said she saw me watching them. She figured it out. She guessed."

"And, of course, you confirmed her suspicions."

He swallowed. "Yeah."

"You dumb-ass dickhead. Who said it first?"

"Who said what first?"

"Who mentioned 'killing.' Who mentioned 'murder.'"

His cheek twitched. "Well...me, I guess. She kept saying she knew why I was here. And then she said, I'm why you're here. I hired you."

"And you copped to it. God. I'm on the next bus."

"Quarry! Listen...this is better this way. This is much better."

"What did she do, fuck you?"

He blanched; looked at his feet.

117

"Oh God," I said. "You did get lucky last night. Fuck. You fucked the client. Did you tell her there were two of us?"

"No."

"She's seen us together."

"I told her you're just a guy I latched onto here to look less conspicuous."

"Did she buy it?"

"Why shouldn't she? I say we scrap Plan A and move to Plan B. It's better."

"Plan B being…?"

"Quarry, she's going to leave the door unlocked. She'll wait for him to get back from the bar, and when he's asleep, she'll unlock the door, go out and pretend to be looking for him, and come back and find him dead, and her jewels gone. Help-police-I-been-robbed-my-husband's-been-shot. You know."

"She's being pretty fucking helpful, you ask me."

His face clenched like a fist. "The bastard has beat her for years. And he's got a girlfriend a third his age. He's been threatening to divorce her, and since they signed a pre-marital agreement, she gets jackshit, if they divorce. The bastard."

"Quite a sob story."

"I told you: we're doing the world a favor. And now she's doing us one. Why shoot him right out in the open, when we can walk in his room and do it? You got to stick this out, Quarry. Shit, man, it's five grand a piece, and change!"

I thought about it.

"Quarry?"

I'd been thinking a long time.

"Okay," I said. "Give her the high sign. We'll do it her way."

THE BAR W Bar was a cozy rustic room decorated with framed photos of movie cowboys from Ken Maynard to John Wayne, from Audie Murphy to the Man with No Name. On a brown mock-leather stool up at the bar, Baxter Bennedict sat, a thin handsome drunk in a pale blue polyester sport coat and pale yellow banlon sport shirt, gulping martinis and telling anyone who'd listen his sad story.

I didn't sit near enough to be part of the conversation, but I could hear him.

"Milking me fucking dry," he was saying. "You'd think with sixteen goddamn locations, I'd be sitting pretty. I was the first guy in the Chicago area to offer a paint job under thirty dollars—$29.95! That's a good fucking deal—isn't it?"

The bartender—a young fellow in a buckskin vest, polishing a glass—nodded sympathetically.

"Now this competition. Killing me. What the fuck kind of paint job can you get for $19.99? Will you answer me that one? And now that bitch has the nerve..."

Now he was muttering. The bartender began to move away, but Baxter started in again.

"She wants me to sell! My life's work. Started from nothing. And she wants me to sell! Pitiful fucking money they offered. Pitiful..."

"Last call, Mr. Bennedict," the bartender said. Then he repeated it, louder, without the "Mr. Bennedict." The place was only moderately busy. A few couples. A solitary drinker or two. The Wistful Wagon Lodge had emptied out, largely, this afternoon—even Betty and Veronica were gone. Sunday. People had to go to work tomorrow. Except, of course, for those who owned their own businesses, like Baxter here.

Or had unusual professions, like mine.

I waited until the slender figure had stumbled half-way home before I approached him. No one was around. The nearest cabin was dark.

"Mr. Bennedict," I said.

"Yeah?" He turned, trying to focus his bleary eyes.

"I couldn't help but hear what you said. I think I have a solution for your problems."

"Yeah?" He grinned. "And what the hell would that be?"

He walked, on the unsteadiest of legs, up to me.

I showed him the nine millimeter with its bulky sound suppressor. It probably looked like a ray gun to him.

"Fuck! What is this, a fucking hold-up?"

"Yes. Keep your voice down or it'll turn into a fucking homicide. Got me?"

That turned him sober. "Got you. What do you want?"

"What do you think? Your watch and your rings."

He smirked disgustedly and removed them; handed them over.

"Now your sport coat."

"My what?"

"Your sport coat. I just can't get enough polyester."

He snorted a laugh. "You're out of your gourd, pal."

He slipped off the sport coat and handed it out toward me with two fingers; he was weaving a little, smirking drunkenly.

I took the coat with my left hand, and the silenced nine millimeter went *thup thup thup*; three small, brilliant blossoms of red appeared on his light yellow banlon. He was dead before he had time to think about it.

I dragged his body behind a clump of trees and left him there, his worries behind him.

I WATCHED FROM behind a tree as Bernice Bennedict slipped out of their cabin; she was wearing a dark halter top and dark slacks that almost blended with her burnt-black skin, making a wraith of her. She had a big white handbag on a shoulder strap. She was so dark the white bag seemed to float in space as she headed toward the lodge.

Only she stopped and found her own tree to duck behind. I smiled to myself.

Then, wearing the pale blue polyester sport coat, I entered their cabin, through the door she'd left open. The room was completely dark, but for some minor filtering in of light through curtained windows. Quickly I arranged some pillows under sheets and covers, to create the impression of a person in the bed.

And I called Adam's cabin.

"Hey, Bill," I said. "It's Jim."

His voice was breathless. "Is it done?"

"No. I got cornered coming out of the bar by that waitress I was out with last night. She latched onto me—she's in my john."

"What, are you in your room?"

"Yeah. I saw Bennedict leave the bar at midnight, and his wife passed us, heading for the lodge, just minutes ago. You've got a clear shot at him."

"What? Me? I'm the fucking lookout!"

"Tonight's the night and we go to Plan C."

"I didn't know there *was* a Plan C."

"Listen, asshole—it was you who wanted to switch plans. You've got a piece, don't you?"

"Of course…"

"Well you're elected. Go!"

And I hung up.

I stood in the doorway of the bathroom, which faced the bed. I sure as hell didn't turn any lights on, although my left hand hovered by the switch. The nine millimeter with the silencer was heavy in my right hand. But I didn't mind.

Adam came in quickly and didn't do too bad a job of it: four silenced slugs. He should have checked the body—it never occurred to him he'd just slaughtered a bunch of pillows—but if somebody had been in that bed, they'd have been dead.

He went to the dresser where he knew the jewels would be, and was picking up the jewelry box when the door opened and she came in, the little revolver already in her hand.

Before she could fire, I turned on the bathroom light and said, "If I don't hear the gun hit the floor immediately, you're fucking dead."

She was just a black shape, except for the white handbag; but I saw the flash of silver as the gun bounced to the carpeted floor.

"What...?" Adam was saying. It was too dark to see any expression, but he was obviously as confused as he was spooked.

"Shut the door, lady," I said, "and turn on the lights."

She did.

She really was a beautiful woman, or had been, dark eyes and scarlet-painted mouth in that finely carved model's face, but it was just a leathery mask to me.

"What..." Adam said. He looked shocked as hell, which made sense; the gun was in his waistband, the jewelry box in his hands.

"You didn't know there were two of us, did you, Mrs. Bennedict?"

She was sneering faintly; she shook her head, no.

"You see, kid," I told Adam, "she wanted her husband hit, but she wanted the hitman dead, too. Cleaner. Tidier. Right?"

"Fuck you," she said.

"I'm not much for sloppy seconds, thanks. Bet you got a nice legal license for that little purse pea-shooter of yours, don't you? Perfect protection for when you stumble in on an intruder who's just killed your loving husband. Who *is* dead, by the way. Somebody'll run across him in the morning, probably."

"You bitch!" Adam said. He raised his own gun, which was a .380 Browning with a home-made suppressor.

"Don't you know it's bad luck to kill a woman?" I said.

She was frozen, one eye twitching.

Adam was trembling. He swallowed; nodded. "Okay," he said, lowering the gun. "Okay."

"Go," I told him.

She stepped aside as he slipped out the door, shutting it behind him.

"Thank you," she said, and I shot her twice in the chest.

I slipped the bulky silenced automatic in my waistband;

grabbed the jewel box off the dresser.

"I make my own luck," I told her, but she didn't hear me, as I stepped over her.

I NEVER WORKED with Adam again. I think he was disturbed, when he read the papers and realized I'd iced the woman after all. Maybe he got out of the business. Or maybe he wound up dead in a ditch, his lucky skull ring still on his little finger. Broker never said, and I was never interested enough to ask.

Now, years later, lounging in the hot tub at Sylvan Lodge, I look back on my actions and wonder how I could have ever have been so young, and so rash.

Killing the woman was understandable. She'd double-crossed us; she would've killed us both without batting a false lash.

But sleeping with that cowgirl waitress, on the job. Smoking dope. Not using a rubber.

I was really pushing my luck that time.

Max Allan Collins is the author of many crime novels, including the Quarry, Nolan, Mallory, Elliot Ness, Nathan Heller, and Road to Perdition series, as well as co-author of several books with the late Mickey Spillane.

COOKIE

Daniel Vlasaty

1
Do the Damn Thing

I WALK INTO the back room, see D talking to the kid.

I seen him around. His name's Willie something, but everyone calls him Cookie. Because he's always eating cookies, crumbs all over his face, chocolate smears on his lips, and also because every motherfucker on the street needs a nickname like they some weak-ass off-brand Batman villain.

He's one of a dozen or so kids D uses for his bullshit. Because kids can do things and get away with things we can't. They can disappear into crowds easier, usually they're not tatted up, and plus a kid caught with a few bags of dope might just get probation and not do any real time behind the charge.

D hands the kid a gun and says, "You ready for this fucking shit, little man?"

The kid holds the gun out and the thing looks like a fucking cannon in his hand. He shifts it from one hand to the other, feeling its weight, never taking his eyes off it.

He nods his head.

D says, "My man," and turns away from the kid, looks at me. "Just drive Cook's ass over to the spot, like we talked about, and let him do his thing. He knows what's got to get done. Come home when y'all through and we'll celebrate my man here busting his cherry."

D told me about the job earlier, told me I'd be driving. Left out that the shooter was going to be a kid.

D sees the shit on my face, asks, "Got a fucking problem with that?"

I been working for D a long time, probably since I was not much older than the kid. And I don't got any problems with a kid getting into the life, know we all got to do some shit to survive on the streets. That's not it.

What I do got a problem with is working with someone as inexperienced as this fucking kid. He's going to bust his cherry tonight, and that's cool and all, but I'm not trying to go down when he fucks his shit up.

Let kids gangbang all they want, but keep me the fuck out of it.

"It is what it is," I say. "Just not super down with driving a baby to do a fucking shooting."

The kid won't look at me, keeps his eyes locked on the piece in his hand. Still holding it out in front of him a bit.

"Ain't no baby," he says.

"You're six and a half," I say. "Fuck outta here."

"I'm thirteen, motherfucker."

He's squeezing tighter on the gun and I'm about to smack the crumbs off his fucking face when D steps between us. He pushes the kid's hand down, so the gun is pointing at the floor, says, "Y'all on the same fucking team, man, shit."

And that's the end of it. D tosses me the set of keys to some stolen car and says, "Can's in the trunk. Torch the fucking thing when it's done."

And I shake my head. "Acting like I ain't never done this before."

2
Blunt Instruments

THE KID IS quiet in the car on the ride over to the spot. Staring out the window, got the piece in his lap, munching on a sleeve of chocolate chip cookies he pulled out of somewhere.

We don't say shit to each other as I drive us out of Rogers Park, get onto Sheridan and take it straight through to the address D gave me. Just some random street corner that I don't know in Uptown.

D told me that the corner's run by some dude named Frank Roy. Told me he's got his own little crew and blah, blah, blah. I stopped listening because it don't fucking matter. It's always the same.

Either he's moving in on turf he has no claim to or he was talking some shit or who fucking cares.

Frank Roy and his crew are just some dumb motherfuckers that don't mean shit to anybody but themselves.

Same thing goes for D and the kid and me too.

None of us mean anything to anybody but ourselves.

We're all the same.

It don't matter what D's beef is with this Frank Roy. I don't need to know. I just need to follow orders. Do what I'm told when I'm told to do it.

Only thing that matters is D wants Frank Roy hit and he's picked the kid to do it.

That's how it is with D, that's how he works. To him we're nothing but tools, weapons. Blunt instruments. Things he can point wherever the fuck he wants to get the shit done he won't do himself.

I think if I was a better person I would stop the car right here in this neighborhood that might as well be a foreign country to me, tell the kid to get the fuck out and to forget all about D and his bullshit, this fucking life. Tell him to go be a kid and grow up to be something.

But fuck that. I ain't no social worker. I don't give a fuck about this kid.

He's got to grow up just like we all did. Shit, thirteen's old enough to know he's got to do what he's got to do.

He finishes off the sleeve of cookies and tosses the empty wrapper out the window. He watches it flutter, looks back down at the piece in his lap.

3
Got That Pandemic

THE STREETS ARE quiet, all the shops and restaurants closed. There's a bar up the way that's jumping, but that's about it.

I turn onto Montrose, follow it down and here it's more lively. Just like Rogers Park. You got people out on the streets, hanging on stoops, drinking and smoking and talking shit, whatever.

It's warm nights like this when no one wants to be inside, sweating with some busted-ass fan just pushing hot air around.

Most of the people we pass follow the car from one end of the block to the other with their eyes. Because it's a car they don't know, have never seen before, and who the fuck are we.

I pull over on the side of the road once we get to Damon and shut off the engine.

There's a small group of corner boys gathered up ahead. Must be a slow night for them because they're mostly just kicking back, not really hustling, just chilling. They got a few girls with them and they seem more interested in them than the action on the street.

Every once in a while one of them will call out: "Pandemic, got that Pandemic." Announcing the product they're pushing. But they're lazy about it.

It don't matter anyway. Junkies don't care what you call the junk. As long as it's junk.

We sit for a minute to wait it out, and I get my phone out and pull up the pic that D texted me of Frank Roy. It's a screenshot from his Facebook page. Close up of his face, mouth open to show his fake-ass grill. He's got a gun in the pic too.

Can't be gangster if you ain't got a piece in you profile pic.

The kid's already seen the pic but I show him again anyway

and then point over to the dude in the crowd.

Frank Roy's rail thin, wearing baggy shorts and a wife-beater. Got some shitty stick-and-poke tattoos covering most of his body.

I say, "Just go out there and do the thing. Don't fuck around. One shot, keep it clean." I point to my own forehead. "And then I'll come and scoop you up."

He looks at me like he's about to say something. But he just palms the piece and slides out of the car.

I watch as he tucks the gun in the front of his pants and walks straight toward them. Head down a bit, hands in his pockets, trying to act natural.

"Pandemic, got that Pandemic."

We're about half a block down from them but they see him almost immediately. They follow his approach even though he's trying to stick to the shadows, go unnoticed.

Another thing about D is he don't like drive-bys. Says they're too messy. Thinks the shooter's more likely to miss or hit some random innocent than to actually get the target.

He wants it up-close-and-personal. He wants them to see that shit coming.

Most important, he wants to make sure the person he wants dead gets fucking dead.

"Pandemic, got that Pandemic."

The kid's almost on them now. I start the car just to be ready. And I'm just watching Frank Roy. He's off to the side, talking to one of the girls, leaning against the brick wall.

"Pandemic, got that Pandemic."

The kid's maybe five feet away from the group when one of the other dudes breaks away and approaches him.

"What up, little bro?" he says. "Whatchu need? You looking for something? We got that Pandemic. Getchu feeling good tonight, son."

Another dude approaches the kid now too, coming right up next to the first. He's laughing, says, "Shit'll put some peach fuzz on them baby nuts of yours."

And this gets the whole crew going. Laughing and bumping fists, rolling with it. But the girls don't get involved, just roll their eyes, shake their heads.

They go back to talking to each other, ignoring the dudes.

Frank Roy pushes away from the wall, leaving his girl standing there. He steps up to see what's going on.

And the kid makes his move. He's right on them all now, sidesteps the two dudes in front of him. He says something that I can't hear and makes a big show of lifting his shirt as he reaches for the piece.

He's got the gun in his hand, pointed right at Frank Roy. But he waits a second too long to pull the trigger.

"Fuck," I say.

And the whole crew see what's going on, gets an eye full of the gun in the kid's hand, and they take off running. Like this is something they're familiar with.

The girls don't move. They don't know what's going on, still not paying attention.

And the kid pulls the trigger twice, the gun crooked in his hand, not even fucking aiming.

His first shot catches one of the corner boys low in the leg and the dude staggers but doesn't stop running.

And the second hits one of the girls, the one Frank Roy was talking to, right in the face.

She crumples to the ground and all the girls start screaming. None of them run though, frozen with fear.

Frank Roy gets away.

The kid stands there another second, just staring at the girl on the ground. She can't be much older than him, and she ain't ever going to get any older now. And then he drops the piece and takes off running down the alley.

In the opposite direction of the car.

4
Give It to Me

"MOTHERFUCK," I SAY and throw the car into gear and head toward the alley. But the kid's already gone by the time I get there.

He's nowhere to be seen. He either jumped a fence to cut through some backyards or he's hiding in one of the dozen or so dumpsters dotting the alley.

I drive through to the other end and spin back around to see if maybe he doubled back to where we were parked. But he ain't here either.

I stop at the stop sign at the corner and try to think where this fucking kid might be. He's scared and running, just killed an innocent. And I don't know this fucking neighborhood, the kid probably don't either.

And I know D's going to blame this shit on me.

Now that the shooting stopped some people are starting to come out of hiding, stepping cautiously back onto the street. Sticking heads out through open apartment windows.

Some of them got cell phones pressed to their ears, calling the cops or telling friends what they seen.

This is fucked.

I drive a few more streets, back and forth. Still don't see the fucking kid anywhere. And then I hear the sirens approaching and that's that.

I'm not trying to get stopped driving a stolen car in the vicinity of a murder. I'm already on papers as it is.

Kid's got to be on his own from here.

I take a few random streets I don't know until I find my way back to Sheridan. Head back north toward Rogers Park.

Turn left on Howard and head west a few miles, torch the car under a viaduct near the train tracks.

I watch it go up, feel the warmth of the fire, stare into the flames a while. And then I walk about a mile to the nearest bus stop.

Fucking bus barely runs this far out and it's late when I get back to D's. Hours after me and the kid left and I'm thinking maybe he already found his way back and we can get this shit squared.

There's a party going on when I walk back in. But there's always some kind of party happening at D's. A decent amount of people gathered, heavy weed smoking hanging in the air, loud house music thumping in the speakers, people dancing, grooving.

Like a lot of D's places, this building's abandoned and he claimed it as his own. Not like anyone's going to say shit. Whole fucking neighborhood's full of empty buildings, got enough of them to go around. The floor is covered by orange extension cords, coming in through every window from all the surrounding buildings.

I find D in the back room, chilling, got a fat blunt in his mouth, some random chick I never seen before in his lap. Got some of his other people around him, but they don't pay me any mind. They're busy with their own shit.

D's miles away, lost in the weed and the music. But his eyes focus when he sees me walking up. And he kind of smirks and hands his blunt off to the chick in his lap. Rubs his hands to-gether and says, "Give it to me. How'd my boy do?"

"Need to talk to you," I say, and nod at all the people in this room with us. "Alone."

He taps the girl's thigh and motions for her to get off him. She slides off and he snatches the blunt back from her. Tells everyone to clear the fucking room. And they all leave without a second thought. They know that when the boss says jump, you better start fucking flying.

When we got the room to ourselves, he says, "The fuck?" and I just ask if the kid made it back yet.

He locks his eyes on me, sucking on that blunt like he needs it to breathe.

5
In the Shit

"SO WHAT YOU'RE telling me is that you done fucked up?" D says after I tell him what happened.

"I didn't fuck up shit, that was your boy. He fucked the job up."

"And it was your fucking job to make sure Cookie didn't fuck up."

I knew D was going to spin this shit on me, and I come back with the only thing I can think to say: "I'm not the one put the fucking gun in a kid's hand and expected everything to go smooth."

D finishes off his blunt, drops the roach to the floor, and grinds the thing down with his heel like it's a personal vendetta. He's pissed, red-faced, and I know D's trying to think about just how bad this fucking thing is.

Thing about Chicago is no one cares when it's bangers doing bangers. We kill each other and it's seen as community service, part of the job. But all that shit goes right the fuck out the window when it's innocents getting pulled down with us.

"We got to clean this shit up," D says. "You, motherfucker, you got to clean this shit the fuck up. The pigs catch Cookie, he'll bring us all down with him. You got to find him before they do."

I nod. "You right. Call the fucking troops in, let's get this kid found."

But he shakes his head. "No, fuck that. This needs to stay quiet. I don't want this getting out at all, no way this fuck-up's coming back to my door. You get out there and you find him and keep it on the down-low."

Makes him look bad if it gets out one of his people fucked a job so bad.

I ask him for anything to go on. I don't know shit about the kid, who his people are, where he stays, anything like that.

D shakes his head again. "The fuck I know? Not like I'm collecting resumes or references on all these motherfuckers I got working for me. He's a Rogers Park kid, from the neighborhood. Fuck else you need to know?" He thinks about it for a bit. "You know, I think he got a grandma stays over on Seeley. Maybe. But I don't think he in contact with her much. He mentioned her once when he first started coming around, but she might have thrown his little ass out."

Like any of that's supposed to help.

I tell him I'm going to need a car so I can hit the streets, and he steps over to the closed door, opens it a crack, and shouts for Ray to bring his ass the fuck over.

Ray steps into the room and D tells him to give me the keys to his ride. And dude just reaches in his pocket and throws them to me like it ain't no thing.

D shuts the door again and turns back to me. "And you know what you need to do after you find Cook, right?"

"Man, I ain't trying to kill no kid."

"Fuck else are we supposed to do with him?"

"Maybe we can just like get him out of the city, send him somewhere else until this shit dies down."

"Oh, we WITSEC now? Fuck that. The kid fucked up, he's got to go." He opens the door again and steps to the side for me to leave. "Do what needs doing or you might find yourself right there in the shit with him."

6
One of the Good Kids

I SPEND THE rest of the night driving around aimlessly, but it's bust. I don't know where the kid hangs when he not doing D's shit. I don't know where he lays his head at night.

I cruise up and down Seeley as the sun's starting to rise, but D didn't know the grandma's address and there's nothing else I can do with this.

And then it hits me.

Only one person I know even in the kid's age range at all. Vicki's son Ivan. He's one of the good kids, maybe fourteen or fifteen, but he's not about the life. More into video games and nerdy shit like that. But he knows people. He might know about the kid, or maybe he knows someone who does.

I got nothing else to go on.

It's just after seven a.m. when I pull up in front of Vicki's building on Bosworth, and it's been a while since I been around here.

Me and Vicki used to fuck around until she got tired of all my bullshit, kicked me out, told me to lose her number. And I get it. She got a kid to think about. She got a career, and it's not like I was ever going to marry her, adopt her son, live a normal life with them.

Shit just happens sometimes.

I step up to the door and ring the buzzer. A few seconds later, a third-floor window's screeching open and Ivan sticks his head out, says, "Who's that?" But then he sees it's me and says, "Oh shit, man, hang on. The buzzer's broken again, I'll be right down."

He opens the door about ten seconds later and holds his fist out for me to bump.

"Haven't seen you in a while," he says. "Mom's not home though. She picked up an early shift at the hospital."

And I tell him that's fine, that I'm actually here to see him. Because I need his help with something.

His mom don't want to see me anyway.

I follow him up to his apartment and we go back to his bedroom. He's got some video game paused, big-ass explosion on the screen. Bunch of Red Bull cans scattered around the room. His bloodshot eyes, another video game all-nighter for him and his online friends. He was always doing that back when I was coming around. Something him and Vicki were forever fighting about. He sits down and picks up his controller but doesn't start playing yet, asks what I need his help with.

"Some work shit," I say.

And he nods his head, knows what that means. Knows that's why me and his mom stopped kicking it.

I ask him if he knows the kid. Keep it simple.

"Yeah," he says. "Everyone knows Cookie, man."

Ask him what he knows about him.

He shrugs his shoulders. "Just that he's like some badass kid, man, been stealing cars since he was like eight, always robbing and fighting everyone, people twice his age."

Tells me that Cookie's the kind of kid other people go out of their way to avoid. He shows up at the skatepark or the playground, the bus stop, wherever, the whole place clears out because he's always on some bullshit.

"Why you asking after Cookie?"

And I just tell him I need to find the kid. Leave it at that. Again, he doesn't press.

"You know where he hangs, who his friends are, anything like that? Anything that can help me find him."

"Pretty sure Cookie don't have friends. But I know he hangs around the skatepark sometimes, the one over by Leone Park." He flips the controller around in his hands, thinks on it some more. "There's this like maintenance shed or whatever over there. It's abandoned—basically falling apart. But I know some of the dudes hang around there broke into it a while ago. Use it to like smoke up in, bring their girls there too, you know. I haven't been around in a while, but I heard Cookie crashes there sometimes."

Tells me the kid's been on the street for a while, but other than that, he's not sure.

I thank him for the info. It's more than I had before, and Ivan knows his shit.

He's a good kid. I know for a while he was getting picked on, getting his ass beat like every day. Vicki was worrying about him. Said he just needs to learn to fight. But I always knew Ivan wasn't about that. That's not who he is.

Some kids just aren't cut out for the neighborhood.

7

Dumbasses and Dead Bodies

I DRIVE OVER to Leone Park, cruise past the skatepark there. It's barely even eight and the place is deserted. And I keep going down the road toward the lake, the beach entrance there, the maintenance shed off to the left.

It's a small brick building, covered in mostly shitty graffiti. The roof looks like it's maybe a few days from falling in on itself.

Leone Park's a shithole.

The beach ain't shit, mostly just rocks and broken bottles, cigarette butts. The only people ever out here swimming are dumbasses and dead bodies.

Kind of beach where you're more likely to get pricked by a discarded needle than you are to get a suntan.

I park the car near the shed and reach into the glove box for the piece D told me would be there. Walk up to the maintenance shed and place my ear against the door, listen to see if anyone's in there.

I hear some movement and it might be the kid. Or it might be some rats or maybe even two junkies bumping uglies. I don't know but I kick the fucking door open and step inside.

And there he is. The kid, Cookie, sitting back on a small metal chair, a hoody bunched up under his head like a pillow.

"The fuck?" he says. Jumps up at the sound of me barging in on him.

Never really sleep sound when you spend your nights out on the street, sleeping under viaducts and behind dumpsters and in abandoned sheds.

Without even really looking at me, he charges and tries to juke around me, but I grab him by his shirt and push him back into his chair. He blinks a few times and finally looks up at me.

Really sees me, who I am, and he seems to calm down a bit.

"What the fuck?" I say. "Got me running all over looking for your fucking ass."

"I fucked up," he says. Breathes deep.

"Yeah, you did. Fucked up bad. Should have come back to the car instead of running. But just grab your shit and let's go. We got to get out of here." I look around the room and there's nothing here, some crushed beer cans in the corner, other bits of trash, food wrappers.

He gets a little sniffly. "Wh...where we going?"

I look down at him, see just how young he is, how small. Fucking sitting here crying. And I feel kind of sorry for him, he's just a kid and he's in over his head.

"Got to get you off the street," I say. "Get you hid."

But he doesn't move and I step forward and grab him by his shirt again, lift him to his feet.

"Come on, man. Fuck you doing? We got to get you off the street," I say again. "Fucking cops are looking for you."

"But I'm off the street already."

"You in a fucking shed. How long you think it'll take the cops to figure out where you hiding? I asked one fucking person and they brought me right to you."

He asks again where we're going.

I push him toward the door. "Gonna go see D. He's working on getting you out of the city until this shit blows over. Until we can get some time to figure this shit out."

8

It's All Good Now

THE KID'S QUIET as we drive away from the shed. We get back onto Sheridan and he's reaching into his pocket, pulling out another sleeve of cookies, ripping the package open.

And I want to ask him where the fuck he keeps getting them bitches from. But I don't.

Let him have his cookies.

We drive for a while and I pull up in front of another abandoned building. It's surrounded by other abandoned and boarded-up buildings in a dead part of Rogers Park. We sit for a second and he finishes off his cookies, looks up at the building.

"D's in there?" he says.

"Yeah. Well, probably not yet, no. But he'll meet us here once he gets you all set up with somewhere safe to go."

He's scared again, I can tell. Breathing heavy, blinking too much.

"It's all good," I say. "We'll be good here while we wait."

I step out of the car and the kid follows me inside. It's dark in here. Only a few streaks of light coming in through holes in the boarded-up windows. Some rats scurry away from us.

The place has been gutted. Piles of torn-up carpet thrown in the corner, floorboards missing. This used to be a home and now it's nothing but a bad memory.

"We'll head down into the basement and wait for D," I say. "Don't want to be up here making noise in case someone happens to come through and hear us."

Tell him it's all part of D's plan. Tell him he's in good hands. D's going to take care of everything. And then we'll get him somewhere nicer, safer where he can breathe while we plan the next step. Tell him that shit will be rough for a bit, that it ain't easy living on the run.

"But I know you got it in you," I say. "That fugitive lifestyle, that ain't going to be shit for someone like you."

We make it over to the basement, and it's just a dark hole in the wall. The door's missing and I tell him to go on ahead.

"I'm right behind you. Just watch your step, them stairs can be a bitch."

He hesitates a second and I give him a little smile. And he nods his head, takes a step down into the dark.

I let him get a few steps down before I pull the piece out of the back of my pants. "It's all good now," I say and put the gun to the back of his head.

He pauses when he feels the gun there, lets out a small breath, and I pull the trigger.

He falls forward and is swallowed by the darkness.

"Fuck," I say, and turn to leave. Trying to think about how many bodies D's got in basements just like this throughout Rogers Park. And how many of them bodies I put down in those basements for him.

Daniel Vlasaty is the author of The Church of TV as God, Amphetamine Psychosis, Only Bones, A New and Different Kind of Pain, *and* Stay Ugly. *He lives outside of Chicago with his wife and daughter.*

SOLITARY MAN

Paul D. Brazill

THE MORNING THAT I killed Charlie Harris, the air tasted like lead and the sky was gunmetal grey. Suddenly exhausted, I slouched in a white leather armchair and gazed out of the grubby window of the East London flat, barely focusing on the rows of concrete blocks being smudged by the winter rain. I was starting to get used to these bouts of mental and physical fatigue, putting it down to my age, but they still draped me in a cloak of gloom. My brief moment of morbid self-attention soon melted into annoyance, however. Annoyance with Charlie, of course, but with myself, more than anything else. I'd been messy.

Eventually, I turned to look at Charlie's corpse and sighed. He was flat on his back on the fluffy white rug, where he'd collapsed five minutes before. His was a big man, dressed in an off-white linen suit and a gaudy Hawaiian shirt. His panama hat and sandals lay on the floor next to him. He gripped a string of rosary beads in his right hand. His attire was certainly at odds with the miserable English weather, but then Charlie Harris had always been a queer fish. And now he was as dead as a duck, a bullet in his forehead and one in each eye. As was my wont.

I had an empty grave over Shoreditch waiting to be filled by Charlie's corpse but there really was no way that I was going to be able to get his dead weight into the rackety lift, get it out of the block, and then into my car without being seen.

The Highgate Estate, like most council estates, was full of

mercenary eyes, even at this time of the morning. It was riddled with drug addicts who would sell their grandmothers to get their next fix. Or bored pensioners looking for a cheap thrill to enliven their dreary fall towards the grave.

Why Charlie had chosen to live on the thirteenth floor was beyond my ken. The lifts in those old blocks were notoriously unreliable and so, when they were broken, Charlie was presumably trapped on the ground floor. He was far too heavy to manage the stairs easily, that was for sure.

Still, as I looked around the spartan, pristine living room, I could see that Charlie had used his time in the witness protection programme well, cleanliness being next to godliness and all. The place seemed to have very little to signify the presence of a personality. Nothing to give away who Charlie really was, or, more to the point, the person he had been before The Ministry had ensnared him.

There was an old plasma screen television with a DVD player next to it. A stack Clint Eastwood DVDs was piled up next to them. A cursory look around the kitchen showed that Charlie had pretty much lived on takeaway food and pub grub. His wardrobe contained a collection of similar suits to the one that he now wore.

And then there was the safe.

When I'd walked into the flat, I had immediately spotted an old floor safe in the corner of the room. It was rusty and beaten up and looked quite incongruous. I knew I'd have to crack it if I wanted to find The Skull Ring. I sighed.

With Sisyphean resignation, I walked over and knelt in front of the safe. It looked familiar, probably from the 1960s, complete with a dial on the front. My mother would certainly have been able to give me more information about it, since she was such a safe enthusiast. But all I needed was to be able to open the bloody thing, and I really was no safe cracker despite the many arduous lessons I'd endured at the hands of my mother over the years.

I went over to Charlie's body and checked his pockets. I took out a heavy, well-stuffed leather wallet and sifted through it until I found a sheet of pink paper with the numbers '666999'. Hardly a difficult sequence to remember but it was worth a try.

I knelt down in front of the safe and groaned as my aching joints creaked. I held the dial and carefully twisted it, using the number sequence on a pink sheet of paper. I pulled on the door, but it didn't open. I sighed, glanced at the sheet of paper, and put it back in the wallet. I really hadn't expected a safe, though I really should have, of course.

Although I always hated asking for his help, I knew that I'd have to contact Lulu. It would cost me in the long run for sure, but I didn't really have a lot of choice. I sent a text message, then fished in my coat pocket for my blood pressure medication. I popped a pill out of its packet and dry swallowed it. The taste was bitter but comforting. I plugged the earphones into my iPod, put the buds in my ears, and closed my eyes. I listened to Lana Del Rey sing about being young and beautiful and focused on controlling my breathing.

I was lost in the music until a loud banging and a shrill 'HELLO LAD!' pierced my reverie. I opened the front door to see a priest wearing black sunglasses. Unlike Charlie, Lulu had got himself in shape of late. Ever since his marriage to Ashan, he'd started working out again.

"Morning, Lulu," I said.

"Morning, lad," said Lulu, taking off his sunglasses. His eyes were red. "Well, this is a bit of a surprise. You're looking pretty bloody sprightly, considering the last time I saw you, you were knock, knock, knocking on death's door."

I shrugged.

"It's all fake news these days, isn't it? But you should now that. The Ministry spread enough of it."

"What can I say?"

"Quite a lot, usually."

Lulu laughed. He took an energy drink from his jacket pocket, cracked it open and took a swig.

"Had a bit of a night on the tiles?" I said.

Lulu grunted.

"Yes, unfortunately. I had to spend the evening at the Royal Festival Hall, enduring a Radiohead gig just to keep the hubby happy," he said. "And then he dragged me to The Red Kimono, that shitty hipster bar in Whitechapel, for the fancy dress karaoke. Hence the clothing."

"And what particular tune did you massacre this time?"

"Would you believe 'Bohemian Rhapsody', though even I have to admit I was far from *magnifico*. I thought Ashan was going to die with embarrassment."

"Ah, yes. He's such a sensitive soul."

I smiled. Ashan Khan was The Ministry's most successful killer.

Lulu yawned and massaged his temples.

"You look like death cooled down," I said. "Which is actually quite comforting since I always take great pleasure in someone looking much worse than I feel."

"Well, you know where you can stick your schadenfreude, lad."

Lulu stuck out his tongue, and I chuckled.

"So, what's this all about? I thought you were still on sick leave?" said Lulu.

"I was, but as you can see, something came up...dead."

I sighed and nodded towards the corpse.

Lulu shook his head.

"Okay, so who the hell is that bloke, anyway?" he said. "I can't say that he looks familiar. Unless he was in a Hieronymus Bosch painting that I once saw."

"I'm pretty sure you'd have encountered him over the years. It's Charlie Harris. Former enforcer for the Robinson gang. Ring any bells?"

"Oh, like Quasimodo, lad!"

"I had a hunch you'd say that."

Lulu frowned. "So what happened?"

"Well, I'm supposed to croak him and then ransack the place to find a *Totenkopfring*?"

Lulu pulled a face. "And what one of them when it's at home? Is it another brand of tasty Swedish cider that I haven't yet tried?"

"It isn't. It's Himmler's skull ring. What do you know about it?"

"Not a lot," said Lulu.

He took out his iPhone and tapped the screen.

"Now, let me see," he said. "Ah, yes. The *Totenkopfring* was some sort of honour ring. It had a skull and crossbones design and was sometimes known as a death's head ring. Himmler dished them out to the SS elite, back in the day. They're collectible for sure, and Himmler's own is super collectible. Yes, it seems a lot of people really want to get their hands on Himmler's ring."

"Innuendo and out the other," I said. "Anyway, the particular skull ring that I'm supposed to purloin was apparently given by Himmler himself to a senior member of the British government during the dying days of World War Two. It apparently contains a very...damning engraved dedication."

"And I'm guessing that if the ring fell into the wrong hands..."

"The British government would be so far up shit creek, an outboard motor wouldn't help, let alone a paddle."

Lulu knelt over the corpse. "Hey, I tell you, it's a dead-end job this one," he said, with a cheeky grin.

"Arf arf, yes, very sharp," I said. "You'll be cutting yourself if you're not too careful."

"Speaking of which, do you want me to go and get my chainsaw? Sever Charlie's contract."

I waved a hand in the air. "No, not yet. Too messy. Too noisy. I've an empty grave waiting in Shoreditch and there a funeral booked for tomorrow, so they can park someone on him."

"The old bunk bed trick, eh. Reminds me of Robert

Maxwell…but that's another story."

"Hold on," I said. "I need a quick tinkle."

I headed off to the bathroom. The blood pressure tablets that the quack had given me certainly did the trick but their main side effect was that I had to head off to the little boys' room more often than not.

As I urinated, I started to feel dizzy. I was feeling quite worse for wear but since I was a kick in the arse off sixty, that was to be expected. I washed my hands and returned to the living room. Lulu was going through Charlie's pockets.

"Anyway, that's the main reason I called you." I pointed at the safe.

Lulu walked over to it and caressed it. "Ah, now there's an old classic."

"Do you think you can manage it?"

"Of course. Is the pope a bear?"

"Er, no."

Lulu chuckled and knelt down in front of the safe. He fiddled with the dial.

"Open sez me," he said and opened the safe door.

"Wow! That was bloody fast," I said. "Even for you."

Lulu grinned. "It was already open, lad. You didn't pull it hard enough, as the bishop said to the actress."

"Let's have a gander inside, then."

Lulu pushed a hand into the safe. He took out a pink jewelry box.

"Mm, wonder how much I could get for this on the dark web?" said Lulu.

"Well, you know what curiosity did," I said, taking the ring box from him.

"Led to many major scientific breakthroughs and innovations?"

"Aye, there is that. Who's the client, by the way?"

"It's your lot, actually."

"The Ministry?"

"Yep. I got the gig via Loren LaSalle."

Lulu shuddered. "Really? I am surprised. Loren usually likes to keep things in-house rather than use independent contractors such as yourself."

I shrugged.

"Ours is not to reason why and all that," I said.

"Ah, best not botch this then," said Lulu. "She's not exactly known for her laissez-faire approach is our Loren."

The Ministry were Lulu's employers. A shadier than shady government department that dated back to World War Two when they'd been known as The Ministry of Ungentlemanly Warfare. Officially, they no longer existed. I'd worked for them many times and trusted them as far as I could throw Charlie Harris. If there was no honour amongst thieves, Whitehall's spooks were even more dishonourable.

Lulu walked over to the window.

"You know this area is known as Suicide Central, don't you?"

"I didn't. You're a wealth of useless knowledge, aren't you?"

"No, well yes, but, as my old sergeant major used to say, if you can't fix it, smash it. We could just throw Charlie out of the window. I doubt he'd be missed."

Lulu walked over to the corpse.

"You grab the burping end and I'll grab the farting end. Let's get it over and done with."

"Do you think he'll fit? He's a bit on the...lardy side."

Lulu tutted.

"What have I told you before about your body fascism. Come on, let's at least give it a try."

"Yeah?" I said. I shrugged. "Actually, why not."

I went over to the window and opened it up. The room was filled with a sharp, cold wind and heavy rain.

"Bloody hell, let's get this over and done with," said Lulu.

"Heads or tails?" I said.

"Oh, I'll grab the top bit, lad."

I bent over and grabbed Charlie by the ankles. Lulu slipped his hands under his armpits and we lifted him up. We both gasped for air.

"Here we go," said Lulu.

We lifted the body and tried to push it out of the window, but Charlie slipped from my hands and crashed into a glass coffee table which immediately shattered.

"Buggeration," I said. "This is no good."

"So what do you want to do?" said Lulu. "If you want, I can get The Ministry involved but it might get…messy."

"No, thanks but best not. Loren may not be too pleased for one thing. She must have her reasons for keeping this job off the books."

"So what do you want to do with Sleeping Ugly?"

I put on my hat and opened the front door.

"Heel and toe and off we go," I said, as I took hold of Charlie's ankles.

I STRIPPED TO the waist in the morning dew and started to dig. With great effort, I hurled Charlie's corpulent corpse into the grave and then paused for a moment to evacuate my guts. I took a swig of tea from my thermos flask.

"You could help, you know?" I croaked.

Lulu leant against my battered old BMW. He chuckled. "Aw, don't you worry lad. I wouldn't want to get in your way. It looks like you're doing a bloody good job by yourself."

He smirked and lit a joint. As I watched the spectres of smoke drift upwards, I considered my predicament and decided it was best to just get on with it.

Sweating, I finished filling the grave and walked over to the car. The frost-coated grass crackled beneath my heavy feet and I opened the car boot and wiped myself all over with one of the puke-coloured towels that I'd taken from The Marina Hotel.

I took out a clean shirt and put on my jacket, wiped down

the shovel and placed it back against a gravestone where I'd found it. There was nobody there but me, Lulu, and a chewed-up old mongrel that crawled towards a crumbling mausoleum as if seeking sanctuary.

A church bell echoed through the granite winter morning as I got in the car. Lulu put out his spliff and got into the passenger seat.

"All done and dusted then, lad?" he said.

"Aye. I'll just need to wait to hear from Loren to do the exchange."

"Well, since you've time on your hands, you can start paying me back for this little favour."

He smiled.

"I was waiting for that, so?" I said.

"Well, the first thing you can do is buy me breakfast," said Lulu.

I SAT IN the wan light on a damp bench outside a Cabman's Shelter on Embankment Place as Lulu finished his joint. I was starting to feel a fair bit better than I had earlier. The rain had turned to sleet and I actually found it quite refreshing.

I sat listening to the sounds of the of the city come to life, watching its denizens. This was one of the things I liked about living in The Big Smoke. How easy it was to be anonymous.

A car pulled up nearby playing a French hip-hop song loudly. There were shouts and then it skidded off. A few minutes later, two heavily pierced, snivelling, shuffling smackheads wearing identical black hoodies dragged themselves past us. Their ratty, red eyes glared out from sweaty, spotty, green-tinged skin. They were almost identical in their appearance and movements, like a mad scientist's experiment gone badly wrong.

One of them almost slipped over as he spotted Lulu, who was still wearing his priest's dog collar.

"Oh, forgive me Father," he said.

"Yeah, yeah, lad," said Lulu, making the sign of the cross. "Spectacles, testicles, wallet, and watch."

They laughed and stepped over a tattered and torn placard that proclaimed the imminent end of the world.

"More fake news, eh?" said Lulu.

"Indeed," I said.

A couple of ruddy-faced Champagne Charlies staggered out of a nearby casino, swearing like troupers. The smackheads stepped towards them.

"Spare us a quid, guv," said one of the smackheads, a tremor in his voice. "For a bite to eat, like."

"Oh, for god's sake," said a toff wearing the cravat. "Kindly just fuck off and die, will you? I really can't be bothered with…"

The smackhead jabbed him in the throat and punched him in the face.

"Hey, you!" said the toff's friend.

He grabbed the smackhead's arm.

The other smackhead swiftly head-butted him and within minutes, the toff and his companion were on the rain-soaked pavement, groaning with pain, blood bursting from their noses.

"And a Merry Christmas to you, too," said the smackhead, as he removed the toff's cravat. "Ho ho ho."

Lulu chuckled as the smackhead put on the cravat and sauntered down the street singing "Last Christmas I gave you my arse…"

My stomach rumbled.

"I can name that tune in one," said Lulu. "Come on, let's get some grub."

We got up off the bench and went inside the café. It was super-hot and smelt of hot fat. A radio played a phone-in talk show. The only other customers seemed to be a raggle-taggle bunch of hippies nursing their hangovers and whispering to each other in croaky voices.

Behind the counter, Suzy Q was serving a big mug of tea to a

Las Vegas-era Elvis. Suzy was the last woman in London to have kept her beehive hairstyle from the fifties, and she always dyed it an array of bright colours. Today it was a Day-Glo pink.

Elvis chuckled, burped, and knocked his guitar over.

"If it's not one thing, it's another," he said to himself, in a rough Welsh accent. "You just don't know, don't know, you just..."

"Oh, but I do know, pet," said Lulu. "I really do."

"Well, look who it isn't," said Suzy, as we walked through the door. "Tommy bloody Bennett. Long time, no see."

I grinned. "Morning Suzy," I said.

"I haven't seen you around in donkey's years, stranger," said Suzy.

"Yeah, well, I've been abroad," I said.

"Yeah? So, what are you now?" said Suzy, filling a massive plastic tomato with ketchup. "A bloke?" She laughed loudly at her own lame joke. I smiled and winked at her.

We sat down and took off our hats and coats. I took a napkin from the table and wiped the steam from the lenses of my horn-rimmed glasses. I scrutinised a laminated menu that was stained with brown sauce, holding it by my fingertips. I quickly perused the items on the menu.

"The usual, Tommy?" said Suzy from behind the counter. "Veggie breakfast and black coffee?"

"Yes, please," I said.

"And the carnivore's option for me, lass," said Lulu.

I slouched back in my chair and closed my eyes. I yawned as I listened to a news report about a link between the royal family, fox hunting, and Brexit.

"It's all bread and bloody circuses, eh?" said Lulu. "Smoke and bloody mirrors."

I smiled. "You could well be right," I said.

Elvis shuffled closer. I recoiled from his acrid breath.

"You know, gents, they're interesting places, these Cabman's Shelters," said Elvis, taking off his wig.

"It that right, lad?" said Lulu.

"It most certainly is. For example, did you know that they were actually set up at the end of the nineteenth century to give the cabbies somewhere to pop into for a mug of slosh or a bacon sarnie? The law at the time stated that the Shelters could be no larger than a horse and cart, so that they didn't block the traffic. Oh, there is even a legend that Jack the Ripper once turned up drunk at a Shelter in Westbourne Grove at the height of his reign of terror in the East End."

"Is that so?"

"It is indeed. The story goes that the teetotal cabbies convinced Jack to take the abstinence pledge and so ended his wicked ways. Once upon a time were hundreds of the Shelters across London, but these days they are few and far between and usually only in the posher areas."

"Well, well, well, you learn something new every day," said Lulu. "Most of it shite, eh?"

He smiled at Elvis.

Suzy brought over the food and placed the plate on the table.

"Get stuck into that little lot," said Suzy.

"Don't mind if I do!" said Lulu, snowing salt over his food. He smothered it with brown sauce before tucking in.

"So what have you been up to lately?" I said.

Lulu tapped the side of his nose. "Loose lips, sink ships," he said.

"Speaking of which, today is Helen Duncan's birthday," said Elvis, who had been earwigging the conversation.

"And who, pray tell, is Helen Duncan when she's at home? The name rings a bell but then so does Quasimodo," said Lulu.

Elvis pulled a face. "Helen Duncan, I think you'll find, was the last woman in England to be imprisoned under the witchcraft act. In 1944. She was a medium who held seances in Portsmouth during World War Two. She said that a ghost had informed her of the sinking of a Royal Navy battleship. Some people thought that she was a spy and, well, there were all manner of theories but that was Helen Duncan, who was born on this day over a century ago."

"You do say!"

"Yes, I do."

Lulu raised his mug. "Happy birthday to Helen," he said.

Elvis raised his mug.

"To Helen," he said. "The only crime is getting caught!"

Lulu finished off his food and stood up. "Right, I'd best bugger off and get back before Ashan wakes up."

"And what are your plans for this gloriously grey winter day, oh gentleman of leisure and pleasure?"

"Oh, well I'll be indulging in a little liquid lunch with Ashan at Fortnum and Masons, would you believe?"

"Oh, how very la di dah!"

"Probably, but I'll be glad when he heads back to Brighton, to be honest. I really can't keep up with his pace these days. I'm feeling my age, I really am, lad."

I laughed. "Well, grandpa, I hope you're going to get showered and changed. You're a tad too…crumpled and…fragrant for Fortnum and Masons, if you don't mind me saying."

Lulu yawned. "Aye, I'll have to collect my stuff from the launderette on the way home. Good job you reminded me."

Lulu left and I sat watching the streamers of steam rise from my muddy coffee. The café was stiflingly hot and cluttered with its usual hodgepodge of misfits, waifs, and strays. Oddballs and oddfellows. Has-beens and never-beens. The flotsam and jetsam of London life. And I felt pretty much felt at home in such places, most of the time. As snug as a bug in a rug, as my old gran would have said.

Beside me, a gangling, red-haired biker slurped his tea with all the enthusiasm of an ex-con in a bordello. Each sip was like a leaky tap drip, drip, dripping throughout a sleepless night. I closed my eyes and counted to ten.

Everyone in the café seemed to be listening intently to another radio news report about foxes and tutting accordingly. Apparently,

London was now riddled with the vermin and the grubby tabloid I had in front of me told pretty much the same tale of woe. Someone had even suggested a mass fox culling.

"You see, that's not a bad idea, really, is it?" said the biker, to no one in particular. "But, of course, there'll be the inevitable bleating from the bloody bleeding-heart liberals. Foxes are like dogs, a waste of space, if you ask me. Just shitting machines. The world is better off rid of the lot of them."

I was a little surprised by the biker's upper-class accent although I'd been around the block enough times to know that there were arseholes in all walks of life.

My smartphone pinged and I checked the text messages. There was a message from an unknown number giving me a time and a place to meet. It was certain to be from Loren LaSalle. I replied in the affirmative, relieved that everything had turned out right in the end.

I took out my smartphone and put in the earplugs. I took a sip of coffee, closed my eyes, and listened to Amy Winehouse as time slipped away.

Paul D. Brazill was born in England and lives in Poland. His books include Last Year's Man *and* Man of the World.

GOOD SAMARITAN

Nikki Dolson

I WAS PRETTY sure I had at least one cracked rib, but I was also high on oxy, so when I heard the scream, I investigated. Not something someone like me, a regular breaker of the highest rule—thou shalt not kill—should do. I was coming off a job that proved more difficult than usual. I'd gotten worked over a bit before I killed the guy. Now I was bruised and a little battered, but mostly, I needed something in my stomach so I could take more oxy before the final push home and, yes, I was stalling. Home would be more of the same: shadow an actual private investigator as part of my hours required to officially get my license. It's easier to get around when you're licensed, but Frank would be intolerable when he found out I was hurt. Pain was a sign of weakness and he would never allow me to be weak.

I heard another scream, quieter this time, and I imagined a hand going over a mouth. I looked back inside the convenience store where I had just purchased teriyaki beef jerky and an orange soda. The cashier was reading her magazine again like she had been when I walked in. If she heard a thing, she wasn't acting like it. The parking lot in front of me held only my car, and the streets and sidewalks were empty. As I looked around the corner of the building, the Frank in my head was saying, *Laura, never be a hero. Walk away from someone else's fight.*

Please shut up, Frank.

155

Across the alley from the convenience store was Lehman Boys Garage, their name painted in a fading mural on the side of the building. In the alley between the two buildings, next to the garage's open door, was a maroon Oldsmobile. A '70s land yacht. It was huge and glinted in the light. The trunk was open and I couldn't see who or how many were on the other side. I moved closer, set my bag of jerky and soda on the hood of the car, unhooked my baton, and flicked it to its full length. There was scuffling and cursing.

"Get her legs."

"What do you think I'm doing?"

"Fuck if I know. Dammit, get that purse!"

"Purse or legs, what do you want me to hold?"

I peeked around the trunk lid and saw two men struggling with a woman who was admirably swinging her purse and throwing elbows, mostly missing but connecting often enough that the men had a hard time getting her into the open trunk.

The Frank in my head said, *Don't.* Oxy said, *Why the fuck not?* Oxy won.

I ran up and whacked the guy holding her legs across the back of the head with my baton. As he fell forward onto her and the guy in a black shirt sputtered in confusion, I came around the wriggling mass of woman and dumbfounded man and cracked Black Shirt in the face. He let go of her to scream and cradle his nose in both hands. I hit him again and again until he was writhing on the ground. I hit the other man too, but he wasn't actually moving. The woman had scooted out from under him and was watching us, fear and confusion writ clear on her face.

"You okay?"

She only looked at me. Black Shirt moaned and rolled over like he was thinking about getting up. I kicked him in the head once and as my foot lifted to connect again she screamed, "No, stop, please." She asked nicely, so I did.

"Are you okay?" I asked again.

"I think so." Her focus was on the men on the ground, and a bad feeling started to creep up my neck. Or maybe that was the oxy? I should probably not do drugs anymore.

"Do you know them? Please tell me I didn't interrupt some prank or good-natured fun." Fuck me, I did not need to good Samaritan my way into a felony. A string of dead bodies behind me, and this was what I'm gonna go to jail for?

"No, no. I…they were hurting me and—" Her face scrunched up like she was about to cry.

"They tried to kidnap you?"

She nodded. "Yes? Probably?"

"You don't know?"

She shook her head.

"Are they friends of yours?"

"No."

A car backfired on the street and we both jumped. The sun was nearly down, but we were in plain sight of anyone who was as curious as I had been.

"How 'bout we take this somewhere else?" I reached out my hand and she let me pull her to her feet. I tried to walk her away from the prone men, but she pulled away from me.

"I can't leave yet. I have to know."

"Know what?"

"Please just help me with them."

I felt my oxy high turning into something not nice. I closed my eyes and took a deep breath. I heard the blood pounding in my ears and smelled—well, a lot of not nice things. We were in an alley after all—but I was calmer now, floating again. I turned to this stranger, this unknown woman with kewpie doll lips done up in bright red, and said, "What do you want to do?"

The screaming woman was Rebecca Nygaard and what she wanted to do was interrogate the men. The garage was theirs evidently, and so we dragged them in. Well, I dragged one in and then went to help Rebecca because her purse kept slipping down her arm, and she started weeping all over him. Eventually, he was gonna wake up under the deluge of her tears. So she held her purse, and I lugged the other one in. Rebecca let the garage door down.

The garage was long and wide. Concrete floor, metal beams high above our heads, slots for four cars along each wall. In the far corners on either side were yellow-painted steel sawhorses. Three engines hang from hooks on the sawhorse to the right. The hooks on the one to the left were empty. They called to me. They were begging to be put to use. I'd put them to use. Oh, yes I would. At the end of the room, which was actually the front of the shop, were two offices with closed doors and glass windows that let the occupants look in on the work being done in the shop.

I left Rebecca with the unconscious men and jogged to the end of the room. I tried the door on the right. Locked. The door on the left was open though. This must be the customer waiting area. Here I found five chairs in a row in front of me, a door to outside to the left of them, and a window through which I saw a blue compact parked in the lot. On my left was a counter and register. There was a short hallway with a bathroom door on one side and a vending machine on the other.

To my right was another door and it was unlocked. This was the shop office. I found latex gloves and unused blue shop towels, and my favorite thing ever, zip ties! Zip ties could be so helpful in situations like this. I wrestled my hands into the latex gloves and used the towel to wipe down everything I touched as I made my way back to Rebecca. I patted the guys down while she watched, still clutching her purse. Black Shirt had a loaded Glock and a basic phone that I took off him. I zipped their wrists and ankles, then wrapped ropes I found under a counter around and between their hands. I dragged them over to the metal sawhorses and attached each of them to a hook and up, up, up they went. While the good ol' boys slept on, I set out to get to know my new weeping acquaintance.

Rebecca was grateful. I was hungry and it was time to take

my oxy again. We sat on wheeled stools, each of us draping the seats with blue towels to save our clothes from stray car oils. I chugged my orange soda and savored my teriyaki-flavored beef jerky.

She dabbed at her face with another towel. "You just took them on like it was nothing."

I shrugged. "They didn't see me coming. It's easier that way."

She tucked black hair behind her ear. "What do you do?"

Tricky. Oxy was a humdinger of a drug. Coursing through my veins, lifting my brain. I had business cards that said I was an apprentice investigator. I hummed her a little lie, a technicality. "I'm a private investigator. I find people."

"Really?" She brightened. This was the right answer.

"Sure," I said.

"My sister-in-law went missing. Can you find her?"

Well, shit. "I'm headed home. You should find someone local."

"But you're here now. You can help me."

I concentrated on my jerky. "So, who are these guys?"

"I think my brother is a silent partner in this garage with them." She drew a chip from the bag and nibbled on it.

"Why were they trying to stuff you into the trunk of a car?"

"I'm not sure."

I raised an eyebrow and slurped my soda. She took a breath.

"Last weekend was their five-year anniversary. Last weekend was also the last time anyone saw my sister-in-law," she said.

"What happened?"

"She didn't show up for their big dinner. He filed a missing person report the next day. Police searched the house. They checked bank accounts. Her car was found at the airport. There's video of someone matching her description leaving with some man." She shook her head.

"You don't think she would."

"She would never."

"Why are you so sure?"

She lifted her head and tears fell. "She loved me."

She set the scene: five years and six months ago, big brother Thomas brought home his girlfriend for the holidays. Little sister was in the kitchen making her Nygaard-famous snickerdoodles and she turned around to see a vision of loveliness named Emma.

"Lightning," she said. "It was like lightning on a clear day." They touched hands and Rebecca's whole world was made anew. "Can you imagine turning around and falling in love with your brother's fiancée?"

I knew that helplessness in the face of desire. I knew it all too well.

"So you two got together?"

"We ignored it for years. I tried to keep away from her. But last summer we found ourselves alone and she kissed me. I didn't know it was possible to be happy like that."

"Then what happened?"

"We traded text messages. We called each other. Thomas didn't know it was me, but he knew something was up with Emma."

"How do you know?"

"He asked me if she had confided in me. He wouldn't handle it well if she was cheating. My brother is…fragile. He likes to look a certain way—successful. A cheating wife? A divorce? Those are failures, and he wouldn't stand for it."

"Then she disappeared."

"Yes. Plus there's the convenience store you were in. It's an investment. Emma gave him the capital to open it and four others. He manages them, but her name is on everything. Now that she's 'run off,' he has legal control."

"It looks bad. What do you think happened?"

She looked down at her shoes. "I don't know. I hired someone. He traced her cell phone to somewhere near here. Tonopah is the only place that made sense to me. I think those guys did something to her. I think my brother paid them to do it."

"Why were they trying to put you in trunk?"

"I was poking around in the books at the c-store. I think Thomas has been skimming. I saw a reference to this place in some of my brother's paperwork. I came out here to talk to them. They weren't very forthcoming."

"I guess not."

Pasty Legs groaned. That was good sign. I'd been a little afraid he wouldn't wake up. I think he smacked his head on the bumper of the Olds on the way down.

"I told them I'd have the police come investigate them. That I knew my sister had been here. When I tried to leave, they cornered me and dragged me out the back where you found me."

"You won't leave until you know what happened to Emma?"

She nodded.

"But you think she's dead, right?"

Her chin wobbled. "I know she wouldn't leave me. Not without a word."

I looked up at the men hanging from their wrists.

"Well, let's get to it."

"Wait. How?" She gripped her purse tighter.

"We're gonna make them tell us. Everything." I gave her my best smile to reassure her, but she looked afraid. I slapped her knee and giggled. I maybe had too much oxy in me. I bounced to my feet. "Relax. It'll be fun."

I THREW WATER on them. Pasty Legs slowly came around. Black Shirt woke up pissed.

"You fucking bitch."

I hit him sorta softly on the shin with a handy lug wrench. He screamed. Rebecca meeped.

"Be nice," I said to him.

"I can't watch," she said.

"Hold on now, Becky. Ask them your question."

"My name is Rebecca." To the men she said, "Where is Emma?"

"Psst, that's not what you want to know," I stage whispered and spun myself around on the stool.

Rebecca glared at me. "Is Emma alive?"

Pasty Legs and Black Shirt just looked at us.

"Please."

I hated to see her beg. We'd driven the Oldsmobile into the building and hooked up jumper cables to it. I touched the ends of the cables together and we all flinched at the sparks.

"Fellas, whoever talks first gets to walk out of here."

"Tom asked us to deal with her. She came looking at the books just like you did," Pasty Legs said. This one wanted to live. The way he was slurring his speech though was a concern. He probably had a concussion.

"Shut. Up," Black Shirt said.

"Did he ask you to deal with Rebecca too?" I asked.

He nodded and swayed. "He's coming tonight to talk to her first."

I set the jumper cables down and drew Rebecca aside with an arm around her shoulders. "Do you have a dollar?" I asked her.

"What?" She looked at me, then the men, and back to me like I was being rude in front of company.

"A dollar."

She rummaged in her purse. "I have a five-dollar bill."

She handed it to me and for a moment both us were touching it. "You have just hired me to deal with them."

"What do you mean."

I rolled my eyes. "Rebecca, they killed Emma."

I called to Pasty Legs, "Right?"

"He did it. Shot her. She's buried not far from here."

"Fucking snitch." Poor Black Shirt was put out.

"Do you want to let them go? They were probably gonna do the same to you."

I could see she was torn. I let the money go. "Okay. Let's leave then. They can get away with it."

"No, they won't. I'll call the police."

162

"The police must work differently for you, because you don't have any real proof and they aren't going to look kindly on how you got your information."

"They can't get away with it," she said.

"Hire me and they won't."

She settled her big brown eyes on me then stiff-armed the money into my chest. "Take it."

I LET DOWN Pasty Legs first and gently laid him flat on the concrete. I massaged his shoulders and arms. He thanked me and turned his head and I saw one pupil was blown wide, the other eye was normal. Not a good sign. "You still with me?" I asked. He mumbled and I patted his leg.

I let down Black Shirt grudgingly. I stopped when his toes just reached the ground. I stood in front of him. "Your friend's not doing so good. I need you to talk to her brother for us. I need to know when he's coming."

"Fuck you."

Behind me, Rebecca had picked up the jumper cables and scared herself when the ends touched.

"Now, now, I only want to know if he's coming. I only want him. Give me what I want and you won't suffer another minute of indignity."

He looked down at me. He tried to mask the hate in his eyes. He was tired and sore and I was literally bouncing from foot to foot in front of him. He nodded.

First, I had to deal with Rebecca. I pointed Black Shirt's phone camera at her and she talked and cried. She had a flight out of Vegas in the morning. I encouraged her to drive like the devil was chasing her and to check into a hotel or motel near the airport for the overnight. She needed someone to see her. She needed that alibi because I was sure her brother was coming to Tonopah, and I intended to deal with him the same way I was gonna deal with these Lehman boys.

"Remember when the police come calling, those men ran you off when you asked questions about who owned the garage," I said, leaning in through the window of her blue compact.

"You be honest. Don't you dare mention me unless they mention me. And all you know is I was some stranger who helped when they got rowdy with you."

She nodded. I put my hand over hers on the steering wheel and squeezed just this side of painful. "Say it, Rebecca."

"I don't know you." She put her hand atop mine. "You were just a good Samaritan who disappeared out of my life."

Back inside the garage, Black Shirt sat on one stool, his hands still zipped. Pasty Legs was still on the floor. I sat on the other stool and pulled out Black Shirt's phone. He told me the number to dial. I put the call on speaker. I withdrew his gun and smiled at him.

"Scottie?" Thomas Nygaard said.

I nodded at Black Shirt. "Yeah, man. Where are you? It's getting late."

"I'm an hour out."

"Look, don't come to the garage, alright? She caused a little scene before we got her under control. We had some nosy tourists earlier. Meet us out at the old gas station." Scottie sounded convincing.

"The burnt-out one? Okay. See you in an hour," Thomas said.

I hung up the call. "Thank you, Scottie. Where is this gas station?"

"A couple of miles outside of town, toward Reno."

"Is Emma buried there?"

He made a face but nodded. "Behind the building. There's a cactus close to the building. She's buried there. I shot her because he asked me to do it."

"I get it. You had your partner's back. I respect that."

Scottie shoved his wrists at me. "I'm so glad you approve, now get these off me."

I shot him in the face. I waited until he stopped twitching then rolled him onto a tarp and dragged him to the trunk. My ribs were screaming by the time I got him into it. Luckily, I could walk Pasty Legs to the trunk. I shot him in the heart. He fell back into the trunk, half onto Scottie. The bullet nearly made it through the trunk lid, but not quite. I wrapped them up together and slammed the truck closed.

I contemplated taking another oxy. The pain was sharp but receding. I had a clarity now. I wasn't floating anymore. The Frank in my head was like an angry bee buzzing the rules at me. *Don't get involved. Never kill in your own backyard. Don't make side deals. Always be ready for trouble.*

Blah. Blah. Blah. Shut. Up.

First business, then relief.

GENERALLY SPEAKING, good men and bad men look alike. Sometimes they open their mouths and you know exactly which one you're dealing with. Sometimes they are so clever in their sheep's clothing that even I miss seeing them for what they are. Fortunately, Thomas Nygaard was exactly who I thought he was.

Night had fully descended and I was waiting for him in a corner of what remained of Mallard Gas. I watched his headlights cut across the darkness. He parked his BMW under the awning that used to cover the old pumps. He didn't look around for other cars. He didn't watch his back. He was sheep.

Scottie's phone buzzed in my hand. Thomas was calling. I sent him a text message telling him to come around back. I ran to meet him. He stopped his car next to the Oldsmobile. This time he got out and stood with the car door open and the headlights on.

"Scottie?" he called.

I came up behind him. "Sorry, Scottie is not available."

He squinted at me. "Who's that."

"I'm the one with the gun." I shot out the window next to him.

He jumped away and ran around to the front of the BMW and crouched down low.

"I can still see you. Why did you have your wife killed?"

"I...she was cheating on me."

"No, the real reason."

"Why are you doing this? How much are you being paid? I'll pay more. Whatever you want."

"Your sister paid me enough."

"Rebecca did this? No way."

"Yes way," I said.

I found the video on my phone. I turned the screen out for Thomas Nygaard to see. "Stand up. I'm not gonna shoot you. I just need you to watch this." He peeked over the hood of the car. I wiggled the phone at him, then tossed it at him. "Just press play."

He stood up and in the light I saw his soft middle and his "I'm the man" haircut. He fumbled with the phone a moment, and then the screen lit up. I knew Rebecca's face was looking out at him. Her puffy eyes locked him in place. Then she began to speak. Her small voice was hard for me to hear, but it wasn't for me. I was there when she recorded it.

She said, "I knew something was wrong. She wouldn't have just left without a note or phone call. She was too sweet for that." Thomas shook his head. Rebecca continued. "I found a note under your desk calendar. I thought you hired the Lehman Boys to catch us. But you hired them to kill her." At this point there would be tears streaming down her face. "You're my big brother. I never wanted to hurt you, but I love her. I love her more than I love you. So fuck you for taking her away."

I shot him in the shoulder. He flailed and went to his knees. I came around to stand over him.

"You can't do this!"

My phone rang. Timing is everything. "You think about what

it took for Rebecca to do this. To hire me. Don't go anywhere," I said to him. Then into the phone I said, "Hello, Frank."

"Where are you? You should've been in town hours ago."

"You're checking up on me?"

He chuckled. "I had your payment, but if you don't want it, I'll keep it."

"I got held up, but I'll be there soon."

"Held up?"

I waggled the gun at Thomas. He gasped and raised his arm. "More like distracted."

"Cupcake, do I need to come get you?" The real Frank never called me by my name. Only ever Cupcake.

"No, thank you. I just need to kill this guy and then I'm on my way home."

Frank sighed. The bullet made Thomas's head snap back and the rest of his body continued that direction.

"I'm done now."

"I'll come by in the morning."

I could hear the frown in his voice. "Make it noon, please. I need my sleep."

"No rest for the wicked, Cupcake. I'll expect you at the gym by eight. No later." He hung up.

I began my walk back to town, flinging pieces of the gun into the desert as I went. Frank would have me in the gym sparring and running and sparring some more until I couldn't move. Ah, well. No good deed went unpunished.

Las Vegas, Nevada scribe Nikki Dolson is the author of the novel All Things Violent *and the short story collection* Love and Other Criminal Behavior.

NUMBER NINE

Stephen Spignesi

1
Bang

THEY GRABBED HIM by the ankles, pulled him roughly off the bed and onto the floor, and shone a flashlight in his eyes. He was naked and had an erection, which instantly faded.

"Where is he?"

"Where is who?"

Bang. A slam with the flashlight into the left side of his face.

"Where is he?"

"Where is who?"

Bang. Now he was bleeding.

"One more time. And only one more time. And then you'll die. Where is he?"

"Up your sister's ass."

Bang. Only this time, it was from a gun.

"Let's go."

2
Mr. Senior

"UNION PRISONERS OF war in the Andersonville, Georgia Confederate prison had to bathe and drink from a swamp that was also used by the prisoners as a toilet. Let that sink in for a moment."

"Why did you tell me that?" Trunk Persimmon closed the filing cabinet drawer, moved back to his desk, and sat down heavily.

His associate at DDIS—Discreet Details Investigative Services—Elisha Relish, looked up from the book she was flipping through—*Rachel's Wiccan History of the Civil War*—and said, "Why? What's the problem with me telling you that?"

Trunk sighed and opened a manila folder. "Nothing, Eleesh. Nothing at all."

He looked down at the folder in front of him and said, "Have you seen this?" He tapped the top sheet with his pen.

"The Senior family?" Elisha asked. She pulled a box of orange Tic-Tacs out of her right desk drawer and popped a bunch of them into her mouth. She didn't offer Trunk any and put the box back in the drawer.

"Yeah," Trunk replied.

"Yeah, I did. The old man, Mr. Terrence Senior, is being targeted. They want us to see if there's a hitman after him." Elisha paused and smiled. "Does he have a son? Imagine if he had a son and gave him the same first name. He'd be Terrence Senior, Junior."

Trunk did not crack a smile. "What do you think?"

Elisha closed her book. "Why would he be a target?"

"Well, first off, some people think he's a prick, but that's pretty commonplace in the arena in which he works, and it's not something on which we base our client decisions."

"Which area?" Elisha asked.

"He's a pharmaceutical CEO. Elanor Pharmaceuticals. Without the 'e' before the 'a'."

"Ah." Elisha paused a second. "Why no 'e'?"

"The founder is a huge Tolkien fan. Elanor—E-l-a-n-o-r—is the name of Sam Gamgee's firstborn daughter."

"Sam married Rose."

Trunk nodded. "Right. And Elanor Pharmaceuticals raised

the price a while ago of an experimental drug they developed used for lupus, celiac disease, and other autoimmune diseases. There really isn't an adequate substitute for people who cannot take the usual meds, and Mr. Senior raised the price tenfold."

"How bad did it get?"

"People fucking died. And Senior started getting threats."

"Why didn't he go to the police?"

"They did."

"Lemme guess. 'We can't do anything until something happens,' right?"

"Right."

"So that's why they hired us."

"Yes."

"Are any of the threats serious?"

Trunk looked at Elisha and said, "What's our motto, Eleesh? Actually, the private motto we don't tell clients?"

Elisha chuckled and said, "They're all serious until they're not."

Trunk nodded and said with a smile, "Billable hours, Relish. Billable hours."

Elisha grinned and said, "Okay, so where do we start?"

Trunk pulled a sheet of paper out of the folder and handed it to Elisha. "This one."

3
Nine First Fridays

EVERYONE CALLED HIM Uncle Sally, which was funny, since Sal Tarantollo had no nieces or nephews. No one ever brought that up, though. No one would dare.

Uncle Sally was one of the few made men in mob history who had been allowed to leave OC.

Uncle Sally's sister Loretta was a nun, and she personally went to Sally's Boss in New York and pleaded that her brother be allowed to "retire." The reason? Sally wanted to marry Virginia, but Virginia's family would not allow the wedding to take place if Uncle Sally continued to work in organized crime. "He loves her, sir. Surely you can make an allowance for that?"

At first, the Boss was unmoved, although he did jokingly suggest—to Sister Loretta's horror—that they could get rid of Virginia's family for her if that would solve the problem.

But ultimately, the Boss allowed Sally to retire to Jersey and swear to never set foot in New York again, especially Little Italy. "There'll be blood on Mulberry Street, Sister," the Boss told her, "if your brother even *thinks* about ordering some clams from Umberto's."

Sister Loretta smiled and nodded.

"Good," the Boss said. "Please give my best wishes to the happy couple."

Loretta's negotiations with the Boss became a thing of legend. How did she do it? After the Boss was assassinated by a drive-by machine gunning, she told her brother the story.

She had promised the Boss he'd go to heaven.

There's a little-known bit of Catholic dogma that states that anyone who receives Holy Communion on nine First Fridays in a row is guaranteed admission to heaven, no matter what.

Sister Loretta told the Boss that as a sanctified member of the Catholic clergy and a certified bride of Christ, she could assign her First Friday guarantee to someone else. And she swore she'd bestow it upon the Boss. Of course, she didn't tell him that she had lost her faith years ago and become an atheist and that she had stopped going to Mass or receiving Communion altogether. *Fuck him*, she thought. The ruse worked and Sally and Virginia married and moved to Jersey.

Several years after his retirement, Sally was working as an insurance salesman. One morning in the early Sixties, as he was drinking his coffee and getting ready for work, there was a knock on his back door.

What the fuck?

Virginia was still sleeping upstairs. Sally pulled the curtain on the door aside an inch to see who was on his porch.

He saw two men, impeccably dressed in black suits.

Uh oh.

Sally opened the door. He did not open the screen door.

"Good morning, Sal," the man on the right said. He was not smiling. "Have you got a moment?"

Sal remained silent for a few seconds and then said, "What happened?"

The man nodded and said, "I'll get to the point. A friend of ours has been arrested and we're raising money for his legal bills."

"Which friend?" Sally asked.

"I'm sure you can figure that out."

Jesus fuck.

Sally knew his and Virginia's lives depended on what he did next. He nodded and said, "I understand. Would you gentlemen please allow me to run upstairs for a moment? I would ask you in, but my wife is sleeping and I don't want to disturb her."

The men looked at Sally and didn't move a muscle or make a sound for what seemed like an eternity. Finally, the man on the right gave Sally the tiniest of nods and Sally closed the door. He hoped he survived what was an astonishing display of disrespect. You don't leave two mob lieutenants standing on a back porch.

Sally ran into his den, picked up the phone, and dialed a number.

The call was answered on the first ring. Before Sally had a chance to utter a word, the man on the other end said, "Pay them."

Sally hung up the phone. He pulled out his wallet and looked inside. Eighty-seven dollars.

Sally opened the side drawer of his desk, pulled out a telephone book, and placed it on the desk. He then lifted the wooden bottom of the drawer. Underneath was a manila envelope that contained close to five thousand dollars in cash. Sally counted out ten one-hundred-dollar bills, put the envelope back, covered the panel with the phone book, and closed the drawer.

He rushed to the back door. The men hadn't moved an inch.

He opened the screen door and handed the folded bills to the man who had asked for it.

"This is a thousand dollars. It's all I can afford. I hope it's acceptable. Please express my best wishes to our friend and accept my apologies for the insult of leaving you alone on the porch."

The man took the money and, without even glancing at it, slipped it into his overcoat pocket.

He nodded and they both turned and walked down the steps.

Sally closed the door.

4
Pith

ELISHA LOOKED AT the threat letter Trunk had handed her. She read it out loud:

My sister died because of you. I swear to you on the lives of my children that you will pay for her death, and in ways you cannot begin to imagine.

The depth of my hatred for you knows no bounds.

I know where you live, I know where you work, I know the names of every member of your family. I know your Amazon and Twitter and Wine.com and Instagram and Fidelity passwords.

I know where your grave is. I have shit upon it.

I know where your wife's grave is. I have shot my seed onto it.

Elisha looked up from the letter. "This fucking guy jerked off onto Mrs. Senior's grave?"

"Yup."

Elisha continued. "And it concludes."

You are a piece of shit and I will kill you. I will kill you. I will kill you.

"Pithy," Elisha said, and handed the letter back to Trunk. "So?"

"Well, in a perfect world, if we were to glean anything from the letter, we could determine that the stalker has children, and that his DNA is on the Seniors' graves. And that he's internet savvy. But of course, this is not a perfect world and he could be lying about everything except the threat. Plus, it may have rained since he...deposited his leavings on the graves."

"It's not signed," Elisha said.

"No. And there were no fingerprints anywhere on the letter or the envelope."

"It was mailed to him?"

"No. Senior found it under his windshield wiper in his parking garage at work."

"So what do we do now?"

"Mr. Senior posts a video."

5
Elanor

TERRENCE SENIOR SAT behind his desk in his office at Elanor Pharmaceuticals and tried to slow his breathing. A TV news-quality camera stood on a tripod in front of his desk. Elisha, clad in all black, stood next to it. One of Senior's employees—Nancy from accounting—was on the other side of the camera holding large white cardboard cue cards. Elisha

175

had written Senior's statement.

"Okay, Mr. Senior. I want as little emotion as possible from you. This is a declaration of war and, as such, it needs to be dispassionate and calm. Do not think about what this guy said he was going to do to you, or what he claims to have done. Consider him an enemy to be vanquished. He does not deserve your fear or anxiety. Remember what Churchill said: 'Never give in.'"

Senior nodded. "Okay. I think I can do that."

"I'm going to count down from five and the 'two' and 'one' will be silent."

Senior nodded.

"You all set? Want some water? Have to take a piss?" Elisha winked and whispered, "Quick hand job?"

Senior smiled for the first time since they had begun setting up the filming session.

"No, I'm good."

"Roger. Here we go." Elisha held up her hand with her five fingers splayed and folded them down one at a time as she spoke. "Five, four, three..." Elisha folded down her last two fingers and pointed at Senior. "Go," she mouthed.

My name is Terrence Senior and this is an open message to the person who threatened my life.

You blame me for the death of your sister. I do not accept responsibility for such a horrific crime, nor will I allow you to terrorize me and my family any longer.

We will find you, and you will be held accountable for your vile threats.

I am not afraid of you. Please understand that.

Let me reiterate: I am not afraid of you and we will find you.

You have no idea what is happening. You are unaware, and you will pay.

I encourage you to take this message, and me, seriously.

Thank you for listening. And I hope you paid attention.

Elisha made a throat-cutting sign and stopped filming. "That was great," she said to a somewhat shaken Terrence Senior.

She walked behind the desk and placed her hand on Senior's shoulder. "Take a breath. It's over. You did it. This'll go up on your company's website and your Twitter and Facebook pages today. Within an hour, it'll go viral."

Terrence looked up at Elisha and said, "Thank you, my dear. I appreciate your help. But it is nowhere near over. It is actually, like the Carpenters told us, only just begun."

6
Sally Junior

UNCLE SALLY'S SON was named Salvatore Jr. and he was called Sally Junior.

Sally Junior's sister was named Sally and she was called Little Sally.

Sally Junior had a daughter named Selina and she was called Baby Sally.

Little Sally was Baby Sally's godmother.

7
AM-19

SALLY JUNIOR'S FATHER Uncle Sally had been a made guy in the fifties and sixties until he got a dispensation from the *capo di tutti capi* and became one of the few OC guys to be allowed to retire without getting whacked.

After his father died in 2005 at the age of seventy-five, Sally Junior, forty years old, became the man of the house, and that meant taking care of his twenty-five-year-old sister, Little Sally, who suffered from a rare genetic disease. From when she was a kid, she'd get terrible chest pains, raging fevers, blinding headaches, and digestive troubles, and she'd have trouble breathing almost all the time. She took a drug known as AM-19 that mitigated some of the symptoms, but it was an experimental compound that included a new corticosteroid, an ACE inhibitor, a beta blocker, and a new diuretic, and the drug would not be finally approved by the FDA until after Little Sally had died.

AM-19 was the only drug that truly helped her. She had taken all of the components in one form or another individually, but they made her violently sick. What was new, and thus unapproved about AM-10, was that it could be taken twice a day in liquid form. It worked wonders for Little Sally, but because it was still awaiting approval, the cost of the drug was out-of-pocket. Little Sally's health insurance wouldn't pay for it.

And guess who made AM-19?

Elanor Pharmaceuticals.

The cost of AM-19 was around ten dollars a dose. Little Sally needed two doses a day, which came to around six hundred dollars a month. Sally Junior always managed to come up with the money, even if it meant he had to "suggest" (extort) some "modest" (big money) tribute from a soldier (flunky) in his crew.

Sally Junior remembered the news article verbatim:

Terrence Senior, CEO of Elanor Pharmaceuticals, today announced a tenfold price increase for an experimental compound called AM-19 for which the company is awaiting FDA approval. The liquid medication is being used by patients suffering from serious autoimmune disorders, but because of its experimental nature, health insurance plans do not cover its cost and users must pay out-of-pocket for the drug. When asked about this projected burden on patients, Senior said, "No one likes to raise prices, but sometimes, for the good of the company and the shareholders, as well as future beneficial research, it becomes necessary."

So Little Sally's medication jumped overnight from six hundred to six thousand dollars a month. Sally Junior tried valiantly to keep buying it for her, but there were months when he couldn't afford the full load and Little Sally had to make do with less than half her usual dosage. This did not please her heart and lungs.

Sally Junior's daughter Selina helped with caring for her beloved aunt, but without 100 percent of her meds onboard all the time, the most felicitous, meticulous care didn't matter. Little Sally died five months after the price increase.

Sally Junior had kept her alive for many years, but a pharmaceutical company had essentially orchestrated her death. Sally Junior remembered the last thing his sister had said. She had been reading a collection of Jane Austen's letters and she quoted a line she had memorized: "Sickness is a dangerous indulgence at my time of life."

The day after her funeral, Sally Junior declared war on Terrence Senior.

8
Blocked

TRUNK HIT THE spacebar on his MacBook and the Terrence Senior statement stopped playing.

He looked up at Elisha and said, "Good job. How did he handle himself off-camera?"

"He was a little nervous, but overall, okay. CEOs live under high pressure anyway, so he was probably used to the experience."

Trunk's iPhone bleeped. He picked it up off the desk and dragged the lock slider to the right.

"Trunk Persimmon. Oh, hello, Mr. Senior. Elisha's here. Let me put you on speaker." Trunk did so and placed the phone down on the desk.

"What can we do for you, sir?"

"I heard from him."

Elisha and Trunk locked eyes. Elisha spoke first. "What do you mean, Mr. Senior? Who is 'him'?"

"He said he's in the mafia. He said he's a mob hitman, and that he saw my video, and he said that if I succeeded in doing anything by making it, it was to encourage him to move things along even faster." Trunk and Elisha heard Senior deeply sigh. "He said...this is a quote...'You'll be dead before you know it.'"

"Did he give you his name?"

"No. He just said, 'You know who this is.'"

"How did he contact you?"

"He called my office and the switchboard put him through."

"Caller ID?" Trunk asked.

"Blocked call."

"Okay, Mr. Senior. Don't panic," Elisha said calmly. "We've got security on your car and house. And I'll send someone to your office to escort you to the garage and get you someplace safe."

"No way. This asshole is not scaring me out of my house." He paused. "But you can move my wife and kids if you think that's best."

Elisha looked at Trunk, who gave her a quick nod.

Trunk covered the microphone of the phone and whispered to Elisha, "Tell Philly to triple-check the car—front to back, top to bottom."

Elisha mouthed, "Will do."

"Jesus Christ," Senior said with a tremor in his voice.

"I know," Trunk said. "But don't worry. We'll get you through this, sir."

"Will you?" Senior asked.

"We will. Stay calm and we'll be in touch."

Trunk ended the call.

"Balls," Elisha said. "Big, hairy balls. To call him at his office? This guy's got some serious *cojones*. He's committed. We've got to wrap this up. Fast. And we need to find out if this creep knows we're on the job."

Trunk chuckled dryly. "Y'know something, Relish? With this guy, I wouldn't be surprised if he knew about us on the very day Senior hired us."

Elisha chuckled and said, "You're probably right." She smiled. "Speaking of balls...did you know that Larry David considers balls and toes the most disgusting parts of the human body?" She took a sip of her coffee. "I don't know...I kind of like them both."

Trunk looked at his partner and didn't say anything for what seemed like a long time. He then said, "Good to know."

9
Philly

TRUNK GOT THE call about three in the morning. Philly was dead.

Three guys had broken into his house around midnight, tied up his wife, and then shot Philly in the head. His wife was hysterical, but did manage to tell Trunk that they kept asking her husband, "Where is he? Where is he?" before they shot him.

10
Long-term Parking

SALLY JUNIOR SAT in the 1979 Lincoln Continental he had inherited from his father, Uncle Sally, and watched as two guys examined Terrence Senior's car from front to back and top to bottom. Sally was parked on the same level but a row away from Senior's car and, with his tinted windows, he was essentially invisible to anyone passing by—or in the opposite row.

"You won't find anything, assholes," Sally Junior said softly. "That'd be too easy."

What Sally Junior did not know was that Trunk Persimmon was walking the same parking garage level, dressed in a parking attendant uniform, and pretending to check permits of long-term parkers. Trunk had clocked Sally as soon as he got to Senior's level. He walked slowly by each car, making a big show of writing down license numbers on a sheet on a wooden clipboard. Beneath his sunglasses, though, his eyes were on a black Lincoln Continental about fifteen spaces away from the ramp, and one row opposite Mr. Senior's.

It was four p.m., and Trunk knew Mr. Senior had just left his office and was headed for the parking garage.

Trunk and Elisha had invested in a top-of-the-line, state-of-the-art, in-ear communications system for DDIS and they both loved it. It was completely intuitive: you just spoke and anyone with an earpiece heard you and could respond like normal conversation. No lag, and it was crystal clear. Like Steely Dan sang, "No static at all." It had been expensive, but they both felt it was worth every penny. Elisha had a friend who always used to say, "The two greatest decisions I ever made was to see a therapist and buy a GPS system for my old Toyota." Trunk and Elisha found themselves echoing that sentiment after their purchase of the comm system.

"He's on his way, guys," Trunk said without moving his lips.

"Okay, Trunk," Elisha responded.

"Got it," Dominick said as he felt around Mr. Senior's right rear wheel well.

Elisha was parked one level down, right next to the ramp, and monitoring a parking garage security camera she had hacked into that showed Terrence Senior's car. Her laptop was open on the passenger seat. Her gun was right next to it.

Trunk jotted down another license plate number. He was six cars away from Sally Junior's car.

Elisha watched the elevator door from which Senior would exit.

Trunk and Elisha knew Sally Junior's plan. It was obvious. He would wait until Senior and his bodyguard got to the car. He'd then get out of the Lincoln quickly, take a few steps toward Senior and his crew, and open fire. They knew he probably had a MAC-10 automatic machine pistol and would strafe the area until everyone was dead. At 1,250 rounds a minute, it's unlikely any of his targets would survive.

Elisha didn't even blink as she watched her laptop screen. Her heart skipped a beat when the elevator doors opened.

"He's here," she said.

She watched as Mr. Senior and his bodyguard walked across the concrete floor toward his car. Trunk's two men stood formation as Senior approached. Dominick watched Senior; Andy surveyed the garage. Trunk kept his gaze locked on the Lincoln.

Mr. Senior got to his car and Dominick opened the passenger door. Mr. Senior got in and Dominick closed the door.

He then walked around the car, nodded to Andy, and got in behind the wheel.

As soon as he closed the door, he said, "We're secure."

He then backed out of the parking space and drove slowly toward the exit ramp.

Trunk walked a little more quickly toward the Lincoln. He stopped one car away. "No movement," he said to Elisha.

"Nothing to report, Trunk. Dommy and Senior are gone. Andy's walking to his own car."

What should I do? I know Sally Junior is after Senior. And Elisha confirmed he owned the Lincoln from an MVD check on the plates.

"Fuck it," Trunk said out loud and ran toward the Lincoln. He was wearing body armor and the thought went through his mind, *I hope he doesn't aim for my head if he starts shooting.*

He drew his Glock, reached the Lincoln and shouted, "Tarantollo! Come out with your hands up!"

Nothing.

He moved to the driver's door, yanked it open, and Sally Junior fell sideways out of his seat, ending up halfway out of the car, his body stopped from hitting the ground by the steering wheel.

He was dead.

An autopsy would determine cause of death to be a massive cerebral embolism. He was dead in less than a heartbeat. He was dead before he knew he was dying. The coroner said embolisms like the one that took out Sally Junior were like flipping a switch.

11
We Done?

THREE DAYS LATER, Trunk and Elisha sat in Mr. Senior's living room, small glasses of Fernet-Branca on the table before them.

Mr. Senior sat opposite them in the biggest single-person chair either of them had ever seen.

"So?" Senior began. "We done?"

Trunk and Elisha looked at each other and Elisha spoke first. "That's up to you, sir."

"What does that mean?"

It was Trunk's turn. "It depends on how safe you feel now that the man who targeted you is dead."

Senior smiled and said, "I feel pretty fucking safe, truth be told. And please excuse my vulgarism."

"I see," Trunk replied. "Well, then…"

"Hang on," Senior interrupted. "Should I feel *un*safe? Is there something you're not telling me?"

Elisha chuckled and said, "No, sir, not at all. Salvatore Tarantollo was on a mission of personal vengeance. This was not business. Thus, it is highly unlikely that any members of his crew, or any of his lieutenants would consider you to be, shall we say, 'unfinished business,' and seek to finish what Sally Junior didn't."

Senior furrowed his brow, took a sip of his Fernet, and said, "I see." He leaned forward. "But what about the rest of his family? Is there anyone who would feel a responsibility to wrap up this 'personal business,' as you describe it?"

"Unlikely," Trunk said. "His sister is dead, he has no brothers, and cousins would not presume to make such a decision on their own. His sister had a daughter, Selina, but she's not involved at all in 'family' matters."

"What does she do?" Senior asked.

"She's an English professor at the University of New Haven. Tenured."

Senior nodded and leaned back, the chair almost swallowing him whole. "I see. Yes, it's unlikely that a woman poetry teacher would take out a hit on me," he said with a palpable air of condescension.

Senior stood. Trunk and Elisha immediately did the same.

"Well, then, I guess it's over. I want to thank you both for your excellent work. Please send my final bill at your earliest convenience. I will take care of it immediately and would like to add a little something extra for your superior efforts."

"That's not necessary, Mr. Senior," Elisha said. She then winked at him and said, "But we'll take all the help we can get."

Hands were shaken, cordialities were exchanged, and the case of "Terrence Senior: Stalking, Threatening" was officially concluded.

12
Nine Months Later

FRIDAY MORNING. EARLY.

Terrence Senior was alone in the house. The maid had called

in sick, his wife was at a spa, and his kids were away at school. Even the dog was absent, recovering from minor surgery at the vet's. So Senior had to answer the door himself when the doorbell rang at the too-early hour of seven.

He opened the door, prepared to lace into the cretin who had the audacity to disturb him at such an obscene time, but instead froze when he saw a lovely young woman smiling at him.

She was twenty-eight years old but looked younger. She had red hair, was slim, and her complexion was spotless. She reminded Senior of the actress Alicia Witt when she had guest starred on *The Sopranos*.

"Yes?" Senior said. "Can I help you?"

Selina smiled and said, "Hello, Mr. Senior. I'm here from Discreet Details Investigative Services."

"You are?" Senior said with a puzzled expression on his face. "That's odd. Trunk or Elisha didn't call me about anything."

Selina chuckled and said, "Oh, they must have just forgotten. They're so busy, you know."

"Very well. Please come in."

Senior stepped back, Selina walked in, and he closed the front door.

13
"CEO Found Slain"

THE FBI TODAY reported the slaying of Terrence Senior, CEO of Elanor Pharmaceuticals. His body was discovered in his home by his wife upon her return from a trip.

Senior had been found in the bathtub of his private bathroom. He had been bound with duct tape, castrated, and shot once in the head and once in the chest.

Officials said nothing was reported stolen from the Senior residence.

The investigation is ongoing.

14
Number Nine

BABY SALLY WALKED slowly down Senior's driveway to her car, which she had parked on the street four doors down.

She smiled and said, "There you go, Auntie." And then, "Hope I did you proud, Daddy."

She glanced at her watch. She had ten minutes to get to church. She was excited. Today was her ninth First Friday.

Stephen Spignesi is the author of the novel Dialogues. *He has also written more than seventy nonfiction books on topics as diverse as Stephen King, Elton John, the Beatles, and* The Sopranos.

TO THE SURVIVORS

T. Fox Dunham

"I SURVIVED THEM all," Leo said. "The whole fucking family. It was my punishment." He set his cane against the wall of the alley and steadied the Colt 1911 with his right hand. Arthritis in his knuckles throbbed, and his arm trembled.

"You didn't disappoint," Michael said. He sat at peace in the chair, hands folded in his lap. The old man didn't look surprised when Leo stepped out from the alley next to the Boardwalk Chapel, and he went willingly into the shadows out of sight. He didn't fight, try to take off, or call for help to the families walking by.

"You knew I'd come?" Leo asked.

"I played this moment out again and again."

"Congratulations on the book." Michael had to yell over the congregation singing in the church that had setup in the store-front that used to be Cabrini's Pizza. Across the boardwalk, kids fired tennis balls at floating battleships in a tank. No one paid attention to two seniors chatting in an alley.

"I struggled writing it," Leo's old friend said.

"Really? Talking came easily enough for you," Leo said, getting in a barb.

"Not easily enough," Michael said. "Not about the important things. I always figured I'd die in prison or be found in someone's trunk in AC. If I knew I'd survive to old fuckery, I would have done things differently."

"Yeah. I get that." Leo's parched tongue tripped up his words, and he needed some cool water to wet his sandy mouth. In the distance, the surf roared as it reached out to the beach then dragging its foamy fingers down the firm wet sand. His body ached in some places, burned in others. Reminiscing made him fully aware of his decrepit state. It was time to end this and spare himself the fate of survivors.

"I know it's futile to tell you I'm sorry," Michael said.

"For betraying your family?"

"Fuck no. For not convincing you to betray them too."

Leo carefully knelt down in front of the chair until their eyes met at level. "I don't want to do this," he said. "But all I have is my perfect score. My reputation."

"I'm just glad we're together at the end," Michael said.

Leo aimed, remembering his old mantra, ready for the right moment of intuition when the stars and moon aligned above the Boardwalk Chapel in Wildwood, New Jersey where the two old mafia killers languished in perpetual torment so close to the almighty.

"Set your mark," he recited.

"Just tell me," Michael said. "How long did you know?"

"A reporter showed up at my door this morning," Leo said. "He drove me out here. He's waiting at a bar to hear how this story ends. Before that, I thought I was the last survivor."

EIGHT HOURS EARLIER and sixty-five miles east in South Philly, Leo Leonardo, ex-soldier of the Bruno-Scarfo Philadelphia crime family, waited to die in his shithole of a studio apartment.

"Set your mark," Leo whispered, reciting the mantra. He aimed his piece and steadied his hand. The relic only discharged on occasion—seldom at his command and always at the least desired times. In fifty years, Leo had never lost a mark, and when he died—soon, dear God, soon—he'd wear that sin of pride with pride. Still, it didn't fire. He clenched the flaccid piece of flesh between his fingers. Finally, pain seared through his urethra, but he held steady, keeping his hands in place lest he'd spray the bathroom floor. He dribbled—not enough to give him relief from the constant pressure of his bladder. When no more came, the old man pulled up his underwear, tied his robe shut and resigned himself to the threadbare couch that also served as his bed.

Leo turned on the old television to the end of *The Reverend Johnny Light Show*. He knew Johnny back on South Street when he went by Johnny Cello, and even then he sucked as a two-bit flimflam man.

"Pulling that plug is no act of mercy!" the evangelist yelled, going on about assisted suicide. That reminded Leo. He reached under the pillow, pulled out his piece, and pressed it under his chin.

"Set your mark," he said, hoping his mantra gave him the nerve this time.

"Sin. Sin! Vengeance is mine, sayeth the Lord. He gives life. It is for no man to take it."

Leo's fingers ached, and he squeezed the gun to keep it steady; still, it slipped. He had done this twenty-three times during his career, and it came so naturally to him—the only time he ever felt real in this world. For fifty years he had lied to everyone, especially himself, but taking a life made an honest connection. Nothing could be more intimate than the binary transition between life and death.

Someone knocked, and Leo aimed at the door. No one came to visit him. The super never fixed anything, so she wouldn't need to get into the apartment. "If you're from the church," he yelled. "I don't want any of your fucking meals!"

"Leo Leonardo?" spoke a voice through the door. It sounded like a young man. Maybe it was Bobby or Lee—one of his grandkids looking to learn about their family history. He'd seen it on television, and he'd played out the scene in his mind again and again. Leo slid the Colt under the couch then propped himself up to get to the flimsy door.

A young guy, college student maybe, sporting a patchy and thin black beard stood in the doorway holding up his phone. "Mr. Leonardo?" A door slammed shut down the hall, and the kid jumped. He was either really brave to walk into this junkie's den or really stupid. Leo bet on the latter. "I'm Toby Williams with Philadelphia Media News. I wanted to get your comment on—"

"I don't talk to reporters," Leo said.

"Did you know this man?" the kid asked, pulling a book out of his bag and showing him the cover. The image smacked Leo in the head, and he stepped back, leaning against the wall to stay standing. "The picture is of Michael 'The Angel' Anzio." Leo didn't say anything, just stared at the cover. The photo was taken nearly thirty years ago in August of '91 not more than a block over at the Italian Market. He'd just bought that red '89 Camaro with the money from the truck heist on I-95. His youth startled Leo—seeing Michael again in his cutoff jean shorts and sandals, thick arms wrapped over his chest as he leaned back against his new car.

"I took this fucking picture." Leo had to sit down. The kid took that as an invitation and shut the door behind him. "Someone write a book about us?"

"Mr. Leonardo. I'm writing an article about the surviving Mafioso who profit off of their crimes by selling their stories. Henry Hill and the guy who killed Jimmy Hoffa."

"I don't know what the fuck you're talking about," Leo said, reciting the old line, keeping loyal to the code. You never talked about this thing of ours. "Who wrote this?" he asked. He couldn't read the byline without his glasses. "Is this Connie's doing? His sister. She find some old papers of his? Made up a fat story?"

"You haven't heard?" Toby smiled, and Leo recognized the look of ambition on his face. The kid had walked in on one hell of a story.

"I don't hear much these days, kid, and I don't give a shit about what I do hear."

"The Justice Department faked Michael Anzio's death after the botched hit in New Jersey twenty years ago."

"*Cazzata!*" Leo turned the book over to a headshot of the author—same angelic features, though gnarled by age and wrinkled by time. Over the years, Leo often wondered how Michael might look if he'd gotten old, but actually seeing it shocked him. All this time, he was alive, probably stashed in some town out west where he'd gone on with his life. Leo squeezed the book until his fingers ached.

"We'll pay you an honorarium."

"You don't talk about *this thing*," he said. "How much?" It went against the code, but Leo had been left with nothing at the end of it—just his honor and his perfect score—well, maybe not so perfect. And this is where all that got him: a shitty studio apartment, living with junkies, without friends or family and with a gun in his mouth while these guys were writing books and gaining a folk hero status by jerkoffs in cafes who recited lines from the movies over and over again. Who the fuck was he protecting? Everyone talked sooner or later. It had just become part of the life.

"We pay a couple hundred depending on the size of the article."

"You win, kid," Leo said. "But we do this my way. I'll give you something better than a quote."

"Like what?" Toby asked, getting that look again.

"Enough to write my life story then sell it to Netflix, but not until I'm dead. Don't worry. You won't have long to wait. You heard of omerta?"

"The oath you...*made guys* in the mafia took to protect your brothers and always keep silent."

Leo fished some clothes out of his dresser. "It isn't an oath. It's a promise that you'll accept what's coming to you if you break the rules. And stop calling it *the mafia*. We never called it that. It's was *our thing.*" His young eyes lit up like Dante gazing into hell with a pen up his ass ready to write a stanza. "You said this book party was in Wildwood?" Leo asked, pulling his crucifix necklace over his shirt. His pants sagged even with a tight belt, and he felt like a child dressing in his father's clothes.

"He is having his release party at Captain Spitzie's Deck. Limited invites. Every crime reporter in Philly tried to get an invite. I mean, the guy came back from the dead. But I don't think there ever was a hit. The US Marshals faked it so everyone would think he was dead."

"There was a hit." Toby stepped back from Leo, visibly shaken. It must have just dawned on him that he had wandered into the home of one of the most effective syndicate hired killers since Murder Incorporated. "I'm going to make a deal with you, kid. You accept, and you'll have a fucking bestseller."

"You'll tell me everything?" he asked.

"I made a living exploiting people and their weaknesses. Why should I begrudge you the same?"

"A book? Yeah. Okay. And may it bring you the same riches it brought me." Leo waved about the shithole, then searched for a saint card from the pile on the top of his dresser—leftovers from the funerals he had attended. He found one of the Virgin Mary.

"Cup your hands."

"Ahh...I guess?"

Leo dropped the prayer card in his hand then lit it with a cracked plastic liter. The kid nearly dropped it, and Leo grabbed his palms. "And like this card burns may my soul burn in hell if I ever betray my family—well me." The kid repeated and the card burned in his hands. Then he ran to the sink and dropped it.

"You got a car?" Leo asked.

"I borrowed my mom's to drive into the city," he said.

"Go get it, and I'll tell you on the way. Just keep your fucking mouth shut. I don't want to know you, and you don't want to know me. And this gets published when I'm dead. You send thirty percent to my family." Leo knew he didn't need a contract. In his life, all he'd ever had to do was tell someone to do something, and they did it.

"Where are we going?" the kid asked.

"Are you really that fucking stupid?" Leo asked, already regretting this, but how the fuck else was he going to get to east Jersey?

"When's the last time you talked to him?" Toby asked, figuring it out.

"1991."

LEO TOOK THE photo, then Michael released his pose and got into the driver's side of his new Camaro. The camera spit out the photo, and he shoved it into his top pocket. He felt like an idiot wearing the beach clothes, but they planned to use the crowd as cover.

"She's a fine piece of ass," Leo said through the open window. He tossed his bag on the back bucket seat then got in. Michael put out a cigarette in the ashtray then lit up a second. His hands shook. He pulled out of the fire lane then turned left onto South Street, heading away from the onramp onto I-76. "Where are you going? Wildwood is that way."

"Shit," Michael said. "I...had a late night. I was up all night thinking about my trial."

"We all get pinched sooner or later," Leo said. "Forget the trial. If they offer you a deal, take a few months in jail. It's honestly not worth the hassle, and you'll get your stripes. The bosses will remember that you stood up when they open the books, they'll straighten us all out."

Michael switched on the stereo to the new Marky Mark song, turned onto I-76 and rolled all the windows down. They had the world by the fucking balls—two young soldiers rising fast, having proven themselves to be useful and soulless, which was the perfect combination in such an organization. Michael grew his hair out long back then, and a wave of blond fell down along his angelic cheekbones. Often, Leo had reached out to touch it when Michael had his back to him, certain it would feel soft like silk. He always pulled back his hand quickly.

Two hours later, they parked behind an arcade on the north end of the boardwalk. Families arrived, taking their kids to the beach and dragging carts of towels and umbrellas and toys—perfect cover for their pickup. Atlantic City was too important to the operation, so the boss, Nicodemus "Little Nicky" Scarfo, arranged deliveries off a boat anchored in international waters. Charter fishing boats sailed out to pick up the shipments then brought them back to the pier. It was risky shit since the Coast Guard had a base near the shore town, but the feds were watching AC. The two found the Cobia 296, "The Polyphemus," in the marina off the boardwalk. The crew disembarked that morning. Michael and Leo went aboard, dug through barrels of ice and fish for the cargo, then loaded up the packages into his backpack.

"Little Nicky is shitting bricks over this Kuwait thing," Michael said. He stopped packing and scanned the pier, looking for something. "He's worried with everything going down over there the shipments are going to be light from our friends with the poppy fields."

"I brought an electronic scale," Leo said and dug out another package of powder. "We'll weigh it before we leave."

"Smart," he said, checking the dock again.

"Will you relax?" Leo asked. "We weren't followed. We were careful."

"Yeah. Did Mary bitch you weren't bringing her down?" Michael asked, changing the subject.

"She's staying with her mother until she pops. She says I keep her up by coming in every hour of the night."

"Yeah," Michael said. "You're a bastard. Mary must have a lot of Christian charity."

"You have no idea," Leo said and sighed. He tried to come

home after she'd fallen asleep to avoid any chance of sex. Leo felt nothing for her. He never had for a woman, and it was just easier this way. He had trapped her in this life, made her a part of his cover.

After unloading the shipment, Leo grabbed the bag and headed back to the boardwalk. Families crowded the walkway. Couples held hands, strolling together along the shops and arcades. The iconic yellow tram eased by, and an automatic system warned people to watch the tram cars. They always stopped for a slice at Cabrini's Pizzeria before heading back. Leo loved smelling the aroma of baking cheese and grease. When they were done, they'd throw crust pieces to the seagulls.

Michael kept looking around, checking for feds maybe. "We're cool, Michael," Leo said. "You're making me nervous." Michael stepped into an alley between a frozen custard stand and the pizzeria where they kept the garbage cans then grabbed Leo's shoulder, pulling him into the shadows.

"What the fuck, Michael?" He got close to Leo to whisper. "You're not going to kiss me, are you?" He grabbed the silver cross dangling from his neck.

Michael whispered into his ear. Chills spiked down Leo's back. "I have to tell you. Leo, I just...how come you never dated in school?"

"What the fuck?"

"When I was eighteen, I couldn't ask enough girls out. I had a date every Friday and a second every Saturday—and woe if two ever should meet."

"Right," Leo said. "A real fucking ladies' man. What's your point?"

"You never had a date."

"I've always been a one-woman man," Leo said, employing the casual lie, the one he'd polished from use. "What's this about?" Michael leaned in close. Leo felt the brush of his lips along his earlobe, and his heart raced.

"We should sell the shipment and go," Michael said. "Leave

all this shit behind. Go to Spain. We wouldn't have to hide there." Blood rushed through Leo's face. They'd never been this close, and in the dark no one would see. He tried to catch his breath, tried to answer, but he'd been struck mute. Michael's built body rubbed up against his. Their chests touched, and Leo felt hardness pushing against his shorts. Michael's hot breath blew on his check.

"What the fuck's gotten into you? Why are you doing this—?"

"I'm sorry, Leo," he said. "It wasn't stolen stereos. They caught me dealing."

"Michael, what the fuck did you do?" He broke out of his embrace, ran into the sunlight, dodging the happy couples and families and back out onto the pier. He spotted several staties in uniform chasing after him. He made it to deeper water, banging into a group of guys carrying fishing rods. When he spotted an Invincible 36 backing into an open slot, Leo tossed the bag into the green waters. The bag sank in the wake of the boat, and he turned around with his hands up in the air and a shit-eating grin on his face.

THE PHILLY DA had some shit on him for robbing a truckload of LaserDisc players, but they never recovered the shipment he'd thrown into the ocean. The screws on the fishing boat ripped open the bag and the seawater did the rest. Without the evidence, the DEA had to drop their charges, but he was still going to do time. The rest of the family wasn't so lucky. Michael was just one of the guys they'd flipped along with Nicholas "Nicky Crow" Caramandi and Nicky Scarfo's nephew, Philip "Crazy Phil" Leonetti. Over the next two years, the feds took everyone off the street and jammed them up with RICO.

Leo even looked forward to jail. Most of the guys dreaded it. When you were off the street, you couldn't earn, and if you couldn't earn, you weren't much use to your crew or the bosses. Yeah. They promised to take care of your family when you stood up but that only lasted a few months. The DA offered to advise the judge to suspend his sentence if he testified against the family, but Leo knew what to say.

Blow me.

Anyway, prison was the only place he felt some peace. He kept his nose clean, didn't start any beefs, and most of the guys in Lewisburg were wiseguys, so he didn't have to watch his back as much. He slept good at night, did a lot of reading, played cards with guys from the other crews. One prison freed him from another, and he felt relieved that he no longer had to lie to Mary or worry that she knew the truth, that she sensed the real reason for his distance and constant compensation with jewelry and cars and vacations. All that shit was outside the walls, and he didn't have to struggle every day under the weight of the image he'd built.

He got out, and things just got worse at home. He couldn't look at his family anymore. Leo loved them but hated them too. In '93, Mary took their sons and moved out to Indiana to take a job at a bank where her sister worked.

After that, the Philly family was never the same. He ran some book, did a few jobs for New York, but he never stopped looking for Michael. Even after the bosses who had put out the contracts on Michael died, he kept putting money on the street. Most of those guys in the Justice Department were degenerate fucking gamblers or had other appetites he could exploit. Usually the feds planted rats out in Idaho or New Mexico where wiseguys would dry up and die in the sun but sooner or later, the turncoats missed their old turf and always came back. Then, Joey Minnow got his conviction thrown out, and the DA had to try him again. They brought Michael out of whatever desert they stashed him and set him up in a condo in Wildwood—Wild-fucking-wood! It wasn't all that crazy. The feds stashed Phil Leonetti in Ocean City, Maryland. During the summer, vacationers came and went in the shore towns, so a new face wouldn't attract much attention. Some of the New

York guys owned motels and beach houses out there, and word got back. By the end of the week, Leo looked through a telescopic scope on a fishing boat in Sunset Lake on the inlet off the Atlantic, waiting for the waves to settle down.

Michael loved the beach early in the morning, before anyone was out but the joggers and people with metal detectors. Leo got a tip on suspected safe houses on the island then camped on a boat where he could watch the beach. He patrolled the shore, hoping to get lucky. Then one morning, he got a hit. Even from a distance, he recognized Michael's brazen attitude. He really thought no one could get to him, that he'd beaten the system. There was no one left from the families, right? All he had to do was rat on a guy in court again, and he'd go back to his life out west as Mr. John Hanfuck.

Leo struggled to aim his TKiv 85 from this distance, but he had to hurry. He knew he'd be made any moment.

"Set your mark. Wait for your moment."

Michael's FBI keeper ran into view and grabbed his shoulder to get him out of there. Then the moment came. Like a reflex, Leo fired just as Michael turned. Blood burst from the agent's hand, and Michael went down. The shot must have hit him in the back, but Leo couldn't stick around to confirm. The Coast Guard would be out in moments. He wiped down the rifle then dove off the side and swam like hell to the shore. He had a car waiting for him and was on the Atlantic City Expressway while the Coast Guard was checking out the boat he'd borrowed.

That night, Philly CBS news reported that a mob informant had died of natural causes. Leo threw a bottle at the screen. If the feds let it be known that one of their witnesses got whacked under their protection, no one would flip again. At least there wouldn't be a huge manhunt after him, but it also meant he wouldn't get paid.

Then for the next twenty-seven years, he drank himself to sleep every night and grew old alone, always alone, until the morning a reporter knocked on his door.

IN WILDWOOD, nearly twenty-seven years later, the congregation in the Boardwalk Chapel ended their song.

Leo aimed the Colt at a black mole on Michael's wrinkled forehead. His old friend never broke his gaze, looking into Leo's eyes. Though faded and intersected with spidery veins, he recognized the same spirit he'd known since they'd both met as altar boys at Saint Joseph the Worker in South Philly.

"I'm ready," Michael said.

"So am I." He handed the piece to Michael, placing the grip in his hand and aiming the angry end at Leo's own chest.

"Leo…"

Leo's knees ached from kneeling on the gnarled and beaten boards. He lost his balance and pushed the wheelchair into the alley wall. The Colt slipped from Michael's fragile grip and dropped into his lap. "We weren't supposed to survive," Leo said. "We joined the life. Never said we were fucking sorry. I always thought we'd die in jail or get whacked by a friend. We were never going to grow old and rot like this."

"That's why you came here?" Michael asked. "You killed all those people, but you needed me to put you out of your misery?"

"I'm a fucking coward," he said, grabbing onto his dangling crucifix with his left hand and holding onto the arm of the wheelchair with his right. "I can't do the last job. It should be you. I put you in this fucking chair."

"It doesn't have to be this way," Michael said. His nostrils flared like they used to when they were young and defiant.

"Because you want me to keep suffering? How do I make this right?"

"I have a beach house off Park Avenue," Michael said. "We've suffered enough. We still have some time, and I don't give a flying fuck what anyone thinks anymore." Michael let go his hand and cupped Leo's chin in his palm, then he leaned forward and found his lips with his. Leo yanked back by reflex.

His heart pounded, and he nearly blacked out.

"What the fuck are you doing?" Leo asked.

"Living the twilight of my life," he said. "If we'd been born in this time…"

"You know what the guys would do to us if they thought we were—?"

"They're fucking dead, Leo…my only."

Leo wanted to go with him but he didn't know if he could. He'd buried these feelings deep where none of his crew could see, where his parents and his wife couldn't see it, where God couldn't see it, and Leo had spent his life showing how tough he was, whacking people to cloak himself in a tough reputation. He was always terrified someone was going to glean his sinful tendencies.

"They're all burning in hell," Michael said. "We survived. No one cares what we do."

"Go fuck yourself, Michael. I can't just let it all go. We took an oath. We were soldiers, remember? Oh yeah. I forgot. You turned your back on us. You fucking turned your back on me."

"It was the only way I could be free."

"This shit is all new for me," Leo said. "I don't know how to do this."

"Love. Murder. Set your mark. Feel your moment."

And Leo felt it. He let go and kissed him, For the first time, the kiss felt right—not forced or pretended, not a burden or a lie. For the first time, the old killer felt grateful that he had lived this long.

"Come home with me," Michael said while trying to catch his breath.

"For a while," he said. "Promise me that when it gets too much—"

A YEAR LATER, Leo sat on the edge of their bed typing on a laptop in the bedroom of Michael's beach house. He could only type so much each day before his hands ached. Neither of them had slept, still processing the news from the oncologist in Philly, and they'd talked all night, drinking a cabernet and looking at photos they'd taken while traveling together to promote his book. Leo's presence was an added bonus, and the world had fallen in love with their story.

"It feels right?" Michael asked.

Leo tried to answer him, but a violent coughing fit choked him. He grabbed his inhaler to calm the fit. His left lung ached through his chest. "Yeah. This guy's got to go."

"I don't want to be here with you out," Michael said. "I tried that for a while."

Leo attached the last document. They'd written it all down without prevarication or deception. This was the way it happened and that's how it turned out. Then he sent the email to that reporter kid like he'd promised. It was all his shit now.

"Could you get me my—"

"Yeah." Leo got their pieces from the night table, handed one of them to Michael, then he wrapped his arms around his love's frail and broken body. Then he joined his beloved in a toast. "Well fuck," he said. "To the survivors."

They finished their wine, set down the glasses then picked up the tools of their trade.

"One last job," Michael said. "At least your perfect record is secure."

"Set your mark..."

He aimed at Michael's chest, and Michael aimed at his.

Philadelphia's T. Fox Dunham is the author of The Street Martyr, Destroying the Tangible Illusion of Reality; or, Searching for Andy Kaufman, Mercy, *and* Dr. Kevorkian Goes to Heaven.

THE FIRST HORSEMAN

Clark Roberts

"HE'S DEAD, RAPHE," Sylvia said into the disposable cell phone. "You better send some of your goons over pronto."

"You check his pulse? Put a mirror beneath his nose?" Father Raphe asked.

"I did check!" she spat, and a split-second later winced at the sharpness of her sudden outburst—almost like a gunshot.

The piled-up stress from everything—the lifestyle, the affair, and now the murder—had reached a breaking point inside her. She seriously didn't need to be taken to task right now with questions insinuating she was too dense to know a dead body staring back at her. No, what she desired was a sense of trust to come from the man she'd been screwing the past year. For crying out loud, she'd knocked off her husband to demonstrate her loyalty to Father Raphe.

"Sylvia," Father Raphe's voice went low and serious. "Nobody talks that way to me, not even my new arm candy."

Is that what she was to him? Arm candy?

Did she even care as long as it moved her up the social ladder a rung or two in this crazy-ass life?

The internal answer might have been different except it wasn't just a rung or two climb; it was a jump all the way to the top of the city's crime scene.

She knew how Father Raphe operated, knew he didn't keep women around forever, but he rarely left them high and dry either.

Certainly he discarded them, but as long as they didn't cross him, as long as they took being cast aside with a little dignity, he'd always made certain they landed in much comfier circumstances than prior their time as his girlfriend.

The couple girls that hadn't accepted a clean break from Father Raphe? Well...Sylvia had heard the stories of muzzle flashes in the dark and concrete shoes.

Still, she'd secretly hoped it could be different for her, that she could prove she was the true ride-or-die kind of woman fit for the position of Father Raphe's queen of the gangster world, but also brimming with enough class for the religious facade.

Wasn't that her entire life packed neatly into a bullet casing?—the constant drive to prove she was worthy of more than her trailer trash childhood determining all life's meaningful decisions.

"I'm sorry," she mumbled. There was no other choice at this point. Her husband of thirteen years' legs were in view on the other side of the dining table. He was crumpled on the floor, his dinner plate broken in half and spaghetti splashed next to his head.

"Now that it's done, do you regret it?" Father Raphe asked.

"No." The firmness of her response surprised even herself. It was true, but there was little to no joy either. "Please don't have me killed for what I'm about to say, Raphe, but I did love Dean, and I still don't regret it."

"I'm not having you whacked. This proves you're all in, and I can live with that even if ole Deano couldn't."

"Okay," Sylvia sighed. "I'm not trying to be bitchy, but will you please send somebody over for clean-up?" *Jesus, that's all my husband is now, a mess that needs a good wiping away.* "I'm shaking, and having him stare back at me isn't helping."

"I got some boys on the way as we speak. And, sweetie...?" Father Raphe paused, a silent prompt demanding a response. It was a part of his authoritarian makeup, a skill that always gave him the upper hand.

"Yes?" she asked.

"You made the right choice. Dean was of great service to me over the years, but you did the right thing. If you hadn't, right now you'd be lying next to him."

The connection cut off.

Sylvia shivered. Lord almighty, Raphe was as cold blooded as a reptile.

SHE STEPPED PAST Dean's body, her heels clicking on the mahogany flooring of their dining room. Mahogany was nice, but it wasn't bocote, which she knew Raphe had in his compound outside the city where he stayed part of the time.

In the kitchen she took down a wine glass and filled it. Drank.

She closed her eyes.

You made the right choice.

But had she?

Her confession to Father Raphe was true. She *had* loved Dean, even over the last few months while feeding light traces of arsenic to him on his dinner plates.

She'd been trailer trash her whole life up to meeting Dean one night in the strip bar. She hadn't been on stage, rather serving tables, and when the man with slicked-back hair and a professional shave—something he always paid for on a *hit* night Sylvia later learned—had flicked his grey eyes to hers, it might as well have been a match to gasoline for the flaming heat it created between them. She'd sat with him near the end of the night, and he'd confessed what he was. She hadn't believed his hitman story, but the next day when she went to work, the place was swarming with cops. Her boss's car had never left the parking lot after closing time. The boss's body had been found slumped over his steering wheel, a clean shot from the back seat that exited his forehead and punched through the windshield. Debts to the wrong people. The ridiculously simple questions asked by the onsite detective had made it easy for Sylvia to play dumb that morning. After five minutes she'd been sent away, and she left with the impression the detective hadn't wanted to hear any real evidence; that deep down he already knew the truth but was content, maybe even desired, to let it all fly to the wind.

You made the right choice.

But the affair with Father Raphe, the top dog, had been hot—so skin-scorching hot that even with her dead husband one room over goose bumps sprang alive to her flesh.

Plus, feelings of true love or not toward Dean, the pull to move up in class was too damned tempting. Why continue to be tail for the boss's right-hand man when you could be tail for the boss?

You made the right choice.

She downed the wine quickly, needed another, and even on the second pour her nerves still tapped the bottle against the rim of her glass.

She needed space between her and Dean. Dead Dean.

Dead Deano.

Deano, that's how Father Raphe had referred to him whenever calling in a favor. Cute plays on people's names was definitely a display of dominance. Dean probably hadn't given a shit though, because the money for being the boss's number one hitman paid well, and truthfully, Dean loved the work, loved what all the extra pay provided for him and Sylvia.

Provider—that was Dean to a tee. He'd have been an excellent father if Sylvia had ever desired children.

Dean the provider.

Dean the should've had the chance to be a father.

Dead Dean.

Deano.

She exited the kitchen out the opposite side to avoid the dining room and dead Deano.

In the spacious living room, she fell back into the leather sofa, clicked on the TV simply for comfort.

When the doorbell rang two hours later, it shook her awake. The clock on the wall said it was well past ten p.m., so Raphe must have lied earlier. He hadn't at that moment already ordered "boys on the way." Sylvia slid her feet out of the heels—hard to believe she'd fallen asleep with them on—smoothed her skirt, and padded to the front door.

The night air was cooler by degrees. She recognized the two faces staring back at her from the porch: Mike "Guttermouth" Spitzer and Bones, the lanky sidekick whose complexion could make chalk jealous.

Guttermouth's white Mustang, so pristinely clean it nearly glowed in the dark as much as the moon's face, was parked perfectly straight in the driveway, engine humming. Sylvia recalled Dean commenting on the muscle car more than once—*that's one fine piece of American machinery for such a POS like Guttermouth to be steering.*

Before Sylvia could say hello, Guttermouth greeted her with a question, "Where's the cold son-of-a-bitch at?"

"Dean wasn't cold," Sylvia scolded back, and shook her head. She squinted at the men before her. The sudden urge to defend the man she'd loved yet killed suddenly rose up in her like a wakened tiger. She wasn't about to let these two dipshits talk down on him when he wasn't alive to defend himself. "He might've been your outfit's best hitman, but damn it, he was a really warm husband, more caring than me or either of you two dolts."

These two men on her porch were dangerous, maybe not as much as Dean had been, but they were certainly muscle that belonged to Father Raphe and that counted for something in these parts. However, Sylvia also knew *they* knew the game between her and Father Raphe and dead Deano—*shit, she had to stop thinking of him that way.* Since she was now Father Raphe's flower, she didn't think the goons would do her harm.

"He means dead," Bones said, in a voice as dry as desert dust. Over his shoulder, Bones carried a roll of clear industrial plastic wrap. As if in a spelling bee, he continued. "Cold. D-E-A-D. Cold."

Sylvia blinked. She'd been in the company of these two goons at social gatherings when they were acting as Father Raphe's bodyguards, and they were always present whenever she'd snuck over to the church to offer Father Raphe a little action.

Guttermouth wasn't exactly gregarious. Whenever he did talk he proved the nickname fit him like a glove, but Sylvia couldn't recall ever hearing Bones breathe let alone make a joke.

Guttermouth snickered, sliding his eyes with disbelief at his partner's sudden sense of humor. The toothpick in his mouth rolled from one side to the other. "Bitch, just tell us where the fucking body is."

She glanced around the neighborhood—a few front porch lights on and a dog barked in the distance. Besides that, the subdivision slept.

She stepped aside, inviting the goons in.

Guttermouth entered first, then Bones with the plastic wrap. Bones winked as he passed, but his long face never changed from its deadpan expression.

"Down the hall and to the left," Sylvia said to their backs.

Next to the body, Guttermouth booted dead Deano in the ribs, firm enough the body rolled completely over onto the back. An arm flopped heavily against the floor.

"They don't come any deader than this fucker," Guttermouth said, chewing away on the toothpick.

"Nope," Bones agreed.

Astonishment crossed Guttermouth's face. "You're a regular chatty-fucking-gabby tonight. The hell has gotten into you, Bones?"

Bones shrugged, and this time stayed quiet.

Guttermouth nudged the body one more time with his boot. To Sylvia he said, "Yes, ma'am, you killed the Christ outta ole Dean here, and good riddance. I never was a fan of your dickshit husband. Alright, Bones, let's get this job fucking cleaned up and done."

Both men knelt. They grabbed onto limp wrists and ankles.

"Heave-fuckin'-ho," Guttermouth said in a tone suggesting they'd performed this task dozens of times.

They lifted and dropped dead Deano onto the plastic.

In under two minutes Sylvia's husband was wrapped tight like a cold burrito, the ends of the plastic bunched and sealed with the heaviest-duty zip ties Sylvia had ever seen.

Bones hefted the body up to his shoulders, and Sylvia showed both men to the door.

At the bottom of the porch, Guttermouth turned back to her. He pulled the toothpick out of his mouth and gazed up, something profound on his mind.

"I understand you're Father Raphe's new piece of ass and all, and that's a spot for any bitch to envy. Fuck, it's like hitting the goddamn jackpot, but I still can't believe you pulled it off. You got the best of the most efficient hitman probably to ever walk the earth. You killed the Dean of Death. A prissy little bitch like yourself, I wouldn't believe it if I wasn't carting his cold ass away."

The two partners didn't bother with the trunk, just threw dead Deano in the shiny white Mustang's back seat.

Sylvia stood on the porch and watched as the red taillights receded, listened until the powerful engine was out of earshot. She turned and shut the door on the night.

Upstairs, she stripped and changed into a silk slip; she slid beneath the eiderdown duvet and jacquard bed sheets and slept.

"LET ME SEE those baby blues, Sylvia."

The bedside lamp clicked on.

Something cold and metal pressed into her forehead, and she was awake instantly. She opened her eyes and the sight before her immediately tripped her internal flight mode. She bunched her legs up in an effort to scramble backwards, but her crab walk was halted by the bed's solid headboard. She squeezed her eyes shut again, but this time tightly, as if the *see no evil* trick might make the nightmare disappear.

It didn't work. The gun pressed with even more force.

Uncontrollably her head shook. She'd been in a similar predicament one other time in her younger days before Dean, and the business end of a handgun pressing into the brow and threatening to splatter her brains wasn't a feeling she'd ever shake.

But this was worse, because it couldn't be happening. She knew the man's voice giving the directive—as implausible as it was, it was Dean's.

The almighty fear kept her eyes shut.

"This isn't a dream," Dean said, his tone dead flat. "And I ain't no Casper the friendly ghost. I'm not saying it a third time. Open those fucking baby blues or I'll kill you, Sylvia."

That was all the persuasion she needed. Dean was a natural born killer; she knew as much as anyone still taking breaths.

He was her husband for Jesus's sake—or had been.

At one time the fortitude to waste a woman, let alone his wife, wouldn't have been a part of his DNA, natural born killer or not.

That was before Sylvia had slowly fed arsenic to him over a three-month period, just enough sprinkled into his dinners here and there to give him a mild case of the runs and some headaches and do some internal damage over time. Then tonight, she'd dumped the whole shebang into a heaping plate of spaghetti and in minutes he'd had Xs for eyes.

She knew damn near everything about Dean, certainly knew his only morals when it came to killing for Father Raphe—never women or children.

Never.

Dean would've smoked his own grandfather without batting an eye for the right amount of bankroll from the right person, but long ago he'd promised Sylvia—not that she'd cared—never women or children.

She blinked open her eyes.

"Even brimming with fear they sparkle like sapphires," Dean sighed. He withdrew the gun so it now pointed at the bedroom ceiling. "Those beauties always were a balm to my wounds; I guess they still are."

He was naked as the day he was born, showing off his muscular yet lean build.

They stared at one another, a marital standoff of sorts.

After what seemed an interminable time, Dean broke the silence. "I know what you did to me. I know the score."

Sylvia's heart pounded against her chest too forcefully for this to be a nightmare. She thought she was opening her mouth to apologize—instead, "You can't be here. You're supposed to be dead."

"Well fuck me sideways," he replied, and patted over his chest as if checking, even grabbed his nut sack and shook it. His bottom lip stuck out and he shrugged. "It's all real."

"Are you back for revenge?" Sylvia trembled.

"Kind of—now get dressed." Dean motioned with the gun, ordering her out of the bed.

At first she didn't move, worried he was going to put her on her knees and do her execution style.

The loudest boom she'd ever heard suddenly sounded off and a brilliant flash of orange lit up the room. The headboard next to her cheek exploded, and she cowered away from the hole. Flames licked the broken and splintered wood. A straight rope of smoke tied the damaged headboard all the way back to the gun's eyehole.

It had happened so quickly, but she knew it hadn't been a normal bullet. When Sylvia closed her eyes, the afterimage burned the backs of her lids.

An arrow, her mind confessed. *Good Christ, it wasn't a bullet but an arrow of flames!*

"I don't want to do it," Dean said, "but the next one is

headed straight between your eyes. Get some clothes on."

No more motivation was necessary. When she squatted and reached for the skirt and blouse she'd earlier discarded to the floor, Dean shook his head.

"Not those," Dean said. "I liked the look and all, but date night ended when my throat sealed like a tomb. Put on something sensible." Again, he used the gun, but this time directed her over to the walk-in closet.

She pulled out some jeans and a hoodie.

"Shoes too," Dean said. "We're taking a ride. Gotta make a visit."

She slid her feet into a pair of sneakers and asked, "How come you're not wearing clothes?"

"I'll explain in the car. Follow me."

Dean hesitated in the bedroom doorway, reached for something on the dresser and tossed it back to Sylvia.

She jerked her hands up in time to catch it. The weight of the cross pendant dangled the necklace from her fingers—ten sets of amethyst beads all connected by a sterling silver chain. The rosary was one of her dearest possessions, an inheritance from her dead grandmother, and the only thing of real value she'd ever received during her dirt poor childhood.

"Keep that on you from here on out," Dean said. "A word of advice, stick with me and you'll be on the right side."

He peered back over his shoulder, and Sylvia swore his eyes had turned obsidian dark save for the flame of orange that danced where the pupils should've been.

GUTTERMOUTH'S MUSTANG PURRED with mechanical life in the driveway. This time it was askew and skid marks trailed behind it as if the driver had chaotically whipped it into a parked position.

"Passenger seat," Dean said, and again gestured with the pistol. Apparently that was dead Deano's new thing. Despite his nakedness, the cool night air seemed not to play any effect on him.

There were three bodies propped up in the back seat, crammed together like sardines. The two wasted goons flanked either side of Dean's earthly but lifeless flesh and blood, which was still encased by plastic. With the interior light on, Sylvia could make out Dean's dead gaze somewhat blurred as it eternally stared out from the plastic.

It was obvious what had happened to both Guttermouth and Bones. The obliterated tops of their heads and the scent of gunfire smoke still lingering in the air told their stories. Both sides of the front windshield featured holes, and with her mind's eye, Sylvia envisioned two fiery arrows bursting through glass.

She sat and gasped. Blood and cranial gore were plastered to the Mustang's dashboard.

The Mustang rocked on its frame as Dean dropped in and slammed the door. He nonchalantly tossed the handgun on the dashboard.

"I know it's not an ideal ride for a lady," Dean said, acknowledging the brain splatter. He turned the rotary shifter between them and the car reversed so quickly Sylvia had to brace her hands to keep from slamming her forehead. "We'll have to give her a good cleaning eventually, but this is *my* battle horse now." Backed into the street, Dean leveled his gaze on Sylvia who was staring at the tacky blood on her palms. "Get used to it. There'll be a lot more of that on your hands in the future."

The car shot forward, and they sped out of the subdivision where they'd carved out thirteen years of life together.

Out on the main road, Dean turned to head into the city. The moon was full and high, a polished round bone suspended against the celestial stars. There was no traffic and the Mustang rushed forward causing everything in the periphery to blur.

Sylvia wiped her soiled palms down the front of her jeans smearing the blood in streaks. This was real; this was happening.

"Dean?" Sylvia said. She peered intensely, studying his features. Lit up in the dashboard lights, his skin was the opposite of waxen, actually looked as healthy as ever before. His complexion damn near cast a glow back against the car's interior. There was no rise and fall to his naked chest indicating even the slightest breath. "Can you explain how you're steering the car while your dead body is in the back seat?"

"You fucking killed me," Dean said. He put both hands on the wheel and must have really pressed the accelerator, because engine locked into a higher gear and the Mustang screamed considerably faster. "How's that for an answer?"

The digital speedometer climbed into triple digits.

"That's probably not what you meant though," Dean conceded. "I believe the proper term is *discorporate.*"

"You're a ghost."

"Not exactly." He braked, and the Mustang slowed with the same smoothness it had just moments before accelerated. Dean steadied the car into a turn, and then they were racing down a lonely yet familiar stretch of road—the back route to the outskirts of the city. With a cool head, Dean continued, "I've held council with God, Sylvia. How is that for a shocker? And God sent me back with a job."

"He gave you a job?"

"Not a *he,* but just God. My orders come from the absolute highest power."

"What are your orders?"

"*Ohhh,*" Dean purred. "This is where the story really takes a twist. You're a good Catholic girl. So let me pose a question to you. Did you notice what shot from my gun?"

"An arrow." She wasn't certain if she approved of the crazy confidence in his voice, like there was nothing that could possibly defeat him.

"A *flaming* arrow," he corrected her. Dean slapped his palm atop the panel indicating the Mustang. "Who in the good book shoots fiery arrows from his perch upon a white steed? Revelations

6:2: 'And I saw, and behold a white horse: and he that sat on him had a bow; and a crown was given unto him: and he went forth conquering, and to conquer.'"

"Oh my God," Sylvia said. So much of the bible was symbolic but the real pieces started clicking together in her mind. The white Mustang, the gun that shot arrows like a bow, the position of power God had bestowed Dean was his crown. She clutched the rosary necklace. "We're going to—"

"The church," Dean cut off her sentence. "Raphe's church. God has agreed to let me have this one small and personal reckoning before unleashing the apocalypse."

In ten minutes they were parked in front of the Golden Domed Cathedral. Built in the early 1900s the church was a monolithic mass of white stone with stained windows standing tall and sentry. For the span of a century it had been a proper place of worship, but since Father Raphe had taken over, it now also carried an overture of ill-repute. It was where Father Raphe openly coordinated with the drug dealers, where he made deals with the cops, where he often passed a judgment of death to those that had crossed him.

"You're gonna kill Raphe," Sylvia said.

"Not I," Dean answered, his tone heavy with suggestion. He reached for the gun on the dash, held it out to Sylvia. The fiery glow had returned to his pupils and the intensity of his stare froze Sylvia's blood. With his free hand, Dean gently lifted her arm by the wrist and wrapped her fingers around the weapon.

The gun was death cold to the touch.

Somewhere deeper in the city a siren wailed.

"You know exactly what I am," Dean intoned.

"The first horseman." Sylvia could barely get her voice above a whisper.

She didn't need any confirmation from Dean, but he did wink, and then the fire behind his eyes grew exponentially.

"Beautiful Sylvia, always on the lookout for the man with the winning hand." With the backs of his knuckles, Dean stroked tenderly down her cheek. "Can't say that I blame you though. Life is a game of choices. I know you're prone to shifting with the wind's gusts, so can you feel it this time, Sylvia?"

A puff of heat washed Sylvia's face. The flames in each of Dean's eyes reshaped into galloping horses. Perched atop those respective horses were burning figures which flung flaming arrows to either side.

She could feel it, looking into those obsidian eyes telling a story of old, it was impossible not to accept the truth of what was unraveling—the judgment.

"Are you a true ride-or-die kinda gal?" His countenance subtly changed, becoming more stoic. He was no longer simply Dean returned from the dead.

He was—without doubt—the first horseman.

They climbed out of the Mustang and with caution silently closed the doors. They quickly bounded up the stone steps. In front of the massive double doors, Dean touched Sylvia's wrist.

"There's no reason to draw it out," Dean whispered. "I don't care for the recognition that'll be in his eyes. I only desire to see him die at your hands. As soon as you see him shoot. The weapon will be true."

Sylvia nodded.

Dean opened the door a crack and they slipped inside.

It was dark, save for the altar where lights beamed up at a massive wooden cross. There was Father Raphe, knelt on a knee, and with bowed head.

Behind Sylvia, Dean cleared his throat.

Father Raphe rose to his feet, already yelling an obscenity at what he thought was the arrival of his two best goons. "What the fuck took so long, and why aren't you answering your—?" Dressed in a black button down shirt and slacks, he wheeled on his heels. When his eyes found Sylvia rushing forward and pointing the gun, his face drained, turning the color of the collar he adorned during ceremonies. He reached for his sidearm, the same one he concealed beneath his robe through every Sunday worship he conducted.

Sylvia didn't hesitate. She pulled the trigger, and the entire interior of the cathedral lit the color of fire. There was no reason for a second shot. Although she'd been running, causing the sights to bounce wildly, the gun was as true as Dean had prophesied.

A hole the size of an immortal's fist had been punched through Father Raphe's chest.

Sylvia approached and stared down at the body. She could smell cooked meat. Smoke coiled heavenward from the hole that had replaced Father Raphe's dark heart.

It was completely different this time. Whereas with Dean she'd felt hollow inside afterwards, this time satisfaction resided in the pit of her stomach.

She footed the body, firm enough to test it—much like Guttermouth had earlier in the night with Dean's corpse—but not strong enough to flip the defunct body.

"There's something I don't understand," she confessed to Dean.

"What's that?"

"Revelations doesn't mention a partner with the first horseman."

The horseman grinned. "Let's just say not only was I the greatest hitman to ever grace this world, but I'm also a hell of a negotiator."

That was enough for Sylvia. For now, it had to be.

Hand in hand they exited the church.

Back outside, they watched a running crack rip through outer space—like the night sky was constructed of a giant sheet of black ice. From somewhere up there, a great horn sounded, and then, the floor of the earth shook.

Windows all over the city shattered.

Hearts stopped dead like they'd been squeezed in a vise.

Those that didn't immediately die screamed awake.

There would be more death.

There would be judgment.

"And so the ending begins," Dean intoned.

The fissured night sky actually yawed open and what raced in descent was every representation of celestial beings imagined by man.

Sylvia knew somewhere there were demons crawling up from the bowels of the Earth.

"Shotgun," she called and jogged to the Mustang's passenger side.

She turned back to the horseman—her husband—saw him displaying his pearly whites within a great big smile. His eyes burned orange.

She couldn't recall the last time she'd seen him looking so proud.

Was she on the right side?

She knew from as far back as her grandmother's teachings there had been a timeless debate of whom exactly the first horseman's allegiance resided. That debate right now didn't mean squat.

She'd made a decision in the present, and that choice was keeping the blood pumping through her veins. If need be, she'd switch teams in the future.

In their white steed, husband and wife raced away from the church and into the depths of the city to deal death.

Sylvia leaned out the window. She peered down the sights of the pistol, practicing her aim and thinking to herself, *I'm a ride-or-die kinda gal—for now.*

Clark Roberts is the author of the short story collection Led By Beasts. *His stories have appeared in more than twenty publications.*

KILLER

Paul Heatley

THE SUN SHINES through threadbare curtains, hits Bruce square in his waking eyes. Someone is trying to rouse him. Hands upon his shoulders rock him. Bruce rolls onto his side, pulls the blanket up over his head.

"Fuck-sake, Bruce." The voice is sharp, angry, familiar. A foot kicks him. "Wake your ass up, will ya?"

Bruce forces one eye open, sees a blurred outline fill the window where the sun blinded him, the light behind making the golden hair glow, like a halo. Bruce knows it is no angel. He smacks his lips, his mouth dry. Whatever time it is, it's too early. There is a throbbing pain behind his eyes as they struggle to bring the face of his ex-girlfriend into focus.

The blur begins to clear. The softened features sharpen into nose, cheekbones, chin, the eyes become blue and narrowed. "Lucy," Bruce says. He lifts his head, checks the room for Maddie. She isn't present. "Where's—"

"She's not here." Bruce awake, Lucy crosses the room, away from him, to a chair in the corner. She dumps the pair of jeans there onto the floor, and sits in their place. She stretches out her long legs, clad in tight, faded denim, and folds her arms. "You need to shower. You stink."

Bruce sits up, pulls the blanket tight around his shoulders. "I ain't that bad."

"You smell fuckin rancid, Bruce. You smell like you're dyin."

Bruce shrugs. "Who'm I tryin to impress?" He runs his sawdust tongue over his peeling lips, feels the familiar urge beginning to settle in. He needs a drink, something stronger than water. He needs Lucy to leave so he can find himself one. "How'd you get in?"

"The door wasn't locked."

"Well, shit. Guess that happens sometimes. How'd you find me?"

"I asked your mother."

"Still talk to her, huh?"

"More than you do."

On the windowsill near his bed there is a beer can, part crumpled with indentations from his fingers. Bruce reaches for it, keeps the blanket tight round his shoulders. Beneath it he is naked. He grabs the can, gives it a shake to see if there is anything left. There is, and he drains it off in one long gulp. It isn't satisfying. Lucy watches him with one raised eyebrow. "Why are you here?" Bruce says.

He crushes the can and she watches it fall. Her lip curls. "I came to talk."

"Uh-huh. You already said plenty, few years back. Got a lot off your chest that night you kicked me out, and I ain't seen you since. Can't imagine what you'd have to say now."

"You wanna hear it, or you just wanna bitch some more about how I got fed up of your bullshit?" Lucy runs her tongue round the inside of her mouth like there's a bad taste in it. "Y'know, looking at this place, it don't seem like anything's changed, has it? I reckon you don't even spend much time in this shithole, right? Every night in the bar, huh?"

"I see a lot of your brother."

Lucy snorts. "I'm sure you do. He's a fuckin good-for-nothin, too."

Bruce looks her over. Lucy scratches behind an ear. She has a tattoo there. Three small black stars. She is dressed in jeans and a leather jacket, her skin covered, but he knows the tattoos beneath her clothes. Wonders if she's gotten any more since he saw her last, or if she's kept to her word when she said she was done with them. She called them evidence of her misspent youth, and she was putting those days behind her. Same way she'd decided to put Bruce behind her.

Bruce remembers, though. The way she'd been when they'd first met, introduced through her brother. *Shit, I reckon the two of you'll get on like a house on fire.* He wasn't wrong. They took real quick to getting drunk and high together. Lucy used to hit it harder than Bruce did. Stopped when she got pregnant, though. Got herself clean, but the ink won't fade—the pin-up girl on her left shoulder, the snake wrapped around her right arm. Bruce has always been especially fond of the little purple butterfly on the inside of her panty line, visible only when her pussy is on show.

Bruce grabs the jeans Lucy shoved onto the floor, tries not to think too much about her intimate areas as he pulls them on. He searches the ground for a shirt, picks one up. It's badly creased, and it isn't fresh, smells almost sour, but he isn't going to find any better.

"Nothin to say?" Lucy says. "You wanted to play twenty questions a couple minutes ago. *How'd you find me, how'd you get in, what d'you want.*"

Bruce looks at her, raises an eyebrow. "The fuck d'you expect me to say?"

"Why don't you try askin about your daughter? Other than a cursory glance round the room, and a half-asleep questioning as to her whereabouts, I don't think she's even crossed your fuckin mind."

Maddie was born six years ago. Lucy stopped getting high. Bruce didn't. When Maddie was two, Lucy left, took her with her. Bruce didn't know where they went. Received radio silence from Maddie when he tried to reach out. Depressed, he stopped working then. Killing men for money lost all its luster when all he really wanted to do was sip imaginary tea at teddy bear parties with his young daughter. He kept getting high, though. Kept his mind off his shitty little lonely life. His drug of choice these days is alcohol. It shows in his frame. He's not as firm as he used to be. He's gone soft.

"I think about her every fuckin minute of every fuckin day," Bruce says. "Right now, lookin at you, I'm thinkin about her, the two of you look so damn alike. But what difference does that make? You gonna tell me how she is? Shit, you gonna let me see her?" He snorts.

Lucy bites her lip. "She don't look so much like me no more."

"What?"

Lucy looks away, takes a deep breath.

Bruce gets impatient waiting for her to respond. "What's that mean? Hey, what do you mean?"

Lucy closes her eyes. "Something happened."

LIAM TAKES A drink. "That's what she said?"

Bruce nods. They're in the bar round the corner from where he lives. It's quiet, it's always quiet. They sit at a table, the furthest one away from the bartender, the only person present that could hear them talking.

"A dog?" Liam takes another drink. He's involved in the same work Bruce used to be. He's kept himself in shape, too.

"Put that down, damn it—this is fuckin serious."

"She's my niece, man, I'm upset too. You don't gotta take it out on me."

"Maddie is my fuckin *daughter*. You didn't know anything about this?"

"Of course not—you think I would've kept it from you? Shit, I'd known my sister was shackin up with some Nazi, you think I would've kept *that* from you?"

"When'd you see her last?"

"Who—Maddie? Lucy?"

"Either of them."

Liam shrugs. "I dunno. 'Round the same time you last did. Longer, maybe. How bad's it, anyway? The scarring."

"I dunno, she didn't have a picture."

"Alright, run it by me one more time."

"I already told you."

"You told me stop-start. Come on, from the top, linear fashion. I wanna get it clear in my head. Go."

Bruce grunts. "Lucy gets with this guy Michael. He ain't a good guy, she thinks he looks like a gang-banger type, but she wasn't lookin for a husband so she didn't think nothin of it."

"She was lookin for a dude to fuck."

Bruce shoots him a look. "It was stop-start cos you kept interrupting."

Liam makes a gesture across his lips, zipping them shut.

"So. Michael had a dog with him, nearly always. Pitbull. When he was at her place he left it outside, tied up. Lucy said it seemed well-behaved, and it was always outside the house, she never really thought about it. She knew he used it for dog fights, but that was none of her business. Then one night she couldn't get a sitter for Maddie and Michael was already heading over. Maddie was in her room, supposed to stay in there, then Lucy hears a lot of screaming. Best she can figure, Maddie tried to play with the dog. For whatever reason, the dog took a chunk outta her face. Lucy's gonna kill the dog, Michael backhands her. She calls the cops, Michael's gone to ground. She don't know where he is."

"And she wants you to find him. Instead of the cops."

"That was a few weeks ago now. She don't want cop justice anymore. She wants *real* justice. Revenge."

"The kind people usually pay for?"

"Exactly."

"What do you want?"

"The motherfucker's hurt my little girl. Disfigured her."

"So you're getting back in the game?"

"Just this once."

Liam grins, like despite everything else this is the best news he's heard in a while.

Bruce sits back, runs his hands through his hair. He leans forward, arms on the table. "Lucy says I can see her again. Maddie. If I do this."

"You believe her?"

"I don't have any other choice. You gonna help me?"

Liam finishes his drink. He grins. "What you think? Course I'm gonna fuckin help you. Let's go get this motherfucker."

LUCY HAS GIVEN Bruce the name of a few bars, but told him Michael is most likely to be at The Leaking Tap. Bruce and Liam go into the backroom, stand at the rear of a crowd gathered round a mesh enclosure, the floor within coated in sawdust.

"I don't see him," Liam says.

"I don't see anyone ready to fight," Bruce says. "But everyone's waiting. Let's give it a minute, huh?"

The room is a poorly lit concrete box that hurts Bruce's eyes. The men in front of them are tightly wedged, jostling against each other, looking for the best position to see.

Liam sighs at his side, stands on the tips of his toes to try and peer over the gathered shoulders. "I dunno what they're all so eager to see," he says. "There ain't nothin there."

Bruce looks round the room. He can't see any dogs, but it looks like there is a door off to the side, a back door, through which the combatants will likely enter.

A murmur ripples through the crowd, two fast-talking men moving among the bodies to take bets. The back door opens. The crowd moves and Bruce can't see. There are a couple of cheers, but mostly the mumblings just increase.

"You see anythin?" Liam says.

Bruce waits for the crowd to settle, for the bet-takers to get out the way. He peers through bodies, over shoulders, sees into the enclosure. There are two pitbulls. They strain at their leads, already snarling and desperate to get at each other. Their owners hold them tight. Bruce feels his heart skip a beat.

"He's here," he says.

Liam leans on Bruce's shoulder, strains his neck for a better look. "I see him. You reckon that's the same dog, or he's got a few of em?"

"Lucy said it was called Rocky. You hear him say *Rocky*, then that's the fuckin dog."

Liam spits.

Bruce gets a good look at the men as another man, the 'referee', goes over the rules.

Michael has a shaved head, a tattoo across his throat, big, done in a spiky, gothic style, all black. Bruce can't make out what it says. Michael grins at the other guy with the corner of his mouth.

Bruce spares the opponent a quick glance. A Hispanic guy, he wears a vest, has a moustache and a tuft of hair on his chin.

Bruce doesn't care about the Latino. He stares at Michael, at his smug smile and intense eyes.

The guy playing referee gets out the way. Clear, he blows a whistle. The dogs are let loose.

They clash, mouths snapping. Frothy saliva sprays. They snarl as they tangle, rolling with each other across the hard ground, their bodies a mass of seething, pulsing muscle. Both dogs have dark fur, and it becomes impossible to tell which is which in the scuffle.

It isn't long before drops of blood begin to mark and smear the ground, dark and red. The dogs continue to fight. Bruce doesn't watch. His eyes are on Michael. He stands on the side-lines. Michael watches the dogs, smiling and confident.

The fight comes to an end. One of the dogs holds the other, pins it to the ground, its teeth in its neck. The other dog whimpers. The referee calls it. Michael, still smiling, says, "Rocky, *heel*!"

Bruce feels his heart skip another beat, feels his mouth go dry, sees Liam looking at him out the corner of his eye, checking he's heard it. Bruce nods.

Rocky lets go but continues to growl. Michael steps into the square, hooks the leash back onto Rocky's collar. The other dog stays on the ground, beaten and bleeding. Rocky is marked but is unaffected. Michael leads him through the mumbling crowd, winners and losers celebrating and commiserating. The Latino stays in the enclosure, strokes the flank of his beaten dog.

"How d'you wanna do this?" Liam says.

"Give him some distance, so he don't see us." Bruce counts to five in his head. "Come on. Either he's in the parking lot or he's still walkin, either way we'll find him."

They hurry through the bar, stop at the front, look round the lot for any sign of Michael and his dog. "Round the back?" Liam says.

They go down the side of the building. Bruce hears whistling. He sees Michael ahead, the dog trotting obediently by his side. They get into a car. Bruce pulls on Liam's arm. They go back to Liam's truck. Michael tears out of the parking lot before they're in the cab. Loud music blasts from his open window, heavy metal.

Liam starts the truck, follows, keeps a safe distance. Bruce eyes the taillights ahead of them, keeps a lock on them as they turn left and right, ensuring Liam doesn't lose them.

Lights behind them catch his eye in the side mirror. They come up fast, then pull back. Bruce makes sure it isn't a cop, then pushes them from his mind, forgets about the car behind them and focuses on Michael up ahead before his dim lights can disappear into the darkness.

He leads them to a shitty neighbourhood with overgrown front lawns, boarded-up windows, graffiti on lampposts and fences, overflowing trashcans sitting out on the sidewalk. The other houses look to be in darkness. Michael pulls to a stop. Bruce and Liam hold back.

"You think this is his?" Liam says.

There is already a light on in the house Michael and Rocky walk up to. He lets himself in.

"You reckon this is where he lives, or this is just some side-bitch?" Liam says.

"I don't know," Bruce says.

"The lights were already on."

"Doesn't mean anythin."

Liam looks up and down the street. "How much meth you think they're cookin in this neighbourhood?"

"I'm pretty sure I've scored here before," Bruce says. He winds his window down, listens to the night. He hears sirens in the distance, howling dogs. Somewhere, a child is crying. It isn't close enough to be of concern.

"Lucy said he always kept the dog tied up outside when he went round to her place," Bruce says. "He ain't done that here. So either it *is* a side-chick's place and she ain't as bothered about having a dog inside her home, or it's *his*."

"You think the dog's gonna be indoors with him?"

"I dunno. Most dogs live indoors, right?"

"Most dogs don't rip the throats outta other dogs in the backrooms of dirty bars. Pass me the gun."

Bruce reaches into the glove box, passes it over. A colt .45. Liam handles it, checks the barrel, the clip. It's his gun. He bought it last night, for tonight. The serial number is filed off. He didn't buy it from a store. Bruce can't remember the last time he handled a gun. It was before Lucy and Maddie left.

"I'll lead the way," Liam says.

"I figured as much."

"If the dog's indoors, I'm taking it out. I ain't gonna give it a chance to chew on my fuckin balls."

"Been a while since somebody was last interested in doing that for you," Bruce says.

"Fuck you."

Bruce chuckles, tries to disguise his nerves. It's been a long time. Tonight feels like it's his first time all over again. He doesn't know when the last time was for Liam. Bruce doesn't ask him about his work. Doesn't need those memories brought back, and a big part of him worries he might be drawn to it. Feel the urge to get back into it. He's out of that life. Tonight is a one-off. Tonight is for Maddie.

Liam shifts his weight in the seat. The gun dangles between his thighs. "Nearly time."

Bruce looks. The lights are off. Five more minutes, tops. If this was a professional job, if they were getting paid for this, they would have scoped the house out. Watched it for a few nights. Check the comings and goings, make sure it's clear, make sure it's going to be clean.

This isn't a job. This is personal.

The minutes crawl by on the dashboard clock, slow, painful. Bruce tries not to focus on them too much. Watches the house instead.

The time comes. Liam gets out, keeps the gun low, pressed to his leg. "Come on."

They stride up to the house. Bruce looks up and down the block. It's quiet. The other houses remain in darkness. Liam's assumption that this is a meth neighbourhood is likely accurate. There aren't many signs of life, other than the trashcans and the litter-strewn front yards. There are a few bicycles that look rusted in amongst overgrown lawns. There are some cars, too, and the ones that are present, with a couple of exceptions, don't look like they can move very far, or fast.

"What're you lookin at?" Liam says. "C'mon, man, head in the game."

They try the front door but it's locked. They aren't surprised. They move to the rear but stop at the gate.

"Dog lives outdoors," Liam says, backing away.

Bruce can see the dog through the slats in the fence. It has its own enclosure, a wood outhouse with a metal grate front. It lies on the ground, looks like it's sleeping.

"We're gonna have to bust the door," Liam says. "You're heavier. Put your shoulder into it."

"It ain't gonna be quiet."

"When he comes running, I'll stick this in his fuckin face." Liam holds up the gun.

Bruce takes a grip on the door handle, puts his shoulder up against the wood. He braces himself, then throws his weight into it. His arm jars, his teeth chatter. He grimaces.

"Again," Liam says. "Don't let up, man, get that fuckin thing open." He keeps his voice low, but Bruce can detect the urgency in it.

He ignores the pain and strikes the door again, keeps his weight close to the frame, to the lock. He does it again. Something splinters. Spurred on by the sound, he does it again, and again.

"Come on, man, bust it down," Liam says. He raises a boot and thrusts it at the door as Bruce throws his weight into it one more time.

The door flies open. Bruce almost loses his balance, drops to one knee but manages to catch himself before he can go flat on his face. Liam raises the gun.

Michael does not come running. The house is dark. Bruce and Liam wait, then look at each other. Liam frowns, cocks his head. "You hear that?"

Bruce listens. "I think he's got the TV on."

Liam nods. "And he's got it fuckin *loud*." He indicates the stairs. "Up," he says.

Liam goes first, gun raised, pointing. Bruce follows. He holds his breath, fearing that it sounds too ragged and harsh when he breathes normally.

They reach the top. The TV sounds have quietened. They creep along the hall, sticking close to the walls to avoid creaking floorboards. What Bruce assumes to be the bedroom door is closed. The door to the bathroom is open, as is a nearby room with a weight bench and a couple of dumbbells scattered upon the floor. They near the closed door. There are footsteps. Bruce feels his heart leap into his throat. He holds his breath still, his lungs burn. The footsteps near the door. Liam has the gun levelled at head height. Bruce almost wants to close his eyes.

The door opens. Liam squeezes the trigger. The bullet catches the girl between the eyes. Blood sprays out the back of her head and piss squirts down the inside of her bare legs. She falls back, hits the ground. She's naked. Michael is naked, too. He leaps up from the bed, arms raised. "Hey, *hey*—hold up, wait!" He falls down the side of the bed, stays there.

Liam glances down at the dead girl, the blood spreading out from under her head. He grunts, but doesn't lament it too much. Coming in this fast, without scoping out the house first, just trying to get it over and done with, there were bound to be mistakes, and mess, and collateral casualties.

There's an explosion, and Bruce feels warm blood splash upon him. Liam is thrown to the side, his face gone. Bruce looks into the room to see Michael has risen with a sawn-off shotgun in his hands. Bruce throws himself back as the next round tears a chunk out the doorframe.

"Whatcha gonna do, motherfucker—you gonna run?" Michael is laughing, unperturbed by the death of the girl.

Bruce can hear him reloading.

"Where you gonna run, huh? You think I don't know who you are? Two white guys, one fat, one thin—you gonna run and tell Lucy I said hi? You run and tell her I'll come see her real soon, too."

Bruce sees the gun Liam has dropped. He grabs it, fires it into the room. Michael opens up with the shotgun. Bruce falls back, stumbles. Another blast rings out, it sounds close. He dives, reaches the top of the stairs, falls. Hits every step on the way down, knocks himself dizzy. The room spins when he reaches the bottom. He can hear Michael coming down after him. Can hear him reloading the shotgun. Bruce sees him, sees his face twisted into a smile, sees that he hasn't bothered to pull on any clothes, and his dick is hard.

"Oh, she told me all about you, man. That's all she did—she'd suck my dick, and once her mouth was empty she'd fill my ears with all the stories of what a deadbeat you were. I don't know if she was tryin to scare me with stories of what a tough guy you usedta be, or if she was just that pissed off at how pathetic you've become. Don't surprise me she went runnin to you, though. Poor little bitch, who else she gonna see? And now she's down a brother. And she's about to be down another man. And poor little Maddie, well, she's about to be down a daddy, ain't that right?" Michael grins. He runs his tongue across his teeth. Bruce can read the tattoo across his neck now. It says KILLER. Michael raises the shotgun.

Bruce stares into the barrel of it. Waits. Michael doesn't fire. Bruce looks higher. Michael has frozen. There is a gun pressed to his temple. Bruce follows the hand that grips it, along the arm. It's Lucy.

"Fuck you, Michael."

She squeezes the trigger. He crumples. The shotgun hits the ground with a thud, but no explosion.

Bruce looks up at Lucy. The scant light from the streetlights outside that manage to catch her hair light it up like a halo, really do make her look like an angel. She drags Bruce to his feet.

"What're you doin here?"

"Followed you."

"What?"

"You thought I wouldn't want to see? And then the two of you went and fucked it up. I thought you were supposed to be professionals?"

"It's been a while," Bruce says. "Your brother's dead."

"And I'll mourn him, but not right now. Let's go."

Bruce stays where he is.

Lucy hovers in the doorway. "You can leave with me, or you can wait until the cops arrive. They'll take their time, but they'll get here eventually."

Bruce grabs the shotgun. He heads to the back of the house, out the door there. Lucy calls after him, asks where he's going.

Rocky has woken. He paces the floor of his pen, claws scratching on the hard ground. He sees Bruce, growls low in his throat. Bruce presses the shotgun to the gaps in the grating. Rocky comes forward, growling still. He sniffs the barrels. Bruce gives him both, then dumps the gun.

Lucy is in the doorway still, waiting to leave, watching him. Bruce brushes past her. "Now take me to see my fuckin daughter."

Paul Heatley is the author of Fatboy, Guillotine, *the Eye For An Eye series,* Bad Bastards, *and more. He lives in the northeast of England.*

GET BORN AGAIN

Mark Slade

"I WON'T BE home tonight, Harry," Dee called out to me as I ushered Tony to the car. We stopped at the mailbox just a few feet from the Focus. Her Outback was parked too close to my Focus again. Good thing no one was parked behind me. I turned and looked at her blankly, trying to comprehend what she had told me.

She stood on the front step of our modest ranch-style home, putting on the earrings I bought her for our anniversary last year. Dee of course loves the house and the neighborhood. I like the city. I like brick and mortar. Decay. The neighborhood is so nice and dull. Our house sticks out like a sore thumb among white houses and white picket fences. The only house on the block that is brown, and why that fucking color? Why not green or blue?

"Why is that, honey?" I yelled back. Tony and I inched closer to the car.

"Dad," Tony said, pushing his long brown bangs out of his eyes. "I don't wanna go to school."

"Shut up and get in the car," I told him.

Tony made a face at me. God strike me down, I was going kill the little fucker. Ten years old and already too much of a pain in the ass.

Dee finished with her earrings and her hands found their way to those ample hips of hers. God, she looked great in that floral print dress and open-toed heels. "The girls and I have that thing we've been planning for months. Oh! And I'm going to be late meeting Helen!"

"Ah, right," I said, giving Dee a fake smile that I was okay with it. I wasn't.

Whatever that "thing" was, I wish it didn't involve Helen Spencer. She's a liar, a braggart, and her face looks like the upside of a downturn ass. Why on earth my wife had to attach herself to the one person the entire neighborhood hates is beyond me.

I wasn't in the best mood this morning. I had a meeting with Sheldon and before each meeting I could feel my arteries harden, and it wasn't because of eating too much like my doctor always says.

"You guys will have to find your own supper," Dee said and went back inside the house, letting the screen door slam.

"I don't want to go to school!" Tony kicked the front tire.

"Hey!" I screamed. "Go easy on the car, kemosabe!"

"I hate it when you call me that," Tony hissed as he climbed into the passenger side.

I stood with the door open to my Focus just as one of our neighbors in a grey Chevy pickup nearly took me out as it sped by. I shook my fist at them and cursed under my breath. I got in the car and slammed the door.

"Dad," Tony said. "Mom says you're not supposed to say motherfucker in public. It makes you sound ignorant."

"Yeah, well," I said as I started the car. "That's why you need to go to school—so you won't be as ignorant as your dad."

Tony groaned and sank into the seat.

I DROVE TO a car park on Fortune Road. Hardly anyone used it. Lots of people write articles wondering when the car park will change ownership. The answer is never. Sheldon and his connections own the car park. And those connections I never ask about. To the public, Sheldon Leonard is a real estate magnate. I work for him as a real estate agent. In truth, Sheldon deals out the contracts to me.

In reality, I exterminate humans.

"Harry Anchor," Sheldon greeted me warmly on the top floor of the car park. He'd been looking over the concrete railing thinking of better times, when the city was different and his father's candy shop sat where the art gallery was now. "So good to see you, my boy." Sheldon gave me a firm handshake and a pat on the shoulder.

"What's new, Sheldon?"

"Oh," he chuckled. "Just standing there...thinking about the old days."

"You do that every time we meet here. Maybe we should go back to the dog park."

"No, no," he said, waving the suggestion off. "That will only remind me of Martha." His face suddenly looked grey. Sad. Martha was Sheldon's first wife. She was killed in a car accident in Georgia with their Jack Russell. Legitimately killed. No foul play was present. I have to admit I've always thought karma was involved.

I had to get his mind off the past.

"How's Tina and the kids?"

Sheldon rolled his eyes. "Harry," he said, wagging a cautionary finger. "No matter how lonely you get, don't start a family at seventy. If you do, make sure to find a woman who isn't so controlling. She told me this morning I spend too much money on Starbucks coffee! Imagine that." He chuckled.

That was funny. Hell, Sheldon might be the third richest man in the state.

"Yeah," I said, nodding. "Dee is always on me to lose weight."

Sheldon looked at me incredulously.

"How much do you weigh?"

I was reluctant to tell him. Finally I sputtered: "305."

Sheldon raised an eyebrow. "The hell? In my day, a real man was big boned. He was thought of as a man's man." He wagged his finger again. "And back then, it didn't mean what it means now! Those people stayed in the closet!"

"Okay, okay," I laughed. "No speeches about the good old days of being racist, misogynistic, and homophobic, Sheldon."

"We were not!" he said, exasperated at my silly ignorance of the past. "Everyone just...knew their place. That's all. Simpler times."

"Uh-huh. Sure," I said. "What do you have for me Sheldon?"

He handed me a manila envelope. I started to unravel the string around the button that kept it sealed and Sheldon placed his hand over it.

"What are you doing?"

"What?"

"What are you doing?"

He ripped the envelope from my hands, looked around to make sure no one was watching. He placed the envelope back in his coat and got in my face. "Fucking moron! How many times do I have to tell you? Don't open these things until I'm gone!" He turned and started to walk away.

"Sheldon, come back!"

He turned to me and screamed: "You're trying to put us both in the gas chamber!"

"I'm sorry. Hey, come back over here. C'mon, Sheldon. Look, I've been a little distracted lately. C'mon."

"You pull a stunt like this again," Sheldon said, his bottom lip trembling, "I'll be forced to sever business ties with you, my boy." He sniffed the cool spring air. "And we both know what that means."

Yeah. A vacation home in an unmarked grave under the Jersey Turnpike.

I didn't get mad. I couldn't. I fucked up and Sheldon was right. So I gave him my signature goofy smile à la Randy Quaid from the National Lampoon's Vacation movies. Sheldon glared at me. The goofier my smile was, the more he loosened up. He eventually broke into a hearty laugh.

"You fucking moron!" He reached into his coat and produced the envelope, smacking me across the face with it.

"Ah, quit it, daddy!" I screeched and ran after he hit me a few more times.

"I got your daddy right here, asshole!"

Sheldon chased me around his car, calling me a mental midget and a moron until we were out of breath. Then we both leaned against his Cherokee and slid down to a squatting position, trying to catch our breath, giggling like two boys sneaking a peek at a dirty magazine.

Suddenly, Sheldon stopped laughing. His face became gloomy again. He waved the envelope in my face.

"We need to be careful, Harry." The lines on his face disconnected and reconnected with a grimace. "More now than ever. We've been living a charmed life."

"You think so?"

"I know so. No complications. No cops. No one asking questions."

"Except Tony."

"Keep lying to him and Dee. Let them keep thinking you sell houses. All for the best."

I thought about it. "Yeah," I said after a long pause. "You might be right."

"Fuck you. I know I'm right."

"You're always right."

Sheldon stood, dropped the envelope on the cement at my feet.

"Get in your fucking car and drive down to the pier and look in the envelope. Don't be a moron, eh?"

That's exactly what I did.

The dock was strangely quiet. No fishermen. No boats coming or going. Even the seagulls were elsewhere.

I opened the envelope, saw the tear sheet. A woman. Thirty-two, blonde, green eyes. Seems like lately it's always a woman. The last three. I know I'm not Sheldon's only professional. He let it slip I had a compadre in this business. I said rival. Sheldon said in his company there are no rivals. Teammates is the term he used.

A woman, though? That's all he gives me anymore. Has he lost all confidence in my abilities? He says he doesn't look at the files that come his way. Once a month he goes to his mailbox at the post office. If two envelopes arrive for a Conrad Hopewell, he gives one to me and the other to my compadre. I asked him what happens if there's only one. Sheldon just smiled and said, of course you get it, buddy.

I read the tear sheet more.

Hmm. This woman lives on my street. 4292 Fowler.

"That's gotta be a mistake," I said to myself, chuckling. "That's my address."

I stopped laughing when I removed the tear sheet and saw Dee's picture behind it.

SHELDON'S MAID WAS surprised to see me at the door. I'd only been to his house once. That was when I married Dee. Sheldon heard my voice and came from the study.

"Thank you, Helga," he said, giving her a fake smile. "I can handle it from here."

The maid shrugged, sashayed away from the foyer.

Sheldon closed the front door and stepped out on the cobble walkway.

"The fuck are you doing here?" he asked.

"I've got a big problem."

"Then you call me on my burner and we set up a place and a time."

"I'll never do that if the problem hits home," I said.

"So, you can't take care of personal situations, and you have to run to daddy?"

"No fucking joke, Sheldon."

I showed him the eight-by-ten glossy of Dee from the envelope. His jaw dropped. Sheldon shook his head and urged me to come inside the house. He took me to his study and sat me down. He poured two glasses of brandy, handing me one. He sat his glass on his desk. He walked over and the shut the door of his study to drown out a television, his wife's voice on her phone, and Helga vacuuming.

He sat on the edge of his desk and sipped the brandy. I just held the glass. I wasn't in the mood to drink. I was too furious.

"Before you ask," he said after a while, smacking his lips. "I don't know who put the hit out. I have no way of knowing, and I don't want to know."

"Then I'm screwed," I said.

Sheldon sighed.

"There's no way for me to find out, is what you're saying?"

"Not without endangering yourself or anyone else close to you," Sheldon said. "Including me."

"Fuck."

"Hold on," he said. "Don't get excited. The game is not up. There is a way you can find out and…possibly substitute."

"Dee's life for someone else's?"

"Maybe. But it has to be special circumstances. Who I deal with would need the story. The whole story. Not necessarily the truth, mind you."

"If this 'person' you deal with thinks I'm going to kill my own wife—"

Sheldon held up a hand and I stopped talking.

"I'm going to give you an idea of solving this matter," he said and stood. "You follow her like normal. Do everything you are supposed to do. At the same time, you gather the intelligence and maybe, just maybe, you get an idea of who put the hit out. Facts are facts, and usually the ones closest to the target are the ones who are behind the job."

I nodded, computing everything he was telling me.

"You offer up that person. I'll come up with the reason. Again, do not vary from your routine. Do what you are trained to do. Don't let emotions get in the way."

"Okay," I said. "They're watching?"

"They're always watching, my boy," Sheldon said.

I KNEW WHERE Dee always met her friends. Pauli's Café. Dee and I used to go the old location when we first married. He had the best blueberry pie. I went inside and saw Pauli was doing pretty good in his new location. Customers were sitting at tables or at the counter. Anthony, his brother was chatting up two business ladies, and Celia, his daughter, was serving two tables at the same time. This building was okay. Didn't have the same atmosphere, but nice. The old place on 21st Street mysteriously burned down last year.

When I walked in, he called out to me. "Harry Anchor! Can I get you some coffee, buddy?"

Pauli Dugre had been a local weight-lifting champion and had made a name for himself, but never competed nationally. Some days you could tell he had been fit one time in his life. Other days he looked like a man whose body had been compressed like an accordion by a cardboard bailer. Today was that day. He moved like an android losing his battery charge.

"No, no, Pauli. I'm looking for Dee."

"Yeah, she and the girls were just here."

"How long ago?"

"I don't know," Pauli said, tapping a pencil on a table he'd just wiped down. "Anthony came in…punched in…about twenty minutes ago?"

"Shit. I don't know where she was going after this."

"Oh, I know." He smiled hugely. "I was pouring them all a second cup and they were talking about going to the Ronettes."

"Say what?!" I screamed.

Pauli was a little shaken by my response. He dropped his pencil and his rag.

"Ronettes. The strip club on 5th and Collins."

"Why the hell would they go there?"

Pauli shrugged. "I don't know. I don't judge anymore. Whatever anybody wants to do is okay with me, as long as it don't hurt me, my family, or others—Hey! Where you goin'?"

I went out the door just as Pauli was telling me his new creed.

"Hold on!" He stuck his head out the door. I stopped at the Focus, my hand gripping the door handle. He trotted over to me as fast his old muscled legs could carry him. "I got something to tell you."

"Okay, Pauli." I rolled my eyes, thinking it was another speech.

"A gray Chevy Suburban was sitting there, watching the whole time."

"Is that so?"

"At first," Pauli said, looking around to make sure no one was listening. He brought his gaze back to mine. "I thought they were here for me."

"That a fact, Pauli?" I smiled. Thinking about that mysterious fire at his other café. Maybe he missed a payment.

"Yeah," he said, swallowing hard. "I, uh, have a bit of gambling problem. Shit, man. I could've sworn the Cavaliers had the Celtics at 3.5 seconds. That asshole Kemba Walker only scored twelve points all game and the twelfth point he hit was a three pointer at the buzzer! Can you fucking believe it?"

I laughed. "Yeah, maybe you shouldn't bet on basketball."

"I know, right? I do better on baseball and bowling. Well...turns out, the guy in the gray Suburban wasn't out there watching me. He was watching Dee."

That worried me tremendously. What had she done for anyone to put an eye on? Dee was a typical housewife, caring for me and Tony. She didn't drink, except for the occasional glass of wine. She didn't spend money unless she really had to.

The whole thing was surreal. Up until forty-five minutes ago, everything had been normal. Now my life had been turned upside down.

"Maybe he was a cop," I said. My voice trembled. Thinking of all kinds of consequences, mostly selfishly thinking what they were for Sheldon and me.

"Naw," Pauli chuckled, placing a hand on my shoulder. "I'm good at spottin' cops. Being in this business so long. Especially undercover. That guy definitely wasn't a cop. Too nervous. Too sleazy looking."

"What'd he look like?"

"Ah. Well. He was tall, skinny—skinny like he did a lot of cocaine, y'know? Sickly lookin'. Dark hair. Pencil-thin mustache."

"How do you know he was looking at Dee?"

"She came and left in her car by herself. The others left with that tall loud-mouthed lady. When Dee left, that gray Suburban left."

I NODDED AND thanked Pauli. I got in the car and sped off, headed to the Ronettes. It was about eleven a.m., so the club hadn't opened yet. There were, however, a few cars on the employee side. Two I recognized. Dee's Outback and the gray Suburban. I parked next to a little old man in glasses and a polo shirt. He was impatiently waiting for the club to open.

I heard a car door slam shut. I looked up and saw the man Pauli described to me get out of the gray Suburban. Pauli was right. He did look sickly. He walked the length of the parking lot and instead of going to the door, the man cut through a small rock garden and headed to the back. I quickly got out of the Focus and did the same thing, only pacing myself so I wouldn't spook him.

I stayed close to the dumpsters behind the building and

watched. The man coughed every other step. He took careful steps that reminded me of astronauts walking on the moon. When he got to the back door, he tried the handle. The door creaked open. He started to enter when his phone rang. He shut the door and found a spot under a bent over, dying tree.

"Hey," the man said and coughed. "I just got here." He listened and answered: "Been following this lady and her friends all morning." He listened for a lengthy time, looking annoyed, appealing to God with his hands to end the conversation. "You really want me to do that?" He gave a few "Uh-huhs" and then said, "Look, I'm not worried. You guys are worried. I just do what I'm told." His facial expression morphed from overconfident annoyance to extreme fear. "Consider it done," he said with a shaky voice and hung up.

Just as he was about to pocket his cell phone, I had my hands on his shirt sleeve, jerking him around to face me.

"*Hey! What the fuck*—" he wheezed and coughed.

I clipped him with a right hook. He landed flat on his back.

"Who the fuck are you?" I screamed.

The street came out of me. Dee could never completely rid me of it and from time to time that other guy from the streets would rage, and I would have to pay the price for "his" actions. This time I wasn't worried about it.

"Why are you watching that woman?" I loomed over him.

The man coughed and wheezed, trying to roll away from me. I kicked him in the ribs and he cried out, sounding like a screech owl. He rolled back toward me and I kicked him on that side. A scream was stifled by repeated coughs. On the ground beside him was an inhaler. He reached for it. I kicked it away from him, then snatched it up.

I bent down and showed it to him.

"Please," he wheezed. "I—I need it."

"Tell me what you're doing here," I said. "And why you're watching that woman inside."

"I'm not…"

"I know you are. You were in my neighborhood! You watched her from Pauli's Café!" I placed my boot over his face. "Tell me something, or I swear to God, I'll obliterate your face!"

He reached in his jacket and I objected.

"My…my card…," he wheezed.

He threw it at my feet. I scooped it up. "The Train Station" the card said. Another strip club.

"So?"

"Let-let me get a hit…I'll…I'll tell you…"

I thought about it. Shit. If he tried anything, I'd just snap his neck and throw him in the bushes. So I tossed him his inhaler, helped him up. He sucked air from the contraption and staggered to the dying tree. I followed closely. He didn't go anywhere. Just leaned against it, glaring at me.

"I work for the owners of the Train Station," he said after a few moments.

"Who owns the Train Station?"

"Carlton Brothers, of course."

Crap. I heard that they were somehow tied into the same people who employ Sheldon and me. Fuck it. Dee is my wife. Mother of my child. If they put the hit on her, I'll become their nightmare.

"They put a hit out on that woman?"

The man scoffed. "What? No. God, no." He shook his head slowly. "They just want me to cause damage to the place. I told them that was a bad idea."

"So how does that lady fit into things?"

"She and those cows bought that fucking place!" he said. "My employers wanted to buy it. Fucking making my life miserable. I just keep the books, damn it!"

I laughed and said, "I think you need to find a new job, kemosabe."

The man agreed. He walked to his Suburban, got in, and drove off.

I went back to the Focus and sat there for a bit. I noticed the old man had left his car and other vehicles were starting to arrive. The bright neon sign was on, telling the world that the Ronettes Gentleman's Club was open for business.

I needed to go inside, but I didn't want to be recognized. I remembered I had that old Celtics cap in the glove compartment, a pair of thick dark sunglasses. Behind the seat was an army coat I bought at the VA store a few days ago. Not much of a disguise, I know. I had to do something. I needed more intel. Had to make sure Dee was safe in there. I didn't exactly buy the story the Carlton Brothers didn't put a hit on her. They were known to protect their territories, and this club sat in their domain.

For it to be just midday, the club was lively. All the dancers were on stage except three who, wearing leopard print body stockings, waited tables. Five businessmen were at the stage, already whooping and hollering. The little old man I'd seen earlier was off by himself to the right of the stage getting a show of his own by a very tall, muscled black woman. She was grinding on his lap and he kept handing her twenties.

Go, Grampa go.

I found a table in the back corner. A strawberry blond woman giggled as she glided toward me, a server's plate in her hand.

"Can I get you anything, honey?" Her Chicago accent was evident. Her rapid delivery between chewing gum was humorous. Of the three servers, she was the cutest.

"Well," I chuckled. "I'm not in the mood for anything to drink."

She leaned in, rested her medium, but nice compact breasts on my shoulder, whispered, "You have to order an alcoholic drink, baby. House rules."

Holy shit, she smelled like strawberries.

"I'll take a rum and Coke, then?"

"Good choice, honey." She shook her tail feather to the bar, looked back at the stage, and made googly eyes with a short, dark-haired naked girl, who did the same to her. Twenty seconds later, the strawberry blonde was back, set my glass on a coaster on the table.

"Thanks," I said.

She didn't respond. Too busy watching her dark-haired friend dance badly on stage.

Dee and her friends had a table in the middle left. Five women talking over the top of each other, Helen being the loudest. All five I'd met. Suzy Carmichael was a former school teacher, now a columnist for the local paper. Geraldine Smalls was the oldest in the group, who had left a very successful engineer husband to be with her girlfriend Jessica Gaunt, who sat beside Dee. Gaunt owned the pawnshop on Maddison and had met Geraldine five years ago on Facebook. Of course, the aforementioned devil dog bitch herself, Helen Spencer, sitting on Dee's left.

Suddenly, there was a new face in Dee's group of friends. A mousy blonde woman in a plain white dress to her ankles and large black purse, pulled a chair next to Suzy.

My waitress came back and asked if everything was okay.

"Oh sure," I said.

"The bartender wants to know why you aren't drinking." She turned her gaze toward the only woman working for the club fully clothed, in jeans and a Garth Brooks t-shirt standing behind the bar with her arms folded, a stern look on her face. "She's sensitive that way."

"Oh!" I raised my glass to the bartender, took a sip. "Mmm." I showed her the glass again. "Very good," I said. The waitress started to saunter off, but I caught her by the wrist and said, "Wait." She giggled, nervously removed her wrist from my grasp. "Oh. I'm sorry. I just have a question for you."

"Uhhh…I don't dance, mister." She was creeped out. "I most certainly will not go into the MVP room with you."

"Oh. No. That's not…not what I was going to ask. Who are the women over there?"

She looked hurt that it wasn't a pass at her, and at the same time relieved. Women are complicated.

She moved a strand of yellow-pink hair behind her left ear. "Ummm. They are the new owners. Well, five of them are. The other is a protester who just came here two weeks ago and is drinking with them."

"Protester?"

"Yeah. From the Northside Baptist congregation."

"For real?"

"Yeah. Weird."

"Which one?"

"The mousy blonde," the waitress said, pointing to the woman who'd just sat down.

"Interesting," I said.

The waitress giggled. "It's always the prudes you can't trust," she said and walked to meet the dark-haired dancer coming from the stage for a break. The waitress dipped the dark-haired dancer and kissed her. They ran off backstage, holding hands.

The mousy blonde excused herself from table, telling everyone goodbye. They yelled goodbye back. I watched her head for the front door. I jumped from my chair and trailed her. What was so urgent she had to leave? All the evil running rampant in the club made her skin crawl? Or did she not want to be around when something happened to Dee?

In the parking lot I saw her get in a gray Chevrolet pickup. Not a Suburban, but a Yukon. The same truck that almost ran me over outside my house. I recognized the driver now.

Reverend Uele Gold of the Northside Baptist congregation. Interesting fella. Served a sentence for racketeering ten years go. Found Jesus and the state let him out. I wouldn't doubt if he was behind the hit on Dee. A month ago I saw him on the news professing he'd rid the area of all filth, including gambling houses and, in particular, strip joints.

I got in the Focus. When the Yukon pulled out, I tailed them. You wouldn't believe where they led me. The car park where Sheldon and I conducted business, and it was still vacant. I drove by the car park as the Yukon entered. I went down Copper Lane, which actually took you to the backside of the car park, and parked near a wooded area. There was a back door where the part-time guard entered. Luckily, he was nowhere in sight.

I reached under the front seat, found my .38 Special wrapped in a sock. I placed the gun in my coat pocket. I went through the door that led me to a flight of stairs that took me to the top floor where Uele and the mousy blonde sat in the Yukon. I kept my distance, staying hidden behind a column. I could see they were engaged in some sort of sexual activity, even from that distance.

I moved two more columns and could see the mousy blonde was riding Uele, grinding away. I took a chance. All I wanted to do was talk to them. Make sure they were not the ones who put a hit on Dee.

I walked around the driver's side and made my presence known.

"Having a good time?"

Uele got spooked. The mousey blonde yelped. Uele pulled out a .45 and fired at me. The bullet whizzed by my head, struck a column, shot back to the Yukon and went through the windshield, into the mousy blonde's right temple. Blood and brain drenched Uele.

I ran.

"THIS IS SO horrible," Dee said. A picture of the mousey blonde, aka Thomasine Rodgers, and Reverend Uele Gold flashed on the TV set. Dee and I were in bed, watching the news.

"She was a good friend?" I had my innocent face on.

"No." Dee shook her head. "Hardly knew her. I don't think anyone will believe Reverend Gold's story about a man trying to assault them."

"No?" I asked with sly smile on my face. "Do you?"

"I'm not so sure." She looked at me coolly. "Hmmm. I swear

I saw you today."

I laughed. "C'mon, Dee. Y'know I was out hawkin' houses."

"Hmmm…"

Mark Slade is the author of the Barry London and Evelina Giles series, as well as the host of the Twisted Pulp Radio Hour on KKRN 88.5.

COMPANY MAN

Tom Pitts

"SO YOU'RE BASICALLY a serial killer."

"I'm not a serial killer," Jerry said. "I'm not anything like a serial killer."

"I think, by definition, you are. At least statistically you are, for sure."

"How would you know?"

"I read it somewhere," Rico said. "It's like three or more makes somebody a serial killer. That puts you way over the top, right?"

"What're you, a cop now? You taking a poll? Fuck you if you think I'm answering that." Jerry smiled and took a moment to light his cigarette.

Rico looked at the chip on Jerry's tooth. With all the scars and bruises on Jerry's face, it was hard not to wonder how each of them got there—and what happened to the poor bastard fool enough to leave their mark. Jerry took a deep pull and blew the smoke at Rico. In the midday sun, the billows of smoke filled up the car.

"It's a job, that's all. I mean, if someone is a whore, that doesn't make her a nymphomaniac, right? It's a job."

Rico didn't want to discuss it much further. He knew better than to upset Jerry when he was gearing up for a piece of work. There was a psychological hurdle he needed to pass and it wasn't going to happen if Rico kept talking. But Rico was nervous. This

253

kind of work wasn't his thing. He agreed to come along to the pawn shop and positively ID the guy, but he didn't like being in a car with Jerry, let alone on a job. Nervous energy always seemed to come out of Rico's mouth.

"For a job, it sure don't pay too well."

Jerry pursed his lips. The comment pissed him off. Rico knew better.

"It's not about that. You know how we make our money. But in our business, if you wanna move up, you gotta have an impressive resume." He pointed at the pawn shop. "The way to do that is work like *this*. You got a resume like mine and the money-making shit just seems to fall into place. No one gives me shit or owes me cash, I'll tell you that much."

Rico shifted in his seat. "With the problems I got, maybe I should beef up the ol' resume."

"Yeah, you should. Fuck yes. I can show you how to do it."

Rico laughed and shook his head. "No, I ain't that guy. I've never been good at the tough guy thing. Never won a fight in my life."

"It don't matter. You don't gotta be a tough guy. That's what the gun is for."

"Ah, it just ain't me," Rico said. "It's a little late in life to switch careers."

Jerry wasn't listening. He was pointing at the front door of the pawn shop. A short man stood by the entrance putting on a pair of sunglasses. "There he is. That's him, right?"

Rico said, "Yeah, that's him."

Jerry reached across Rico's lap and opened the glove box. Inside a rubber-gripped .38 Special sat wedged between a stack of old tickets and napkins.

"That's a terrible place to keep that thing. What if a cop pulls you over? You reach for the registration and, bam, you're done."

Jerry ignored him. "Let's go," he said with a wink.

"No, man. I'll wait here. In fact, you go and I'll walk back to the bar and meet you there."

"You wanted to learn? Now's your chance."

There was a long moment between them. Jerry watched the man from the pawn shop walk down the block. He turned and looked Rico in the eye and said, more forcefully this time, "Let's go."

Rico didn't have to look down at the gun pointed at his belly, the tone of Jerry's voice was enough. He climbed out of the car and Jerry did the same. They both started up the block, Jerry keeping a quickening gait and Rico following behind.

"C'mon, c'mon. He's going to slip away."

Rico sidled up to Jerry and said, "I can't do this, man. I fingered him, that was my part. I ain't getting nothing for this shit. I'll see you when it's done."

Again Jerry ignored him. "The trick is to keep moving, but not too fast. Keep the gun down at your side. Nobody'll look twice if you act like you belong, like you know where you're going."

Rico hadn't noticed, but Jerry had the .38 in his right hand, holding it close to the seam of his jeans. Rico looked over his shoulder. The block was nearly empty. A couple of bums, a few passing cars. Nobody to really take notice. Jerry rounded the corner ahead of him. The side street they stepped onto was completely vacant. Except for the man they followed.

"Better to wait till he gets into the car. If you catch him before he starts it up, you don't have to leave a body on the street."

The man stepped through the wide gate of a tall chain-link fence and pulled a set of keys from his pocket. He was in a private parking lot behind the pawnbrokers they'd spent the afternoon watching.

"Perfect timing. It's like he's asking us to shoot him."

When Rico and Jerry reached the chain-link fence, Jerry asked, "You wanna do it? It's easy. You can be the man. Fuckin' show those dickheads downtown who's got balls."

Rico felt Jerry's gun nudge his thigh.

"Here. Take it. Just walk up, point it at the back of his head, and squeeze two off."

"No way. I'm not even sure if that's him."

Jerry stopped. He grabbed Rico by the arm and spun him around. "What'd you mean, you're not sure?"

The man they were following got into his car. The door slammed shut and the engine started.

"I mean I'm not sure. It looks like the guy, but I'm not sure if it *is* the guy."

"You know what? You're a fucking chickenshit. That's your problem."

Jerry walked up to the running car, the .38 still clutched in his right hand. The windows were tinted and rolled up. Rico plugged his ears. Jerry knocked on the driver's window and it powered down.

Rico heard the man inside say, "Oh, hey Jerry, how're you doing?"

"Good, Richard. Listen, I got a question for you." Jerry gestured with the gun toward Rico. "Is this the guy that came into the club that night?"

The man in the car leaned out the window and squinted at Rico. "Yeah, that's him."

"You're sure?"

The man, with his eyes still fixed on Rico, said, "Oh, I'm very sure."

Jerry straightened up, pointed the .38 at Rico and said, "You, my friend, are going on my resume."

Canadian-American writer Tom Pitts is the author of such novels as Coldwater, 101, American Static, Hustle, *and* Piggyback.

SIX-FINGER JACK

Joe R. Lansdale

JACK HAD SIX fingers. That's how Big O, that big, fat, white, straw-hatted son-of-a-bitch, was supposed to know he was dead. Maybe, by some real weird luck a man could kill some other black man with six fingers, cut off his hand and bring it in and claim it belonged to Jack, but not likely. So he put the word out whoever killed Jack and cut off his paw and brought it back was gonna get one hundred thousand dollars and a lot of goodwill.

I went out there after Jack just like a lot of other fellas, and one woman I knew of, Lean Mama Tootin', who was known for shotgun shootin' and ice pick work. She went out there too.

But the thing I had on them was I was screwing Jack's old lady. Jack didn't know it of course. Jack was a bad dude, and it wouldn't have been smart to let him know my bucket was in his well. Nope. Wouldn't have been smart for me or Jack's old lady. He'd known that before he had to make a run for it, might have been good to not sleep, cause he might show up and be most unpleasant. I can be unpleasant too, but I prefer when I'm on the stalk, not when I'm being stalked. It sets the dynamics all different.

You see, I'm a philosophical kind of guy.

This was, though, I'd been laying the pipeline to his lady for about six weeks, because Jack had been on the run ever since he'd tried to muscle in on Big O's whores and take over that business, found out he couldn't. That wasn't enough, he took up with Big O's old lady like it didn't matter none, but it did. Rumor was, Big O put the old lady under about three feet of concrete out by his lake boat stalls, put her in the hole while she was alive, hands tied behind her back, lookin' up at that concrete mixer truck dripping out the goo, right on top of her naked self.

Jack hears this little tidbit of information, he quit foolin' around and made with the jack rabbit, took off lickety-split, so fast he almost left a vapor trail. It's one thing to fight one man, or two, but to fight a whole organization, not so easy. Especially if that organization belonged to Big O.

Loodie, Jack's personal woman, was a hot-flash number who liked to have her ashes hauled, and me, I'm a tall, lean fellow with a good smile and a willing attitude. Loodie was ready to lose Jack because he had a bad temper and a bit of a smell. He was short of baths and long on cologne. Smell-good juice on top of his stinky smell, she said, made a kind of funk that would make a skunk roll over dead and cause a wild hyena to leave the body where it lay.

She, on the other hand, was like sweet wet sin dipped in coffee and sugar with a dash of cinnamon: God's own mistress with a surly attitude, which goes to show even God likes a little bit of the devil now and then.

She'd been asked about Jack by them who wanted to know. Bad folks with guns, and a need for dough. But she lied, said she didn't know where he was. Everyone believed her because she talked so bad about Jack. Said stuff about his habits, about how he beat her, how bad he was in bed, and how he stunk. It was convincin' stuff to everyone.

But me.

I knew that woman was a liar, because I knew her whole family, and they was the sort like my daddy used to say would rather climb a tree and lie than stand on the ground and tell the truth and be given free flowers. Lies flowed through their veins as surely as blood.

She told me about Jack one night while we were in bed, right after we had toted the water to the mountain. We're laying there lookin' at the ceilin', like there's gonna be manna from heaven, watchin' the defective light from the church across the way flash in and out and bounce along the wall, and she says in that burnt toast voice of hers, "You split that money, I'll tell you where he is?"

"You wanna split it?"

"Naw, I'm thinkin' maybe you could keep half and I could give the other half to the cat."

"You don't got a cat."

"Well, I got another kind of cat, and that cat is one you like to pet."

"You're right there," I said. "Tellin' me where he is, that's okay, but I still got to do the ground work. Hasslin' with that dude ain't no easy matter, that's what I'm tryin' to tell you. So, me doin' what I'm gonna have to do, that's gonna be dangerous as trying to play with a daddy lion's balls. So, that makes me worth more than half, and you less than half."

"You're gonna shoot him when he ain't lookin', and you know it."

"I still got to take the chance."

She reached over to the nightstand, nabbed up a pack, shook out a cigarette, lit it with a cheap lighter, took a deep drag, coughed out a puff, said, "Split, or nothin'."

"Hell, honey, you know I'm funnin'," I said. "I'll split it right in half with you."

I was lyin' through my teeth. She may have figured such, but she figured with me she at least had a possibility, even if it was as thin as the edge of a playin' card.

She said, "He's done gone deep East Texas. He's over in Marvel Creek. Drove over there in his big black Cadillac that he had a chop shop turn blue."

"So he drove over in a blue Caddy, not black," I said. "I mean, if it was black, and he had it painted blue, it ain't black no more. It's blue."

"Aren't you one for the details, and at a time like this," she said, and used her foot to rub my leg. "But, technically, baby, you are so correct."

THAT NIGHT LOODIE laid me out a map written in pencil on a brown paper sack, made me swear I was gonna split the money with her again. I told her what she wanted to hear. Next mornin', I started over to Marvel Creek.

Now, technically, Jack was in a place outside of the town, along the Sabine River, back in the bottom land where the woods was still thick, down a little trail that wound around and around, to a cabin Loodie said was about the size of a postage stamp, provided the stamp had been scissor trimmed.

I oiled my automatic, put on gloves, went to the store and bought a hatchet, cruised out early, made Marvel Creek in about an hour and fifteen, went glidin' over the Sabine River bridge. I took a gander at the water, which was dirty brown and up high on account of rain. I had grown up along that river, over near a place called Big Sandy. It was a place of hot sand and tall pines and no opportunity.

It wasn't a world I missed none.

I stopped at a little diner in Marvel Creek and had me a hamburger. There was a little white girl behind the counter with hair as blond as sunlight, and we made some goo-goo eyes at one another. Had I not been on a mission, I might have found out when she got off work, seen if me and her could get a drink and find a motel and try and make the beast with two backs.

Instead I finished up, got me a tall Styrofoam cup of coffee to go. I drove over to a food store and went in and bought a huge jar of pickles, a bag of cookies and a bottle of water. I put the pickles on the floor board between the backseat and the front. It was a huge jar and it fit snugly. I laid the bag with the cookies and the water on the backseat.

The bottoms weren't far, about twenty minutes, but the roads were kind of tricky, some of them were little more than mud and a suggestion. Others were slick and shiny like snot on a water glass.

I drove carefully and sucked on my coffee. I went down a pretty wide road that became narrow, then took another road that wound off into the deeper woods. Drove until I found what I thought was the side road that led to the cabin. It was really a glorified path. Sun hardened, not very wide, bordered on one side by trees, and on the other side by marshy land that would suck the shoes off your feet, or bog up a car tire until you had to pull a gun and shoot the engine like a dying horse.

I stopped in the road and held Loodie's hand-drawn map, checked it, looked up. There was a curve went around and between the trees and the marsh. There were tire tracks in it. Pretty fresh. At the bend in the curve was a little wooden bridge with no railings.

So far Loodie's map was on the money.

I finished off my coffee, got out and took a pee behind the car and watched some big white water birds flying over. When I was growing up over in Big Sandy I used to see that kind of thing all the time, not to mention all manner of wildlife, and for a moment I felt nostalgic. That lasted about as long as it took me to stick my dick back in my pants and zipper up.

I got my hatchet out of the trunk and laid it on the front passenger seat as I got back in the car. I pulled out my automatic and checked it over, popped out the clip and slid it back in. I always liked the sound it made when it snapped into place. I looked at myself in the mirror, like maybe I was goin' on a date. Thought maybe if things fucked up, it might be the last time I got a good look at myself. I put the car in gear, wheeled around the curve and over the bridge, going at a slow pace, the map on the seat beside me, held in place by the hatchet.

I came to a wide patch, like on the map, and pulled off the road. Someone had dumped their garbage at the end of the spot where it ended close to the trees. There were broken-up plastic bags spilling cans and paper, and there was an old bald tire leaning against a tree, as if taking a break before rolling on its way.

I got out and walked around the bend, looked down the road. There was a broad pond of water to the left, leaked there by the dirty Sabine. On the right, next to the woods, was a log cabin. Small, but well made and kind of cool lookin'. Loodie said it was on property Jack's parents had owned. Twenty acres or so. Cabin had a chimney chuggin' smoke. Out front was a big blue Cadillac El Dorado, the tires and sides splashed with mud. It was parked up close to the cabin. I could see through the Cadillac's windows, and they lined up with a window in the cabin. I moved to the side of the road, stepped in behind some trees, and studied the place carefully.

There weren't any wires runnin' to the cabin. There was a kind of lean-to shed off the back. Loodie told me that was where Jack kept the generator that gave the joint electricity. Mostly the cabin was heated by the firewood piled against the shed, and lots of blankets come late at night. Had a gas stove with a nice sized tank. I could just imagine Jack in there with Loodie, his six fingers on her sweet chocolate skin. It made me want to kill him all the more, even though I knew Loodie was the kind of girl made a minx look virginal. You gave your heart to that woman, she'd eat it.

I WENT BACK to the car and got my gun-cleaning goods out of the glove box, and took out the clip, and cleaned my pistol and reloaded it. It was unnecessary, because the gun was a clean as a model's ass, but I liked to be sure.

I patted the hatchet on the seat like it was a dog.

I sat there and waited, thought about what I was gonna do with one hundred thousand dollars. You planned to kill someone and cut off their hand, you had to think about stuff like that, and a lot.

Considering on it, I decided I wasn't gonna get foolish and buy a car. One I had got me around and it looked all right enough. I wasn't gonna spend it on Loodie or some other split tail in a big time way. I was gonna use it carefully. I might get some new clothes and put some money down on a place instead of rentin'. Fact was, I might move to Houston.

If I lived closed to the bone and picked up the odd bounty job now and again, just stuff I wanted to do, like bits that didn't involve me having to deal with some goon big enough to pull off one of my legs and beat me with it, I could live safer, and better. Could have some stretches where I didn't have to do a damn thing but take it easy, all on account of that one hundred thousand dollar nest egg.

Course, Jack wasn't gonna bend over and grease up for me. He wasn't like that. He could be a problem.

I got a paperback out of the glove box and read for awhile. I couldn't get my mind to stick to it. The sky turned gray. My light was goin'. I put the paperback in the glove box with the guncleaning kit. It started to rain. I watched it splat on the windshield. Thunder knocked at the sky. Lighting licked a crooked path against the clouds and passed away.

I thought about all manner of different ways of pullin' this off, and finally came up with somethin', decided it was good enough, because all I needed was a little edge.

The rain was hard and wild. It made me think Jack wasn't gonna be comin' outside. I felt safe enough for the moment. I tilted the seat back and lay there with the gun in my hand, my arm folded across my chest, and dozed for awhile with the rain pounding the roof.

IT WAS FRESH night when I awoke. I waited about an hour, picked up the hatchet, and got out of the car. It was still raining, and the rain was cold. I pulled my coat tight around me, stuck

263

the hatchet through my belt and went to the back of the car and unlocked the trunk. I got the jack handle out of there, stuck it in my belt opposite the hatchet, started walking around the curve.

The cabin had a faint light shining through the window that in turn shone through the lined-up windows of the car. As I walked, I saw a shape, like a huge bullet with arms, move in front of the glass. That size made me lose a step briefly, but I gathered up my courage, kept going.

When I got to the back of the cabin, I carefully climbed on the pile of firewood, made my way to the top of the lean-to. It sloped down off the main roof of the cabin, so it didn't take too much work to get up there, except that hatchet and tire iron gave me a bit of trouble in my belt and my gloves made my grip a little slippery.

On top of the cabin, I didn't stand up and walk, but instead carefully made my way on hands and knees toward the front of the place.

When I got there, I leaned over the edge and took a look. The cabin door was about three feet below me. I made my way to the edge so I was overlooking the Cadillac. A knock on the door wouldn't bring Jack out. Even he was too smart for that, but that Cadillac, he loved it. Bought a new one every year. I pulled out the tire iron, laid down on the roof, looking over the edge, cocked my arm back and threw the iron at the windshield. It made a hell of a crash, cracking the glass so that it looked like a spider web, setting off the car alarm.

I pulled my gun and waited. I heard the cabin door open, heard the thumping of Jack's big feet. He came around there mad as a hornet. He was wearing a long sleeve white shirt with the sleeves rolled up. He hadn't had time to notice the cold. But the best thing was it didn't look like he had a gun on him.

I aimed and shot him. I think I hit him somewhere on top of the shoulder, but I wasn't sure. But I hit him. He did a kind of bend at the knees, twisted his body, then snapped back into shape and looked up.

"You," he said.

I shot him again, and it had about the same impact. Jack was on the hood of his car and then on the roof, and then he jumped. That big bastard could jump, could probably dunk a basketball and grab the rim. He hit with both hands on the edge of the roof, started pulling himself up. I was up now, and I stuck the gun in his face, and pulled the trigger.

And, let me tell you how the gas went out of me. I had cleaned that gun and cleaned that gun, and now...It jammed. First time ever. But it was a time that mattered.

Jack lifted himself onto the roof, and then he was on me, snatching the gun away and flinging it into the dark. I couldn't believe it. What the hell was he made of? Even in the wet night, I could see that much of his white shirt had turned dark with blood.

We circled each other for a moment. I tried to decide what to do next, and then he was on me. I remembered the hatchet, but it was too late. We were going back off the roof and onto the lean-to, rolling down that. We hit the stacked firewood and it went in all directions and we splattered to the ground.

I lost my breath. Jack kept his. He grabbed me by my coat collar and lifted me and flung me around and against the side of the lean-to. I hit on my back and came down on my butt.

Jack grabbed up a piece of firewood. It looked to me that that piece of wood had a lot of heft. He came at me. I made myself stand. I pulled the hatchet free. As he came and struck down with the wood, I sidestepped and swung the hatchet.

The sound the hatchet made as it caught the top of his head was a little like what you might expect if a strong man took hold of a piece of cardboard and ripped it.

I hit him so hard his knees bent and hot blood jumped out of his head and hit my face. The hatchet came loose of my hands, stayed in his skull. His knees straightened. I thought: What is this motherfucker, Rasputin?

He grabbed me and started to lift me again. His mouth was

partially open and his teeth looked like machinery cogs to me. The rain was washing the blood on his head down his face in murky rivers. He stunk like roadkill.

And then his expression changed. It seemed as if he had just realized he had a hatchet in his head. He let go, turned, started walking off, taking hold of the hatchet with both hands, trying to pull it loose. I picked up a piece of firewood and followed after him. I went up behind him and hit him in the back of the head as hard as I could. It was like hitting an elephant in the ass with a twig. He turned and looked at me. The look on his face was so strange, I almost felt sorry for him.

He went down on one knee, and I hauled back and hit him with the firewood, hitting the top of the hatchet. He vibrated, and his neck twisted to one side, and then his head snapped back in line.

He said, "Gonna need some new pigs," and then fell out.

Pigs?

He was lying face forward with the stock of the hatchet holding his head slightly off the ground. I dropped the firewood and rolled him over on his back, which only took about as much work as trying to roll his Cadillac. I pulled the hatchet out of his head. I had to put my foot on his neck to do it.

I picked up the firewood I had dropped, put it on the ground beside him, and stretched his arm out until I had the hand with the six fingers positioned across it. I got down on my knees and lifted the hatchet, hit as hard as I could. It took me three whacks, but I cut his hand loose.

I PUT THE bloody hand in my coat pocket and dug through his pants for his car keys, didn't come across them. I went inside the cabin and found them on the table. I drove the Cadillac to the back where Jack lay, pulled him into the backseat, almost having a hernia in the process. I put the hatchet in there with him.

I drove the El Dorado over close to the pond and rolled all the windows down and put it in neutral. I got out of the car, went to the back of it and started shoving. My feet slipped in the mud, but finally I gained traction. The car went forward and slipped into the water, but the back end of it hung on the bank.

Damn.

I pushed and I pushed, and finally I got it moving, and it went in, and with the windows down, it sunk pretty fast.

I went back to the cabin and looked around. I found some candles. I turned off the light, and I went and turned off the generator. I went back inside and lit about three of the big fat candles and stuck them in drinking glasses and watched them burn for a moment. I went over to the stove and turned on the gas. I let it run a few seconds, looked around the cabin. Nothing there I needed.

I left, closed the door behind me. When the gas filled the room enough, those candles would set the air on fire, the whole place would blow. I don't know exactly why I did it, except maybe I just didn't like Jack. Didn't like that he had a Cadillac and a cabin and some land, and for a while there, he had Loodie. Because of all that, I had done all I could do that could be done to him. I even had his six-fingered hand in my pocket.

By the time I got back to the car, I was feeling weak. Jack had worked me over pretty good, and now that the adrenaline had started to ease out of me, I was feeling it. I took off my jacket and opened the jar of pickles in the floor board, pulled out a few of them and threw them away. I ate one, and had my bottle of water with it and some cookies.

I took Jack's hand and put it in the big pickle jar. I sat in the front seat, and was overcome with a feeling of nausea. I didn't know if it was the pickle or what I had done, or both. I opened the car door and threw up. I felt cold and damp from the rain. I started the car and turned on the heater. I cranked back my seat and closed my eyes. I had to rest before I left, had to. All of me

267

seemed to be running out through the soles of my feet.

I slept until the cabin blew. The sound of the gas generator and stove going up with a one-two boom snapped me awake.

I GOT OUT of the car and walked around the curve. The cabin was nothing more than a square dark shape inside an envelope of fire. The fire wavered up high and grew narrow at the top like a cone. The fire crackled like someone wadding up cellophane.

I doubted, out here, anyone heard the explosion, and no one could see the flames. Wet as it was, I figured the fire wouldn't go any farther than the cabin. By morning, even with the rain still coming down, that place would be smoked down to the mineral rights.

I drove out of there, and pretty soon the heater was too hot, and I turned it off. It was as if my body was as on fire as the cabin. I rolled down the window and let in some cool air. I felt strange. Not good, not bad. I had bounty hunted for years, and I had done a bit of head-whopping before, but this was my first murder.

I had really hated Jack and I had hardly known him.

It was the woman that made me hate him. The woman I was gonna cheat out of some money. But a hundred thousand dollars is a whole lot of money, honey.

WHEN I GOT home, the automatic garage opener lifted the door and I wheeled in and closed the place up. I went inside and took off my clothes and showered carefully and looked in the mirror. There was a knot on my head that looked as if you might need mountaineering equipment to scale it. I got some ice and put it in a sock and pressed it to my head while I sat on the toilet lid and thought about things. If any thoughts actually came to me, I don't remember them well.

I dressed, bunched up my murder clothes, and put them in a

black plastic garbage bag.

In the garage, I removed the pickle jar and cleaned the car. I opened the jar and looked at the hand. It looked like a black crab in there amongst the pickles. I studied it for a long time until it started to look like one hundred thousand dollars.

I couldn't wait until morning, and after awhile I drove toward Big O's place. Now, you would think a man with the money he's got would live in a mansion, but he didn't. He lived in three doublewide mobile homes that had been lined together by screened-in porches. I had been inside once, when I had done Big O a very small favor, and had never been inside since. But one of those homes was nothing but one big space, no rooms, and it was Big O's lounge. He hung in there with some ladies and some bodyguards. He had two main guys. Be Bop Lewis, who was a skinny white guy who always acted as if someone was sneaking up on him, and a black guy named Lou Boo (keep in mind, I didn't name them) who thought he was way cool and smooth as velvet.

The rain had followed me from the bottom land, on into Tyler, to the outskirts, and on the far side. It was way early morning, and I figured on waking Big O up and dragging his ass out of bed and showing him them six fingers and getting me one hundred thousand dollars, a pat on the head, and hell, he might ask Be Bop to give me a hand job, on account of I had done so well.

More I thought about it, more I thought he might not be as happy to see me as I thought. A man like Big O liked his sleep, so I pulled into a motel not too far from where I had to go to see Big O, the big jar of pickles and one black six-fingered hand beside my bed, the automatic under my pillow.

I dreamed Jack was driving the Cadillac out of that pond. I saw the lights first and then the car. Jack was steering with his nub laid against the wheel, and his face behind the glass was a black mass without eyes or smile or features of any kind.

It was a bad dream and it woke me up. I washed my face,

went back to bed, slept this time until late morning. I got up and put back on my same clothes, loaded up my pickle jar and left out of there. I thought about the axe in Jack's head, his hand chopped off and in the pickle jar, and regret moved through me like shit through a goose and was gone.

I drove out to Big O's place.

BY THE TIME I arrived at the property, which was surrounded by a barbed-wire fence, and had driven over a cattle guard, I could see there were men in a white pickup coming my way. Two in the front and three in the bed in the back, and they had some heavy-duty fire power. Parked behind them, up by the double-wides, were the cement trucks and dump trucks and backhoes and graders that were part of the business Big O claimed to operate. Construction. But his real business was a bit of this, and a little of that, construction being little more than the surface paint.

I stopped and rolled down my window and waited. Outside the rain had burned off and it was an unseasonably hot day, sticky as honey on the fingers.

When they drove up beside my window, the three guys in the bed pointed their weapons at me. The driver was none other than one of the two men I recognized from before. Be Bop. His skin was so pale and thin, I could almost see the skull beneath it.

"Well, now," he said. "I know you."

I agreed he did. I smiled like me and him was best friends. I said, "I got some good news for Big O about Six Finger Jack."

"Six Finger Jack, huh," Be Bop said. "Get out of the car."

I got out. Be Bop got out and frisked me. I had nothing sharp or anything full of bullets. He asked if there was anything in the car. I told him no. He had one of the men in the back of the pickup search it anyway. The man came back, said, "Ain't got no gun, just a big jar of pickles."

"Pickles," Be Bop said. "You a man loves pickles?"

"Not exactly," I said.

"Follow us on up," Be Bop said.

We drove on up to the trio of double-wides. There had been some work done since I had last been here, and there was a frame of boards laid out for a foundation, and out to the side there was a big hole that looked as if it was going to be a swimming pool.

I got out of the car and leaned on it and looked things over. Be Bop and his men got out of the truck. Be Bop came over.

"He buildin' a house on that foundation?" I asked.

"Naw, he's gonna put an extension on one of the trailers. I think he's gonna put in a pool room and maybe some gamin' stuff. Swimmin' pool over there. Come on."

I got my jar of pickles out of the backseat, and Be Bop said, "Now wait a minute. Your pickles got to go with you?"

I set the jar down and screwed off the lid and stepped back. Be Bop looked inside. When he lifted his head, he said, "Well, now."

NEXT THING I know I'm in the big trailer, the one that's got nothin' but the couch, some chairs and stands for drinks, a TV set about the size of a downtown theater. It's on, and there's sports goin'. I glance at it and see it's an old basketball game that was played a year back, but they're watchin' it, Big O and a few of his boys, includin' Lou Boo, the black guy I've seen before. This time, there aren't any women there.

Be Bop came inside with me, but the rest of the pickup posse didn't. They were still protecting the perimeter. It seemed silly, but truth was, there was lots of people wanted to kill Big O.

No one said a thing to me for a full five minutes. They were waitin' for a big score in the game, somethin' they had seen before. When the shot came they all cheered. I thought only Big O sounded sincere.

I didn't look at the game. I couldn't take my eyes off Big O. He wasn't wearin' his cowboy hat. His head had only a few hairs left on it, like worms working their way over the face of the moon. His skin was white and lumpy like cold oatmeal. He was wearin' a brown pair of stretch overalls. When the fat moved, the material moved with him, which was a good idea, cause it looked as if Big O had packed on about one hundred extra pounds since I saw him last.

He was sitting in a motorized scooter, had his tree trunk legs stretched out in front of him on a leg lift. His stomach flowed up and fell forward and over his sides, like four hundred pounds of bagged mercury. I could hear him wheezing across the room. His right foot was missing. There was a nub there and his stretch pants had been sewn up at the end. On the stand, near his right elbow was a tall bottle of malt liquor and a greasy box of fried chicken.

His men sat on the couch to his left. The couch was unusually long and there were six men on it, like pigeons in a row. They all had guns in shoulder holsters. The scene made Big O looked like a whale on vacation with a male harem of sucker fish to attend him.

Big O spoke to me, his voice sounded small coming from that big body. "Been a long time since I seen you last."

I nodded.

"I had a foot then."

I nodded again.

"The diabetes. Had to cut it off. Dr. Jacobs says I need more exercise, but, hey, glandular problems, so what you gonna do? Packs the weight on. But still, I got to go there every Thursday mornin'. Next time, he might tell me the other foot's got to go. But you know, that's not so bad. This chair, it can really get you around. Motorized you know."

Be Bop, who was still by me, said, "He's got somethin' for you, Big O."

"Chucky," Big O said, "cut off the game."

Chucky was one of the men on the couch, a white guy. He got up and found a remote control and cut off the game. He took it with him back to the couch, sat down.

"Come on up," Big O said.

I carried my jar of pickles up there, got a whiff of him that made my memory of Jack's stink seem mild. Big O smelled like dried urine, sweat, and death. I had to fight my gag reflex.

I set the jar down and twisted off the lid and reached inside the blood stained pickle juice, and brought out Jack's dripping hand. Big O said, "Give me that."

I gave it to him. He turned it around and around in front of him. Pickle juice dripped off of the hand and into his lap. He started to laugh. His fat vibrated, and then he coughed. "That there is somethin'."

He held the hand up above his head. Well, he lifted it to about shoulder height. Probably the most he had moved in a while. He said, "Boys, do you see this? Do you see the humanity in this?"

I thought: Humanity?

"This hand tried to take my money and stuck its finger up my old lady's ass...Maybe all six. Look at it now."

His boys all laughed. It was like the best goddamn joke ever told, way they yucked it up.

"Well now," Big O said, "that motherfucker won't be touchin' nothin', won't be handlin' nobody's money, not even his own, and we got this dude to thank."

Way Big O looked at me then made me a little choked up. I thought there might even be a tear in his eye. "Oh," he said. "I loved that woman. God, I did. But, I had to cut her loose. She hadn't fucked around, me and her might have gotten married, and all this—" he waved Jack's hand around, "would have been hers to share. But no. She couldn't keep her pants on. It's a sad situation. And though I can't bring her back, this here hand, it gives me some kind of happiness. I want you to know that."

"I'm glad I could have been of assistance," I said.

"That's good. That's good. Put this back in the pickle jar, will you?"

I took the hand and dropped it in the pickle jar.

Big O looked at me, and I looked at him. After a long moment, he said, "Well, thanks."

I said, "You're welcome."

We kept looking at one another. I cleared my throat. Big O shifted a little in his chair. Not much, but a little.

"Seems to me," I said, "there was a bounty on Jack. Some money."

"Oh," Big O said. "That's right, there was."

"He was quite a problem."

"Was he now...Yeah, well, I can see the knot on your head. You ought to buy that thing its own cap. Somethin' nice."

Everyone on the couch laughed. I laughed too. I said, "Yeah, it's big. And, I had some money, like say, one hundred thousand dollars, I'd maybe put out ten or twenty for a nice designer cap."

I was smilin', waiting for my laugh, but nothin' came. I glanced at Be Bop. He was lookin' off like maybe he heard his mother callin' somewhere in the distance.

Big O said, "Now that Jack's dead, I got to tell you, I've sort of lost the fever."

"Lost the fever?" I said.

"He was alive, I was all worked up. Now that he's dead, I got to consider, is he really worth one hundred thousand dollars?"

"Wait a minute, that was the deal. That's the deal you spread all over."

"I've heard those rumors," Big O said.

"Rumors?"

"Oh, you can't believe everything you hear. You just can't." I stood there stunned.

Big O said, "But I want you to know, I'm grateful. You want a Coke, a beer before you go?"

"No. I want the goddamn money you promised."

That had come out of my mouth like vomit. It surprised even me.

Everyone in the room was silent.

Big O breathed heavy, said, "Here's the deal, friend. You take your jar of pickles, and Jack's six fingers, and you carry them away. Cause if you don't, if you want to keep askin' me for money I don't want to pay, your head is gonna be in that jar, but not before I have it shoved up your ass. You savvy?"

It took me a moment, but I said, "Yeah. I savvy."

LYING IN BED with Loodie, not being able to do the deed, I said, "I'm gonna get that fat sonofabitch. He promised me money. I fought Jack with a piece of firewood and a hatchet. I fell off a roof. I slept in my car in the cold. I was nearly killed."

"That sucks," Loodie said.

"Sucks? You got snookered too. You was gonna get fifty thousand, now you're gonna get dick."

"Actually, tonight, I'm not even gettin' that."

"Sorry, baby. I'm just so mad...Ever Thursday mornin', Big O, he goes to a doctor's appointment at Dr. Jacobs. I can get him there."

"He has his men, you know."

"Yeah. But when he goes in the office, maybe he don't. And maybe I check it out this Thursday, find out when he goes in, and next Thursday, I maybe go inside and wait on him."

"How would you do that?"

"I'm thinkin' on it, baby."

"I don't think it's such a good idea."

"You lost fifty grand, and so did I, so blowin' a hole in his head is as close as we'll get to satisfaction."

SO THURSDAY MORNIN', I'm goin' in the garage, to go and check things out, and when I get in the car, before I can open up the garage and back out, a head raises up in the back seat, and a gun barrel, like a wet kiss, pushes against the side of my neck.

I can see him in the mirror. It's Lou Boo. He says: "You got to go where I tell you, else I shoot a hole in you."

I said, "Loodie."

"Yeah, she come to us right away."

"Come on, man. I was just mad. I wasn't gonna do nothin'."

"So here it is Thursday mornin', and now you're tellin' me you wasn't goin' nowhere."

"I was gonna go out and get some breakfast. Really."

"Don't believe you."

"Shit," I said.

"Yeah, shit," Lou Boo said.

"How'd you get in here without me knowin'?"

"I'm like a fuckin' ninja...And the door slides up you pull it from the bottom."

"Really?"

"Yeah, really."

"Come on, Lou Boo, give a brother a break. You know how it is?"

Lou Boo laughed a little. "Ah, man. Don't play the brother card. I'm what you might call one of them social progressives. I don't see color, even if it's the same as mine. Let's go, my man."

IT WAS HIGH morning and cool when we arrived. I drove my car right up to where the pool was dug out, way Lou Boo told me. There was a cement mixer truck parked nearby for cementing the pool. We stopped and Lou Boo told me to leave it in neutral. I did. I got out and walked with him to where Big O was sitting in his motorized scooter with Loodie on his lap. His boys were all around him. Be Bop pointed his finger at me and dropped his thumb.

"My man," Be Bop said.

When I was standing in front of Big O, he said, "Now, I

want you to understand, you wouldn't be here had you not de-cided to kill me. I can't have that, now can I?"

I didn't say anything.

I looked at Loodie, she shrugged.

"I figured you owed me money," I said.

"Yeah," Big O said. "I know. You see, Loodie, she comes and tells me she's gonna make a deal with you to kill Jack and make you think you made a deal with her. That way, the deal I made was with her, not you. You followin' me on this, swivel dick? Then, you come up with this idea to kill me at the doc-tor's office. Loodie, she came right to me."

"So," I said, "you're gettin' Loodie out of the deal, and she's gettin' one hundred thousand."

"That sounds about right, yeah," Big O said.

I thought about that. Her straddlin' that fat bastard in his scooter. I shook my head, glared at her, said, "Damn, girl."

She didn't look right at me.

Big O said, "Loodie, you go on in the house there, and amuse yourself. Get a beer, or somethin'. Watch a little TV. Do your nails. Whatever."

Loodie started walking toward the trailers. When she was in-side, Big O said, "Hell, boy. I know how she is, and I know what she is. It's gonna be white gravy on sweet chocolate bread for me. And when I get tired of it, she gonna find a hole out here next to you. I got me all kind of room here. I ain't usin' the lake boat stalls no more. That's risky. Here is good. Though I'm gonna have to dig another spot for a pool, but that's how it is. Ain't no big thing, really."

"She used me," I said. "She's the one led me to this."

"No doubt, boy. But, you got to understand. She come to me and made the deal before you did anything. I got to honor that."

"I could just go on," I said. "I could forget all about it. I was just mad. I wouldn't never bother you. Hell, I can move. I can go out of state."

"I know that," he said, "but, I got this rule, and it's simple. You threaten to kill me, I got to have you taken care of. Ain't that my rule, boys?"

There was a lot of agreement.

Lou Boo was last. He said, "Yep, that's the way you do it, boss."

Big O said, "Lou Boo, put him in the car, will you?"

Lou Boo put the gun to back of my head, said, "Get on your knees."

"Fuck you," I said, but he hit me hard behind the head. Next thing I know I'm on my knees, and he's got my hands behind my back, and has fastened a plastic tie over my wrists.

"Get in the car," Lou Boo said.

I fought him all the way, but Be Bop came out and kicked me in the nuts a couple of times, hard enough I threw up, and then they dragged me to the car and shoved me inside behind the wheel and rolled down the windows and closed the door.

They went behind the car then and pushed. The car wobbled, then fell, straight down, hit so hard the air bag blew out and knocked the shit out of me. I couldn't move with it the way it was, my hands bound behind my back, the car on its nose, its back wheels against the side of the hole. It looked like I was tryin' to drive to hell. I was stunned and bleeding. The bag had knocked a tooth out. I heard the sound of a motor above me, a little motor. The scooter.

I could hear Big O up there. "If you hear me, want you to know I'm having one of the boys bring the cement truck around. We're gonna fill this hole with cement, and put, I don't know, a tennis court or somethin' on top of it. But the thing I want you to know is this is what happens when someone fucks with Big O."

"You stink," I said. "And you're fat. And you're ugly."

He couldn't hear me. I was mostly talking into the air bag.

I heard the scooter go away, followed by the sound of a truck and a beeping as it backed up. Next I heard the churning of the cement in the big mixer that was on the back of it. Then the cement slid down and pounded on the roof and started to slide over the windshield. I closed my eyes and held my breath, and then I felt the cold wet cement touch my elbow as it came through the open window. I thought about some way out, but there was nothing there, and I knew that within moments there wouldn't be anything left for me to think about at all.

Prolific author Joe R. Lansdale has written books in just about every genre. He has penned more than fifty novels, including Cold In July, The Bottoms, More Better Deals, *and the Hap and Leonard series.*

BOOKS

On the following pages are a few
more great titles from the
Down & Out Books publishing family.

For a complete list of books and to
sign up for our newsletter,
go to DownAndOutBooks.com.

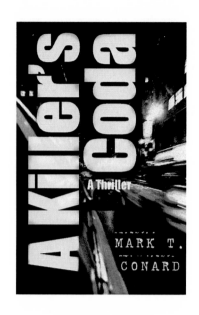

A Killer's Coda
Mark T. Conard

Down & Out Books
May 2021
978-1-64396-180-4

Psychologist Henry Blackwell is living the nightmare of his wife's unsolved murder, when he discovers a series of new killings that may help him track down his wife's murderer.

But Blackwell knows all the victims and his alcohol blackouts coincide with the crimes.

As the body count grows, the race to find the killer just might lead Blackwell to the most shocking suspect of all.

Radicals
Nik Korpon

Down & Out Books
May 2021
978-1-64396-185-9

When a mysterious cyber-terrorist organization begins erasing Americans' medical debt, enigmatic FBI cybercrimes agent Jay Brodsky must focus on an attack threatening to destabilize the US economy.

But when the trail leads to his own family, Jay will be forced to confront everything he never knew about his parents and his long-missing sister and decide where his true loyalties lie.

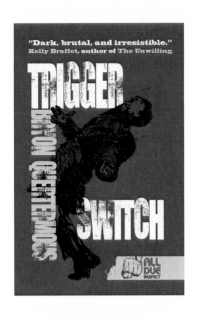

Trigger Switch
Bryon Quertermous

All Due Respect, an imprint of
Down & Out Books
March 2021
978-1-64396-190-3

Dominick Prince has been a magnet for trouble his entire life. A series of poor life choices and their violent consequences have crushed his spirit. Desperate to outrun this burgeoning rage before it fully consumes him, Dominick accepts an offer he doesn't trust from an old high school classmate.

Dutchy Kent says he wants to make one last-ditch effort to prove his acting chops by mounting the New York City debut of a play based on one of Dominick's stories, but the true story involves the real estate empire of a notorious Queens drug dealer and $1.2 million in cash.

Houses Burning and Other Ruins
William R. Soldan

Shotgun Honey, an imprint of
Down & Out Books
May 2021
978-1-64396-115-6

Desperation. Violence. Broken homes and broken hearts. Fathers, junkies, and thieves.

In this gritty new collection, one bad choice begets another, and redemption is a twisted mirage. The troubled characters that inhabit the streets and alleys of these stories continually find themselves at the mercy of a cold, indifferent world as they hurtle downward and grapple for hard-won second chances in a life that seldom grants them.